PE

THIEVES' WORLD

THIEVES' WORLD

EDITED BY
ROBERT ASPRIN

PENGUIN BOOKS

'Sentences of Death' copyright © 1979 by John Brunner
'The Face of Chaos' copyright © 1979 by Lynn Abbey
'The Gate of the Flying Knives' copyright © 1979 by Poul Anderson
'Shadowspawn' copyright © 1979 by Andrew Offutt
'The Price of Doing Business' copyright © 1979 by Robert Asprin
'Blood Brothers' copyright © 1979 by Joe Haldeman
'Myrtis' copyright © 1979 by Christine DeWees
'The Secret of the Blue Star' copyright © 1979 by Marion Zimmer Bradley

Penguin Books Ltd, Harmondsworth, Middlesex, England
Viking Penguin Inc., 40 West 23rd Street, New York, New York 10010, U.S.A.
Penguin Books Australia Ltd, Ringwood, Victoria, Australia
Penguin Books Canada Ltd, 2801 John Street, Markham, Ontario, Canada L3R 1B4
Penguin Books (N.Z) Ltd, 182–190 Wairau Road, Auckland 10, New Zealand

First published in the U.S.A. by Ace Books 1981
Published in Penguin Books 1984
Reprinted 1984

Copyright © Robert Lynn Asprin, 1981
All rights reserved

Printed and bound in Great Britain by
Cox & Wyman Ltd, Reading
Filmset in 9/11 Monophoto Times by
Northumberland Press Ltd, Gateshead

CONTENTS

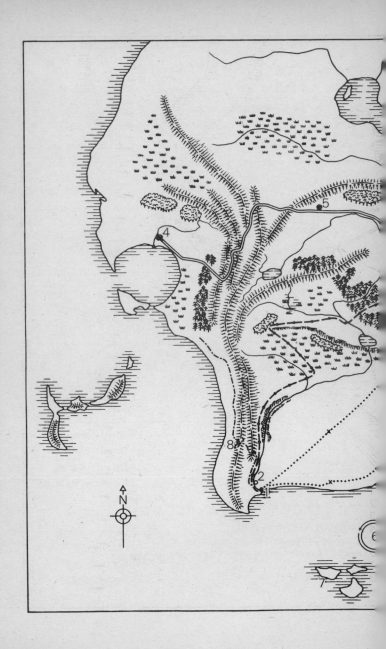

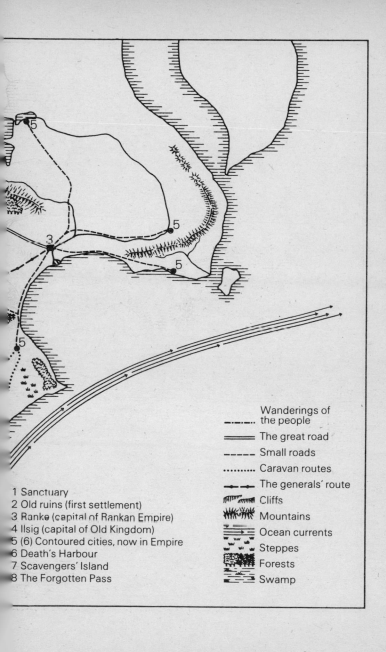

1 Sanctuary
2 Old ruins (first settlement)
3 Ranke (capital of Rankan Empire)
4 Ilsig (capital of Old Kingdom)
5 (6) Contoured cities, now in Empire
6 Death's Harbour
7 Scavengers' Island
8 The Forgotten Pass

	Wanderings of the people
	The great road
	Small roads
	Caravan routes
	The generals' route
	Cliffs
	Mountains
	Ocean currents
	Steppes
	Forests
	Swamp

14

11

N

1 mile

1 Governor's Palace
2 Hall of Justice
3 Servants' Quarters
4 Dungeons
5 Officers' Quarters
6 Armoury
7 Barracks
8 Stables
9 Hanging/Slave
　Auction Block
10 Bazaar
11 (6) Estates
12 (4) Granaries
13 Lighthouse
14 Ford
15 Cave

EDITOR'S NOTE

The perceptive reader may notice small inconsistencies in the characters appearing in these stories. Their speech patterns, their accounts of certain events, and their observations on the town's pecking order vary from time to time.

These are not inconsistencies!

The reader should consider the contradictions again, bearing three things in mind.

First; each story is told from a different viewpoint, and different people see and hear things differently. Even readily observable facts are influenced by individual perceptions and opinions. Thus, a minstrel narrating a conversation with a magician would give a different account than would a thief witnessing the same exchange.

Second; the citizens of Sanctuary are by necessity more than a little paranoid. They tend to either omit or slightly alter information in conversation. This is done more reflexively than out of premeditation, as it is essential for survival in this community.

Finally, Sanctuary is a fiercely competitive environment. One does not gain employment by admitting to being 'the second-best swordsman in town'. In addition to exaggerating one's own status, it is commonplace to downgrade or ignore one's closest competitors. As a result, the pecking order of Sanctuary will vary depending on who you talk to ... or more importantly, who you believe.

INTRODUCTION

1
THE EMPEROR

'But surely Your Excellency can't dispute the facts of the matter!'

The robed figure of the Emperor never slackened its pacing as the new leader of the Rankan Empire shook his head in violent disagreement.

'I do not dispute the facts, Kilite,' he argued, 'But neither will I order the death of my brother.'

'*Step*brother,' his chief adviser corrected pointedly.

'The blood of our father flows in both our veins,' the Emperor countered, 'and I'll have no hand in spilling it.'

'But Your Excellency,' Kilite pleaded, 'Prince Kadakithis is young and idealistic ...'

'... and I am not,' the Emperor finished. 'You belabour the obvious, Kilite. That idealism is my protection. He would no more lead a rebellion against the Emperor – against his brother – than I would order his assassination.'

'It is not the Prince we fear, Your Excellency, it's those who would use him.' The adviser was adamant. 'If one of his many false-faced followers succeeded in convincing him that your rule was unjust or inhumane, that idealism would compel him to move against you even though he loves you dearly.'

The Emperor's pacing slowed until finally he was standing motionless, his shoulders drooping slightly.

'You're right, Kilite. All my advisers are right.' There was weary resignation in his voice. 'Something must be done to remove my brother from the hotbed of intrigue here at the capital. If at all possible, however, I would hold any thoughts of assassination as a last resort.'

'If Your Excellency has an alternative plan he wishes to suggest, I would be honoured to give it my appraisal,' Kilite offered, wisely hiding his feelings of triumph.

'I have no immediate plan,' the Emperor admitted. 'Nor will I be able to give it my full concentration until another matter is settled which weighs heavily on my mind. Surely the empire is safe from my brother for a few more days?'

'What is the other decision demanding your attention?' the adviser asked, ignoring his ruler's attempt at levity. 'If it is something I might assist you in resolving ...'

'It is nothing. A minor decision, but an unpleasant one nonetheless. I must appoint a new military governor for Sanctuary.'

'Sanctuary?' Kilite frowned.

'A small town at the southern tip of the empire. I had a bit of trouble finding it myself – it's been excluded from the more recent maps. Whatever reason there was for the town's existence has apparently passed. It is withering and dying, a refuge for petty criminals and down-at-the-heels adventurers. Still, it's part of the empire.'

'And they need a new military governor,' Kilite murmured softly.

'The old one's retiring.' The Emperor shrugged. 'Which leaves me with a problem. As a garrisoned empire town, they are entitled to a governor of some stature – someone who knows the empire well enough to serve as their representative and go-between with the capital. He should be strong enough to uphold and enforce the law – a function I fear where the old governor was noticeably lax.'

Without realizing it, he began to pace again.

'My problem is that such a man could be better utilized elsewhere in the empire. It seems a shame to waste someone on such an insignificant, out-of-the-way assignment.'

'Don't say "out-of-the-way", Your Excellency,' Kilite smiled. 'Say "far from the hotbed of intrigue".'

The Emperor looked at his adviser for a long moment. Then both men began to laugh.

14

2
THE TOWN

Hakiem the Storyteller licked the dust from his lips as he squinted at the morning sun. It was going to be hot again today – a wine day, if he could afford wine. The little luxuries, like wine, that he allowed himself were harder to come by as the caravans became fewer and more infrequent.

His fingers idly seeking a sand-flea which had successfully found its way inside his rags, he settled himself wearily in his new roost at the edge of the bazaar. Previously, he had frequented the large wharf until the fishermen drove him off, accusing him of stealing. Him! With all the thieves that abound in this town, they chose him for their accusations.

'Hakiem!'

He looked about him and saw a band of six urchins descending on him, their eyes bright and eager.

'Good morning, children,' he grimaced, exposing his yellow teeth. 'What do you wish of old Hakiem?'

'Tell us a story,' they chorused, surging around him.

'Be off with you, sand-fleas!' he moaned, waving an arm. 'The sun will be hot today. I'll not add to the dryness of my throat telling you stories for free.'

'Please, Hakiem?' one whined.

'We'll fetch you water,' promised another.

'I have money.'

The last offer caught at Hakiem's attention like a magnet. His eyes fastened hungrily on the copper coin extended in a grubby hand. That coin and four of its brothers would buy him a bottle of wine.

Where the boy had gotten it mattered not – he had probably stolen it. What concerned Hakiem was how to transfer the wealth from the boy to himself. He considered taking it by force, but decided against it. The bazaar was rapidly filling with people, and open bullying of children would doubtless draw repercussions. Besides, the nimble urchins could outrun him with ease. He would just have to earn it honestly. Disgusting, the depths to which he had sunk.

'Very well, Ran-tu,' he smiled extending his hand. 'Give me the money, and you shall have any story you wish.'

'After I hear the story,' the boy announced haughtily. 'You shall have the coin . . . if I feel the story is worth it. It is the custom.'

'So it is.' Hakiem forced a smile. 'Come, sit here beside me so you can hear every detail.'

The boy did as he was told, blissfully unaware that he was placing himself within Hakiem's long, quick reach.

'Now then, Ran-tu, what story do you wish to hear?'

'Tell us about the history of our city,' the boy chirped, forgetting his pretended sophistication for the moment.

Hakiem grimaced, but the other boys jumped and clapped their hands with enthusiasm. Unlike Hakiem, they never tired of hearing this tale.

'Very well,' Hakiem sighed. 'Make room here!'

He shoved roughly at the forest of small legs before him, clearing a small space in the ground which he swept smooth with his hand. With quick, practised strokes, he outlined the southern part of the continent and formed the north–south mountain range.

'The story begins here, in what once was the kingdom of Ilsig, east of the Queen's Mountains.'

'. . . which the Rankans call the World's End Mountains . . .' supplied an urchin.

'. . . and the Mountain Men call Gunderpah . . .' contributed another.

Hakiem leaned back on his haunches and scratched absently.

'Perhaps,' he said, 'the young gentlemen would like to tell the story while Hakiem listens.'

'No they wouldn't,' insisted Ran-tu. 'Shut up, everyone. It's my story! Let Hakiem tell it.'

Hakiem waited until silence was restored, then nodded loftily to Ran-tu and continued.

'Afraid of invasion from the then young Rankan Empire across the mountains, they formed an alliance with the Mountain Tribes to guard the only known pass through the mountains.'

He paused to draw a line on his map indicating the pass.

'Lo, it came to pass that their fears were realized. The Rankans

16

turned their armies towards Ilsig, and they were forced to send their own troops into the pass to aid the Mountain Men in the kingdom's defence.'

He looked up hopefully and extended a palm as a merchant paused to listen, but the man shook his head and moved on.

'While the armies were gone,' he continued, scowling, 'there was an uprising of slaves in Ilsig. Body-servants, galley slaves, gladiators, all united in an effort to throw off the shackles of bondage. Alas . . .'

He paused and threw up his hands dramatically.

'. . . the armies of Ilsig returned early from their mountain campaign and put a swift end to the uprising. The survivors fled south . . . here . . . along the coast.'

He indicated the route with his fingers.

'The kingdom waited for a while, expecting the errant slaves to return of their own volition. When they didn't, a troop of cavalry was sent to overtake them and bring them back. They overtook the slaves here, forcing them back into the mountains, and a mighty battle ensued. The slaves were triumphant, and the cavalry was destroyed.'

He indicated a point in the southern portion of the mountain range.

'Aren't you going to tell about the battle?' Ran-tu interrupted.

'That is a story in itself . . . requiring separate payment,' Hakiem smiled.

The boy bit his lip and said nothing more.

'In the course of their battle with the cavalry, the slaves discovered a pass through the mountains, allowing them to enter this green valley where game was plentiful and crops sprang from the ground. They called it Sanctuary.'

'The valley isn't green,' an urchin interrupted pointedly.

'That's because the slaves were dumb and overworked the land,' countered another.

'My dad used to be a farmer, and he didn't overwork the land!' argued a third.

'Then how is it you had to move into town when the sands took your farm?' countered the second.

'I want to hear my story!' barked Ran-tu, suddenly towering above them.

The group subsided into silence.

'The young gentleman there has the facts of the matter right,' smiled Hakiem, pointing a finger at the second urchin. 'But it took time. Oh my, yes, lots of time. As the slaves exhausted the land to the north, they moved south, until they reached the point where the town stands today. Here they met a group of native fishermen, and between fishing and farming managed to survive in peace and tranquillity.'

'That didn't last long,' snorted Ran-tu, momentarily forgetting himself.

'No,' agreed Hakiem. 'The gods did not will it so. Rumours of a discovery of gold and silver reached the kingdom of Ilsig and brought intruders into our tranquility. First adventurers, and finally a fleet from the kingdom itself to capture the town and again bring it under the kingdom's control. The only fly in the kingdom's victory wine that day was that most of the fishing fleet was out when they arrived, and, realizing the fate of the town, took refuge on Scavengers' Island to form the nucleus of the Cape Pirates, who harass ships to this day.'

A fisherman's wife passed by and, glancing down, recognized the map in the dust, smiled, and tossed two copper coins to Hakiem. He caught them neatly, elbowing an urchin who tried to intercept them, and secreted them in his sash.

'Blessings on your house, mistress,' he called after his benefactor.

'What about the empire?' Ran-tu prompted, afraid of losing his story.

'What? Oh, yes. It seems that one of the adventurers pushed north seeking the mythical gold, found a pass through the Civa, and eventually joined the Rankan Empire. Later, his grandson, now a general in the empire, found his ancestor's journals. He led a force south over his grandfather's old route and recaptured the town. Using it as a base, he launched a naval attack around the cape and finally captured the kingdom of Ilsig, making it a part of the empire for ever.'

'Which is where we are today,' one of the urchins spat bitterly.

'Not quite,' corrected Hakiem, his impatience to be done with the story yielding to his integrity as a tale-spinner. 'Though the kingdom surrendered, for some reason the Mountain Men continued to resist the empire's attempts to use the Great Pass. That was when the caravan routes were established.'

A faraway look came into his eyes.

'Those were the days of Sanctuary's greatness. Three or four caravans a week laden with treasures and trade goods. Not the miserable supply caravans you see today – great caravans that took half a day just to enter town.'

'What happened?' asked one of the awestruck urchins.

Hakiem's eyes grew dark. He spat in the dust.

'Twenty years ago, the empire succeeded in putting down the Mountain Men. With the Great Pass open, there was no reason to risk major caravans in the bandit-ridden sands of the desert. Sanctuary has become a mockery of its past glory, a refuge for the scum who have nowhere else to go. Mark my words, one day the thieves will outnumber the honest citizenry, and then . . .'

'One side, old man!'

A sandalled foot came down on the map, obliterating its outlines and scattering the urchins.

Hakiem cowered before the shadow of one of the Hell Hounds, the five new élite guards who had accompanied the new governor into town.

'Zalbar! Stop that!'

The unsmiling giant froze at the sound of the voice and turned to face the golden-haired youth who strode on to the scene.

'We're supposed to be governing these people, not bludgeoning them into submission.'

It seemed strange, seeing a lad in his late teens chastizing a scarred veteran of many campaigns, but the larger man merely dropped his eyes in discomfort.

'Apologies, Your Highness, but the Emperor said we were to bring law and order to this hell-hole, and it's the only language these blackguards understand.'

'The Emperor – my brother – put me in command of this town to govern it as I see fit, and my orders are that the people are to be treated kindly as long as they do not break the laws.'

'Yes, Your Highness.'

The youth turned to Hakiem.

'I hope we did not disturb your story. Here – perhaps this will make up for our intrusion.'

He pressed a gold coin into Hakiem's hand.

'Gold!' Hakiem sneered. 'Do you think one miserable coin can make up for scaring those precious children?'

'What?' roared the Hell Hound. 'Those gutter-rats? Take the Prince's money and be thankful I –'

'Zalbar!'

'But Your Highness, this man is only playing on your –'

'If he is, it's mine to give ...'

He pressed a few more coins into Hakiem's outstretched hand.

'Now come along. I want to see the bazaar.'

Hakiem bowed low, ignoring the Hell Hound's black glare. When he straightened, the urchins were clustered about him again.

'Was that the Prince?'

'My dad says he's the best thing for this town.'

'My dad says he's too young to do a good job.'

'Izzat so!'

'The Emperor sent him here to get him out of the way.'

'Sez who?'

'Sez my brother! He's been bribing guards here all his life and never had any trouble till the Prince came. Him and his whores and his Hell Hounds.'

'They're going to change everything. Ask Hakiem ... Hakiem?'

The urchins turned to their chosen mentor, but Hakiem had long since departed with his new wealth for the cool depths of a tavern.

20

3
THE PLAN

'As you already know, you five men have been chosen to remain with me here in Sanctuary after the balance of the honour guard returns to the capital.'

Prince Kadakithis paused to look each man in the face before he continued. Zalbar, Bourne, Quag, Razkuli, and Arman. Each of them a seasoned veteran, they doubtless knew their work better than the Prince knew his. Kadakithis's royal upbringing came to his rescue, helping him to hide his nervousness as he met their gazes steadily.

'As soon as the ceremonies are completed tomorrow, I will be swamped with problems in clearing up the backlog of cases in the civil court. Realizing that, I thought it best to give you our briefing and assignments now, so that you will be able to proceed without the delay of waiting for specific instructions.'

He beckoned the men forward, and they gathered around the map of Sanctuary hung on the wall.

'Zalbar and I have done some preliminary scouting of the town. Though this briefing should familiarize you with the basic lay of the land, you should each do your own exploring and report any new observations to each other. Zalbar?'

The tallest of the soldiers stepped forward and swept his hand across the map.

'The thieves of Sanctuary drift with wind like the garbage they are,' he began.

'Zalbar!' the Prince admonished. 'Just give the report without asides or opinions.'

'Yes, Your Highness.' The man replied bowing his head slightly. 'But there is a pattern here which follows the winds from the east.'

'The property values change because of the smells,' Kadakithis reported. 'You can say that without referring to the people as garbage. They are still citizens of the empire.'

Zalbar nodded and turned to the map once more.

'The areas of least crime are here, along the eastern edge of town,' he announced, gesturing. 'These are the richest mansions, inns, and temples, which have their own defences and safeguards. West of them, the town consists predominantly of craftsmen and skilled workers. The crime in this area rarely exceeds petty theft.'

The man paused to glance at the prince before continuing.

'Once you cross the Processional, however, things get steadily worse. The merchants vie with each other as to who will carry the widest selection of stolen or illicit goods. Much of their merchandise is supplied by smugglers who openly use the wharves to unload their ships. What is not purchased by the merchants is sold directly at the bazaar.'

Zalbar's expression hardened noticeably as he indicated the next area.

'Here is a tangle of streets known simply as the Maze. It is acknowledged by all to be the roughest section of town. Murder and armed robbery are commonplace occurrences day or night in the Maze, and most honest citizens are afraid to set foot there without an armed escort. It has been brought to our attention that none of the guardsmen in the local garrison will enter this area, though whether this is out of fear or if they have been bribed ...'

The prince cleared his throat noisily. Zalbar grimaced and moved on to another area.

'Outside the walls to the north of town is a cluster of brothels and gaming houses. There are few crimes reported in this area, though we believe this is due more to a reluctance on the part of the inhabitants to deal with authorities than from any lack of criminal activity. To the far west of town is a shantytown inhabited by beggars and derelicts known as the Downwinders. Of all the citizens we've encountered so far, they seem the most harmless.'

His report complete, Zalbar returned to his place with the others as the prince addressed them once again.

'Your priorities until new orders are issued will be as follows,' he announced, eyeing the men carefully. 'First, you are to make a concentrated effort to reduce or eliminate petty crime on the east side of town. Second, you will close the wharves to the smuggler traffic. When that is done, I will sign into law certain regulations enabling you to move against the brothels. By that time, my court duties should have eased to a point where we can formulate a specific plan of action for dealing with the Maze. Any questions?'

'Are you anticipating any problems with the local priesthood over the ordered construction of new temples to Savankala, Sabellia, and Vashanka?' Bourne asked.

'Yes, I am,' the prince acknowledged. 'But the difficulties will probably be more diplomatic than criminal in nature. As such, I will attend to it personally, leaving you free to pursue your given assignments.'

There were no further questions, and the prince steeled himself for his final pronouncement.

'As to how you are to conduct yourselves while carrying out your orders ...' Kadakithis paused dramatically while sweeping the assemblage with a hard glare. 'I know you men are all soldiers and used to meeting opposition with bared steel. You are certainly permitted to fight to defend yourselves if attacked or to defend any citizen of this town. However, I will not tolerate brutality or needless bloodshed in the name of the empire. Whatever your personal feelings may be, you are not to draw a sword on any citizen unless they have proven – I repeat, *proven* – themselves to be criminal. The townsfolk have already taken to calling you Hell Hounds. Be sure that title refers only to the vigour with which you pursue your duties and not to your viciousness. That is all.'

There were mutters and dark glances as the men filed out of the room. While the Hell Hounds' loyalty to the empire was above question, Kadakithis had cause to wonder if in their own minds they truly considered him a representative of that empire.

SENTENCES OF DEATH

John Brunner

1

It was a measure of the decline in Sanctuary's fortunes that the scriptorium of Master Melilot occupied a prime location fronting on Governor's Walk. The nobleman whose grandfather had caused a fine family mansion to be erected on the site had wasted his substance in gambling, and at last was reduced to eking out his days in genteel drunkenness in an improvised fourth storey of wattle and daub, laid out across the original roof, while downstairs Melilot installed his increasingly large staff and went into the book – as well as the epistle – business. On hot days the stench from the bindery, where size was boiled and leather embossed, bid fair to match the reek around Shambles Cross.

Not all fortunes, be it understood, were declining. Melilot's was an instance. Then years earlier he had owned nothing but his clothing and a scribe's compendium; then he worked in the open air, or huddled under some tolerant merchant's awning, and his customers were confined to poor litigants from out of town who needed a written summary of their case before appearing in the Hall of Justice, or suspicious illiterate purchasers of goods from visiting traders who wanted written guarantees of quality.

On a never-to-be-forgotten day, a foolish man instructed him to write down matter relevant to a lawsuit then in progress, which would assuredly have convinced the judge, had it been produced without the opposition being warned. Melilot realized that, and made an extra copy. He was richly rewarded.

Now, as well as carrying on the scribe's profession – by proxy,

24

mostly – he specialized in forgery, blackmail, and mistranslation. He was exactly the sort of employer Jarveena of Forgotten Holt had been hoping for when she arrived, particularly since his condition, which might be guessed at from his beardless face and roly-poly fatness, made him indifferent to the age or appearance of his employees.

The services offered by the scriptorium, and the name of its proprietor, were clearly described in half a dozen languages and three distinct modes of writing on the stone face of the building, a window and a door of which had been knocked into one large entry (at some risk to the stability of the upper floors) so that clients might wait under cover until someone who understood the language they required was available.

Jarveena read and wrote her native tongue well: Yenized. That was why Melilot had agreed to hire her. No competing service in Sanctuary could offer so many languages now. But two months might go by – indeed, they had just done so – without a single customer's asking for a translation into or from Yenized, which made her pretty much of a status symbol. She was industriously struggling with Rankene, the courtly version of the common dialect, because merchants liked to let it be thought their goods were respectable enough for sale to the nobility even if they had come ashore by night from Scavengers' Island, and she was making good headway with the quotidian street-talk in which the poorer clients wanted depositions of evidence or contracts of sale made out. Nonetheless she was still obliged to take on menial tasks to fill her time.

It was noon, and another such task was due.

Plainly, it was of little use relying on inscriptions to reach those who were most in need of a scribe's assistance; accordingly Melilot maintained a squad of small boys with peculiarly sweet and piercing voices, who paraded up and down the nearby streets advertising his service by shouting, wheedling, and sometimes begging. It was a tiring occupation, and the children frequently grew hoarse. Thrice a day, therefore, someone was commanded to deliver them a nourishing snack of bread and cheese and a drink made of honey, water, a little wine or strong ale, and assorted spices. Since her engagement, Jarveena had been least often involved in other duties when the time for this one arrived. Hence she was on the street, distributing Melilot's bounty, when an officer whom she knew by name and sight turned up, acting in a most peculiar manner. He was Captain Aye-Gophlan, from the guardpost at the corner of Processional Way.

He scarcely noticed her as he went by, but that was less than surprising. She looked very much like a boy herself – more so, if anything, than the chubby-cheeked blond urchin she was issuing rations to. When Melilot took her on she had been in rags, and he had insisted on buying her new clothes of which, inevitably, the price would be docked from her miniscule commission on the work she did. She didn't care. She only insisted in turn that she be allowed to choose her garb: a short-sleeved leather jerkin cross-laced up the front; breeches to mid-calf; boots to tuck the breeches into, a baldric on which to hang her scribe's compendium with its reed-pens and ink-block and water-pot and sharpening knife and rolls of rough reed-paper; and a cloak to double as covering at night. She had a silver pin for it – her only treasure.

Melilot had laughed, thinking he understood. He owned a pretty girl a year shy of the fifteen Jarveena admitted to, who customarily boxed the ears of his boy apprentices when they waylaid her in a dark passageway to steal a kiss, and that was unusual enough to demand explanation.

But that had nothing to do with it. No more did the fact that with her tanned skin, thin build, close-cropped black hair, and many visible scars, she scarcely resembled a girl regardless of her costume. There were plenty of ruffians – some of noble blood – who were totally indifferent to the sex of the youngsters they raped.

Besides, to Jarveena such experiences were survivable; had they not been, she would not have reached Sanctuary. So she no longer feared them.

But they made her deeply – bitterly – angry. And someday one who deserved her anger more than any was going to pay for one at least of his countless crimes. She had sworn so ... but she had been only nine then, and with the passage of time the chance of

26

vengeance grew more and more remote. Now she scarcely believed in it. Sometimes she dreamed of doing to another what had been done to her, and woke moaning with shame, and she could not explain why to the other apprentice scribes sharing the dormitory that once had been the bedroom of the noble who now snored and vomited and groaned and snored under a shelter fit rather for hogs than humans the wrong side of his magnificently painted ceiling.

She regretted that. She liked most of her companions; some were from respectable families, for there were no schools here apart from temple schools whose priests had the bad habit of stuffing children's heads with myth and legend as though they were to live in a world of make-believe instead of fending for themselves. Without learning to read and write at least their own language they would be at risk of cheating by every smart operator in the city. But how could she befriend those who had led soft, secure lives, who at the advanced age of fifteen or sixteen had never yet had to scrape a living from gutters and garbage piles?

Captain Aye-Gophlan was in mufti. Or thought he was. He was by no means so rich as to be able to afford clothing apart from his uniforms, of which it was compulsory for the guards to own several – this one for the Emperor's birthday, that one for the feast of the regiment's patron deity, another for day-watch duty, yet another for night-watch duty, another for funeral drill ... The common soldiers were luckier. If they failed in their attire, the officers were blamed for stinginess. But how long was it since there had been enough caravans through here for the guard to keep up the finery required of them out of bribes? Times indeed were hard when the best disguise an officer on private business could contrive was a plum-blue overcloak with a hole in it exactly where his crotch-armour could glint through.

Seeing him, Jarveena thought suddenly about justice. Or more nearly, about getting even. Perhaps there was no longer any hope of bringing to account the villain who had killed her parents and sacked their estate, enslaved the able-bodied, turned loose his half-mad troops on children to glut the lust of their loins amid the smoke and crashing of beams as the village its inhabitants called Holt vanished from the stage of history.

But there were other things to do with her life. Hastily she snatched back the cup she had already allowed to linger too long in the grasp of this, luckily the last of Melilot's publicity boys. She cut short an attempt at complaint with a scowl which drew her forehead-skin down just far enough to reveal a scar normally covered by her forelock. That was a resource she customarily reserved until all else failed. It had its desired effect; the boy gulped and surrendered the cup and went back to work, pausing only to urinate against the wall.

2

Just as Jarveena expected, Aye-Gophlan marched stolidly around the block, occasionally glancing back as though feeling insecure without his regular escort of six tall men, and made for the rear entrance to the scriptorium – the one in the crooked alley where the silk-traders were concentrated. Not all of Melilot's customers cared to be seen walking in off a populous and sunny roadway.

Jarveena thrust the wine jar, dish, and cup she was carrying into the hands of an apprentice too young to argue, and ordered them returned to the kitchen – next to the bindery, with which it shared a fire. Then she stole up behind Aye-Gophlan and uttered a discreet cough.

'May I be of assistance, captain?'

'Ah –!' The officer was startled; his hand flew to something stick-shaped under his cloak, no doubt a tightly-rolled scroll. 'Ah ... Good-day to you! I have a problem concerning which I desire to consult your master.'

'He will be taking his noon meal,' Jarveena said in a suitably humble tone. 'Let me conduct you to him.'

Melilot never cared to have either his meals or the naps which followed them interrupted. But there was something about Aye-Gophlan's behaviour which made Jarveena certain that this was an exceptional occasion.

28

She opened the door of Melilot's sanctum, announced the caller rapidly enough to forestall her employer's rage at being distracted from the immense broiled lobster lying before him on a silver platter, and wished there were some means of eavesdropping on what transpired.

But he was infinitely too cautious to risk that.

At best Jarveena had hoped for a few coins by way of bonus if Aye-Gophlan's business proved profitable. She was much surprised, therefore, to be summoned to Melilot's room half an hour later.

Aye-Gophlan was still present. The lobster had grown cold, untouched, but much wine had been consumed.

On her entrance, the officer gave her a suspicious glare.

'This is the fledgling you imagine could unravel the mystery?' he demanded.

Jarveena's heart sank. What devious subterfuge was Melilot up to now? But she waited meekly for clear instructions. They came at once, in the fat man's high and slightly whining voice.

'The captain has a writing to decipher. Sensibly, he has brought it to us, who can translate more foreign tongues than any similar firm! It is possible that it may be in Yenized, with which you are familiar ... though, alas, I am not.'

Jarveena barely suppressed a giggle. If the document were in any known script or language, Melilot would certainly recognize it – whether or not he could furnish a translation. That implied – hmm! A cipher! How interesting! How did an officer of the guard come by a message in code he couldn't read? She looked expectant, though not eager, and with much reluctance Aye-Gophlan handed her the scroll.

Without appearing to look up, she registered a tiny nod from Melilot. She was to agree with him.

But –

What in the *world*? Only a tremendous self-control prevented her from letting fall the document. Merely glancing at it made her dizzy, as though her eyes were crossing against her will. For a second she had seemed to read it clearly, and a heartbeat later ...

29

She took a firm grip on herself. 'I believe this to be Yenized, as you suspected, sir,' she declared.

'Believe?' Aye-Gophlan rasped. 'But Melilot swore you could read it instantly!'

'Modern Yenized I can, captain,' Jarveena amplified. 'I recognize this as a high and courtly style, as difficult for a person like myself as Imperial Rankene would be for a herdsman accustomed to sleeping with the swine.' It was always politic to imply one's own inferiority when talking to someone like this. 'Luckily, thanks to my master's extensive library, I've gained a wider knowledge of the subject in recent weeks; and with the help of some of the books he keeps I would expect to get at least its gist.'

'How long would it take?' Aye-Gophlan demanded.

'Oh, one might safely say two or three days,' Melilot interpolated in a tone that brooked no contradiction. 'Given that it's so unusual an assignment, there would naturally be no charge except on production of a satisfactory rendering.'

Jarveena almost dropped the scroll a second time. Never in living memory had Melilot accepted a commission without taking at least half his fee in advance. There must be something quite exceptional about this sheet of paper –

And of course there was. It dawned on her that moment, and she had to struggle to prevent her teeth from chattering.

'Wait here,' the fat man said, struggling to his feet. 'I shall return when I've escorted the captain out.'

The moment the door closed she threw the scroll down on the table next to the lobster – wishing, irrelevantly, that it were not still intact, so she might snatch a morsel without being detected. The writing writhed into new patterns even as she tried not to notice.

Then Melilot was back, resuming his chair, sipping from his half-full wine cup.

'You're astute, you little weasel!' he said in a tone of grudging admiration. 'Are you quick-witted enough to know precisely why neither he nor I – nor you! – can read that writing?'

Jarveena swallowed hard. 'There's a spell on it,' she offered after a pause.

'Yes! Yes, there is! Better than any code or cipher. Except for the eyes of the intended recipient, it will never read the same way twice.'

'How is it that the captain didn't realize?'

Melilot chuckled. 'You don't have to read and write to become a captain of the guard,' he said. 'He can about manage to tell whether the clerk who witnesses his mark on the watch-report is holding the page right side up; but anything more complicated and his head starts to swim anyway.'

He seized the lobster, tore off a claw, and cracked it between his teeth; oil ran down his chin and dripped on his green robe. Picking out the meat, he went on. 'But what's interesting is how he came by it. Make a guess.'

Jarveena shook her head.

'One of the imperial bodyguards from Ranke, one of the detachment who escorted the Prince along the Generals' Road, called to inspect the local guardhouse this morning at dawn. Apparently he made himself most unpopular, to the point that, when he let fall that scroll without noticing, Aye-Gophlan thought more of secreting it than giving it back. Why he's ready to believe that an imperial officer would carry a document in Old High Yenized, I can't guess. Perhaps that's part of the magic.'

He thrust gobbets of succulent flesh into his mouth and chomped for a while. Jarveena tried not to drool.

To distract herself by the first means to mind, she said, 'Why did he tell you all this . . . ? Ah, I'm an idiot. He didn't.'

'Correct.' Melilot looked smug. 'For that you deserve a taste of lobster. Here!' He tossed over a lump that by his standards was generous, and a chunk of bread also; she caught both in mid-air with stammered thanks and wolfed them down.

'You need to have your strength built up,' the portly scribe went on. 'I have a very responsible errand for you to undertake tonight.'

'Errand?'

'Yes. The imperial officer who lost the scroll is called Commander Nizharu. He and his men are billeted in pavilions in the courtyard of the governor's palace; seemingly he's afraid of contamination if they have to go into barracks with the local soldiery.

'After dark this evening you are to steal in and wait on him, and inquire whether he will pay more for the return of his scroll and the name of the man who filched it, or for a convincing but fraudulent translation which will provoke the unlawful possessor into some rash action. For all I can guess,' he concluded sanctimoniously, 'he may have let it fall deliberately. *Hm*?'

3

It was far from the first time since her arrival that Jarveena had been out after curfew. It was not even the first time she had had to scamper in shadow across the broad expanse of Governor's Walk in order to reach and scramble over the palace wall, nimble as a monkey despite the mass of scar-tissue where her right breast would never grow. Much practice enabled her to whip off her cloak, roll it into a cylinder not much thicker than a money-belt, fasten it around her, and rush up the convenient hand- and toeholds in the outer wall which were carefully not repaired, and for a fat consideration, when the chief mason undertook his annual re-pointing.

But it was definitely the first time she had had to contend with crack soldiers from Ranke on the other side. One of them, by ill chance, was relieving himself behind a flowering shrub as she descended, and needed to do no more than thrust the haft of his pike between her legs. She gasped and went sprawling.

But Melilot had foreseen all this, and she was prepared with her story and the evidence to back it up.

'Don't hurt me, please! I don't mean any harm!' she whimpered, making her voice as childish as possible. There was a torch guttering in a sconce nearby; the soldier heaved her to her feet by her right wrist, his grip as cruel as a trap's, and forced her towards it. A sergeant appeared from the direction of the pavilions which since her last visit had sprouted like mushrooms between the entry to the Hall of Justice and the clustered granaries on the north-west side of the grounds.

'What you got?' he rumbled in a threatening bass voice.

'Sir, I mean no harm! I have to do what my mistress tells me, or I'll be nailed to the temple door!'

That took both of them aback. The soldier somewhat relaxed his fingers and the sergeant bent close to look her over better in the wan torchlight.

'By that, I take it you serve a priestess of Argash?' he said eventually.

It was a logical deduction. On the twenty-foot-high fane of that divinity his most devoted followers volunteered, when life wearied them, to be hung up and fast unto death.

But Jarveena shook her head violently.

'N-no, sir! Dyareela!' -- naming a goddess banned these thirty years owing to the bloodthirstiness of her votaries.

The sergeant frowned. 'I saw no shrine to *her* when we escorted the prince along Temple Avenue!'

'N-no, sir! Her temple was destroyed, but her worshippers endure!'

'Do they now!' the sergeant grunted. 'Hmm! That sounds like something the commander ought to know!'

'Is that Commander Nizharu?' Jarveena said eagerly.

'What? How do you know his name?'

'My mistress sent me to him! She saw him early today when he was abroad in the city, and she was so taken with his handsomeness that she resolved at once to send a message to him. But it was all to be in secret!' Jarveena let a quaver enter her voice. 'Now I've let it out, and she'll turn me over to the priests of Argash, and ... Oh, I'm done for! I might as well be dead right now!'

'Dying can wait,' the sergeant said, reaching an abrupt decision. 'But the commander will definitely want to know about the Dyareelans. I thought only madmen in the desert paid attention to that old bitch nowadays ... Hello, what's this at your side?' He lifted it into the light. 'A writing-case, is it?'

'Yes, sir. That's what I mainly do for my mistress.'

'If you can write, why deliver messages yourself? That's what I always say. Oh, well, I guess you're her confidante, are you?' Jarveena nodded vigorously.

'A secret shared is a secret no longer, and here's one more proof of the proverb. Oh, come along!'

By the light of two lamps filled, to judge by their smell, with poor-grade fish oil, Nizharu was turning the contents of his pavilion upside-down, with not even an orderly to help him. He had cleared out two brass-bound wooden chests and was beginning on a third, while the bedding from his field couch of wood and canvas was strewn on the floor, and a dozen bags and pouches had been emptied and not repacked.

He was furious when the sergeant raised the tent flap, and roared that he was not to be disturbed. But Jarveena took in the situation at a glance and said in a clear firm voice, 'I wonder if you're looking for a scroll.'

Nizharu froze, his face turned so that light fell on it. He was as fair a man as she had ever seen: his hair like washed wool, his eyes like chips of summer sky. Under a nose keen as a bird's beak, his thin lips framed well-kept teeth marred by a chip off the right upper front molar. He was lean and obviously very strong, for he was turning over a chest that must weigh a hundred pounds and his biceps were scarcely bulging.

'Scroll?' he said softly, setting down the chest. 'What scroll?'

It was very hard for Jarveena to reply. She felt her heart was going to stop. The world wavered. It took all her force to maintain her balance. Distantly she heard the sergeant say, 'She didn't mention any scroll to us!'

And, amazingly, she was able to speak for herself again.

'That's true, commander,' she said. 'I had to lie to those men to stop them killing me before I got to you. I'm sorry.' Meantime she was silently thanking the network of informers who kept Melilot so well supplied with information that the lie had been credible even to these strangers. 'But I think this morning you mislaid a scroll . . .?'

Nizharu hesitated a single moment. Then he rapped, 'Out! Leave the boy here!'

Boy! Oh, miracle! If Jarveena had believed in a deity, now was when she would have resolved to make sacrifice for gratitude. For that implied he hadn't recognized her.

34

She waited while the puzzled sergeant and soldier withdrew, mouth dry, palms moist, a faint singing in her ears. Nizharu slammed the lid of the chest he had been about to overturn, sat down on it, and said, 'Now explain! And the explanation had better be a good one!'

It was. It was excellent. Melilot had devised it with great care and drilled her through it a dozen times during the afternoon. It was tinged with just enough of the truth to be convincing.

Aye-Gophlan, notoriously, had accepted bribes. (So had everyone in the guard who might possibly be useful to anybody wealthier than himself, but that was by-the-by.) It had consequently occurred to Melilot – a most loyal and law-abiding citizen, who as all his acquaintance would swear had loudly welcomed the appointment of the prince, the new governor, and looked forward to the city being reformed – it had occurred to him that perhaps this was part of a plan. One could scarcely conceive of a high-ranking imperial officer being so casual with what was obviously a top-secret document. *Could* one?

'Never,' murmured Nizharu, but sweat beaded his lip.

Next came the tricky bit. Everything depended on whether the commander wanted to keep the mere existence of the scroll a secret. Now he knew Aye-Gophlan had it, it was open to him to summon his men and march down to the guardhouse and search it floor to rooftree, for – according to what Jarveena said, at any rate – Aye-Gophlan was far too cautious to leave it overnight in the custody of a mere scribe. He would return on his next duty-free day, the day after tomorrow or the day after that, depending on which of his fellow officers he could exchange with.

But Melilot had deduced that if the scroll were so important that Nizharu kept it by him even when undertaking a mundane tour of inspection, it must be very private indeed. He was, apparently, correct. Nizharu listened with close attention, and many nods to the alternative plan of action.

For a consideration, Melilot was prepared to furnish a false translation designed to jar Aye-Gophlan into doing something for which Nizharu could safely arrest him, without it ever being known that he had enjoyed temporary possession of a scroll which by rights should have remained in the commander's hands. Let him only specify the terms, and it would be as good as done.

When she – whom Nizharu still believed a he, for which she was profoundly glad – finished talking, the commander pondered a while. At length he started to smile, though it never reached his eyes, and in firm clear terms expressed his conditions for entering into a compact along the lines Melilot proposed. He capped all by handing over two gold coins, of a type she did not recognize, with a promise that he would have her (his) hide if they did not both reach Melilot, and a large silver token of the kind used at Ilsig for *him*self.

Then he instructed a soldier she had not met to escort her to the gate and across Governor's Walk. But she gave the man the slip as soon as they were clear of the palace grounds and rushed towards the back entry, via Silk Corner.

Melilot being rich, he could afford locks on his doors; he had given her a heavy bronze key which she had concealed in her writing case. She fumbled it into the lock, but before she could turn it the door swung wide and she stepped forward as though impelled by another person's will.

This was the street – or rather alley. This was the door with its overhanging porch. Outside everything was right.

But inside everything was absolutely, utterly, unqualifiedly *wrong*.

4

Jarveena wanted to cry out, but found herself unable to draw enough breath. A vast sluggishness took possession of her muscles, as though she were descending into glue. Taking one more step, she knew, would tire her to the point of exhaustion; accordingly she concentrated merely on looking about her, and within seconds was wishing that she hadn't.

A wan, greyish light suffused the place. It showed her high stone walls on either side, a stone-flagged floor underfoot, but nothing above except drifting mist that sometimes took on an eerie pale colour: pinkish, bluish, or the sickly phosphorescent shade of dying fish. Before her was nothing but a long table, immensely and ridiculously long, such that one might seat a full company of soldiers at it.

A shiver tried to crawl down her spine, but failed thanks to the weird paralysis that gripped her. For what she was seeing matched in every respect the descriptions, uttered in a whisper, which she had heard of the home of Enas Yorl. In all the land there were but three Great Wizards, powerful enough not to care that their true names were noised abroad: one was at Ranke and served the needs of the court; one was at Ilsig and accounted the most skilful; the third, by reason of some scandal, made do with the slim pickings at Sanctuary, and that was Enas Yorl.

But how could he be here? His palace was on – or, more exactly, below – Prytanis Street, where the city petered out to the south-east of Temple Avenue.

Except . . .

The thought burgeoned from memory and she fought against it, and failed. Someone had once explained to her:

Except when it is somewhere else.

Abruptly it was as though the table shrank, and from an immense distance its farther end drew close and along with it a high-backed, throne-like chair in which sat a curious personage. He was arrayed in an enormously full, many-layered cloak of some dull brown stuff, and wore a high-crowned hat whose broad brim somehow contrived to shadow his face against even the directionless grey light that obtained here.

But within that shadow two red gleams like embers showed, approximately where a human's eyes would be.

This individual held in his right hand a scroll, partly un-rolled, and with his left he was tapping on the table. The proportions of his fingers were abnormal, and one or two of them seemed either to lack, or to be overprovided with, joints. One of his nails sparked luridly, but that ceased after a little.

Raising his head, after a fashion, he spoke.

'A girl. Interesting. But one who has . . . suffered. Was it punishment?'

It felt to Jarveena as though the gaze of those two dull red orbs could penetrate her flesh as well as her clothing. She could say nothing, but had nothing to say.

'No,' pronounced the wizard – for surely it must be none other. He let the scroll drop on the table, and it formed itself into a tidy roll at once, while he rose and approached her. A gesture, as though to sketch her outline in the air, freed her from the lassitude that had hampered her limbs. But she had too much sense to break and run.

Whither?

'Do you know me?'

'I . . .' She licked dry lips. 'I think you may be Enas Yorl.'

'Fame at last,' the wizard said wryly. 'Do you know why you're here?'

'You . . . Well, I guess you set a trap for me. I don't know why, unless it has to do with that scroll.'

'Hmm! A perceptive child!' Had he possessed eyebrows, one might have imagined the wizard raising them. And then at once: 'Forgive me. I should not have said "child". You are old in the ways of the world, if not in years. But after the first century, such patronizing remarks come easy to the tongue . . .' He resumed his chair, inviting Jarveena with a gesture to come closer. She was reluctant.

For when he rose to inspect her, he had been squat. Under the cloak he was obviously thick-set, stocky, with a paunch. But by the time he regained his seat, it was equally definite that he was thin, light-boned, and had one shoulder higher than the other.

'You have noticed,' he said. His voice too had altered; it had been baritone, while now it was at the most flattering a countertenor. 'Victims of circumstance, you and I both. It was not I who set a trap for you. The scroll did.'

'For me? But *why*?'

'I speak with imprecision. The trap was set not for you *qua* you. It was set for someone to whom it meant the death of another.

I judge that you qualify, whether or not you know it. Do you? Make a guess. Trust your imagination. Have you, for example, recognized anybody who came to the city recently?'

Jarveena felt the blood drain from her cheeks. She folded her hands into fists.

'Sir, you are a great magician. I recognized someone tonight. Someone I never dreamed of meeting again. Someone whose death I would gladly accomplish, except that death is much too good for him.'

'Explain!' Enas Yorl leaned an elbow on the table, and rested his chin on his fist ... except that neither the elbow, nor the chin, let alone the fist, properly corresponded to such appellations.

She hesitated a second. Then she cast aside her cloak, tore loose the bow that held the cross-lacing of her jerkin at her throat, and unthreaded it so that the garment fell wide to reveal the cicatrices, brown on brown, which would never fade, and the great foul keloid like a turd where her right breast might have been.

'Why try to hide anything from a wizard?' she said bitterly. 'He commanded the men who did this to me, and far far worse to many others. I thought they were bandits! I came to Sanctuary hoping that here if anywhere I might get wind of them – how could bandits gain access to Ranke or the conquered cities? But I never dreamed they would present themselves in the guise of imperial guards!'

'They ...?' Enas Yorl probed.

'Ah ... No. I confess: it's only one that I can swear to.'

'How old were you?'

'I was nine. And six grown men took pleasure of me, before they beat me with wire whips and left me for dead.'

'I see.' He retrieved the scroll and with its end tapped the table absently. 'Can you now divine what is in this message? Bear in mind that it forced me hither.'

'Forced? But I'd have thought –'

'I found myself here by choice? Oh, the contrary!' A bitter laugh rang out, acid-shrill. 'I said we're both victims. Long ago when I was young I was extremely foolish. I tried to seduce away the bride of someone more powerful than me. When he found out,

I was able to defend myself, but ... Do you understand what a spell is?'

She shook her head.

'It's ... activity. As much activity as a rock is passivity, which is conscious of being a rock but of nothing else. A worm is a little more aware; a dog or horse, much more; a human being, vastly more – but not infinitely more. In wildfire, storms, stars, can be found processes which with no consciousness of what they are act upon the outside world. A spell is such a process, created by an act of will, having neither aim nor purpose save what its creator lends. And to me my rival bequeathed ... But no matter. I begin to sound as though I pity myself, and I know my fate is just. Shall we despise justice? This scroll can be an instrument of it. Written on it are two sentences.

'Of death.'

While he spoke, there had been further changes under his concealing garb. His voice was now mellow and rich, and his hands, although very slender, possessed the ordinary number of joints. However, the redness still glowed.

'If one sentence is upon Commander Nizharu,' Jarveena said firmly, 'may it be executed soon.'

'That could be arranged.' A sardonic inflection coloured the words. 'At a price.'

'The scroll doesn't refer to him? I imagined –'

'You imagined it spelt his doom, and that was why he was so anxious about its loss? In a way that's correct. In a way ... And I can make certain that that shall be the outcome. At a price.'

'What – price?' Her voice quavered against her will.

He rose slowly from his chair, shaking his cloak out to its fullest; it swept the floor with a faint rustling sound.

'Need you ask, of one who so plainly is obsessed by lust for women? That was the reason for my downfall. I explained.'

Ice seemed to form around her heart. Her mouth was desert on the instant.

'Oh, why be so timid?' purred Enas Yorl, taking her hand in his. 'You've endured many worse bedfellows. I promise.'

It was true enough that the only means she had found to cross the weary leagues between Forgotten Holt and Sanctuary had been to yield her body: to merchants, mercenaries, grooms, guardsmen ...

'Tell me first,' she said with a final flare of spirit, 'whose deaths are cited in the document.'

'Fair,' said the wizard. 'Know, then, that one is an unnamed man, who is to be falsely convicted of the murder of another. And that other is the new governor, the prince.'

Thereupon the light faded, and he embraced her unresisting.

5

She woke late, at least half an hour past dawn. She was in her own bed; the dormitory was otherwise empty. All her limbs were pervaded by a delicious languor. Enas Yorl had kept his promise. If he had been equally skilled when he was younger, small wonder his rival's bride had preferred him to her husband!

Reluctantly opening her eyes, she saw something on the rough pillow. Puzzled, she looked again, reached out, touched: green, iridescent, powdery –

Scales!

With a cry she leapt from the bed, just as Melilot marched in, red-faced with fury.

'So there you are, you little slut! Where were you all night? I watched until I could stay awake no longer! By now I was sure you'd been taken by the guard and thrown in jail! *What did Nizharu say?*'

Naked, bewildered, for a long moment Jarveena was at a loss. Then her eye fell on something infinitely reassuring. On the wooden peg over her bed hung her cloak, jerkin and breeches, and also her precious writing-case, just as though she herself had replaced them on retiring.

Seizing the case, she opened the compartment where she hid such things, and triumphantly produced the gold she had accepted from the commander – but not the silver he had allotted to herself.

'He paid this for a false rendering of the scroll,' she said. 'But you're not to make one.'

'What?' Snatching the coins, Melilot made to bite them, but checked.

'How would you like to be scribe by appointment to the governor's household?'

'Are you crazed?' The fat man's eyes bulbed.

'Not in the least.' Heedless of his presence, Jarveena reached under the bed for her chamberpot and put it to its appropriate use. Meantime she explained the plot she had hatched.

'But this means you're claiming to have read the scroll,' Melilot said slowly as he tried to digest her proposals. 'It's enchanted! How could you?'

'Not I, but Enas Yorl.'

Melilot's mouth worked and all his colour drained away. 'But his palace is guarded by basilisks!' he exclaimed at last. 'You'd have been struck to stone!'

'It doesn't quite work like that,' Jarveena said, pulling on her breeches, giving silent thanks that she could do so briskly. That dreadful paralysis would haunt her dreams for years. 'To settle the argument, though, why don't you bring the scroll? I mean, why don't we go and take another look at it?'

They were in his sanctum a couple of minutes later.

'It's perfectly clear,' Melilot said slowly when he had perused the document twice. 'It's very stilted – formal Rankene – and I don't know anybody here or in the conquered cities who would use it for a letter. But it says exactly what you said it would.'

A tremor of awe made his rolls of fat wobble.

'You're satisfied it's the same scroll? There's been no sub-stitution?' Jarveena pressed.

'Yes! It's been all night in a locked chest! Only magic can account for what's happened to it!'

'Then,' she said with satisfaction, 'let's get on with the job.'

Each noon, in the grounds of the Governor's Palace before the Halls of Justice, the ·guard was inspected and rotated. This ceremony was open to the public – to everybody, in principle, but

42

in practice only to those who could afford to bribe the gate guards. Hence most of the spectators were of the upper class, hangers-on of the nobility, or making an appearance at the law courts. Not a few bore a general resemblance, in figure or clothing and in their retinue, to Melilot, who was in any case a frequent visitor when transcripts of evidence were in demand.

Therefore his presence and Jarveena's were unremarkable. Moreover word had got about that today was the last day when the crack imperial guards would perform the ceremonial drill before fifteen of them were ordered back to Ranke. There was a much larger throng than usual awaiting the appearance of the governor, one of whose customary chores this was whenever he was in residence.

It was a warm, dry, dusty day. The sun cast strong dark shadows. Tents, pavilions, stone walls seemed all of a substance. So in a way did people, especially those in armour. Under closed visors, any soldier might have been mistaken for any other of like stature.

Strictly it was not the turn of a guard detachment from the watch-house on Processional Way to take over from the Hell Hounds. But a few bribes, and a sharp order from Aye-Gophlan, and the problem had been sorted out.

Jarveena composed her features and did her best to look as though she were just another casual passer-by impressed by the standard of marching of troops from the capital, rather than a person whose dearest ambition for revenge bid fair to be fulfilled.

But her mouth kept wanting to snarl open like a wolf's.

The relieving guard marched in from the direction of Governor's Walk, exchanged salutes and passwords with the imperial troops, and formed up in the centre of the courtyard. Attended by two armed orderlies, Commander Nizharu formally recognized his successor and took station at his side for the governor's inspection. As soon as it was over, the departing troops would retire by squads and march away with flying colours.

Less than ten minutes later, amid a ripple of applause at the precision drill of the Hell Hounds, the prince was leaving the parade ground arm-in-arm with Nizharu. The latter was being posted back

43

to the capital, but five of his comrades were to establish a body-guard of local soldiers for the governor, trained to imperial standards.

So rumour said. Rumour had been known to lie.

With some care and ingenuity, Melilot had smiled and shoved his way to the front of the crowd, and as the two approached and all were bowing, he said very loudly and clearly, 'Why, commander! What good luck! Now is my chance to return the scroll you dropped yesterday morning!'

Nizharu had raised his visor because of the heat. It could clearly be seen that his face grew pasty-pale. 'I – I know nothing of any scroll!' he barked as soon as he could gather his wits.

'No? Oh, in that case, if it isn't yours, I'm sure the prince will accept it from me with a view to tracing its rightful owner!'

Fat though he was, Melilot could act briskly when he must. He whipped the scroll from under his robe and thrust it into Jarveena's eager hand. A heartbeat later, she was on her bended knee before the prince, gazing up into his handsome, youthful, and somewhat vacuous face.

'Read, Your Highness!' she insisted fiercely, and almost forced him to take hold of it.

The instant the prince caught its tenor, he froze. Nizharu did the opposite. Spinning on his heel, he shouted for his men and broke into a run.

The knife which Jarveena carried in her writing-case served other purposes than the sharpening of reed-pens. She withdrew it with a practised flick, aimed, *threw*.

And, howling, Nizharu measured his length on the ground, pierced behind the right knee where there was only leather, not metal, to protect him.

The crowd shouted in alarm and seemed on the brink of panic, but the incoming guard had been warned. Throwing back his visor, Captain Aye-Gophlan ordered his men to surround and arrest Nizharu, and in a fine towering rage the prince bellowed at the onlookers to explain why.

'This message is from a traitor at the imperial court! It instructs Nizharu to assign one of his guards to murder me as soon as he has found someone on whom the charge can be falsely pinned! And it says that the writer is enchanting the message to prevent the wrong person's reading it – but there's no difficulty in reading this! It's the court writing I was first taught as a child!'

'We – ah – arranged for the magic to be eliminated,' hinted Melilot. And added quickly, 'Your Highness!'

'How came you by it?'

'It was dropped by Nizharu when he inspected our guardhouse.' That was Aye-Gophlan, marching smartly forward. 'Thinking it important, I consulted Master Melilot, whom I've long known to be loyal and discreet.'

'And as for me ...' Melilot gave a deprecating shrug. 'I have certain *contacts*, let us say. It put me to no trouble to counteract the spell.'

True, thought Jarveena, and marvelled at how cleverly he lied.

'You shall be well rewarded,' declared the prince. 'And, after due trial, so shall he be! Attempting the life of one of the imperial blood – why, it's as heinous a crime as anyone might name! It was a miracle that he let fall the scroll. Surely the gods are on my side!' Raising his voice again. 'Tonight let all make sacrifice and give thanks! Under divine protection I have survived a dastardly assassin!'

If all gods, Jarveena thought, are no better than Melilot, I'm content to be an unbeliever. But I do look forward to watching Nizharu fry.

6

'In view of how you must be feeling, Jarveena,' said a soft voice at her side, 'I compliment you on the way you are concealing your emotions.'

'It's not difficult,' she answered with bitterness. The crowd was dispersing around them, heading away from the execution block where, according to the strict form, traitor Nizharu had paid for his many crimes by beating, hanging, and lastly burning.

And then she started. The person who had addressed her was

nobody she recognized: tall, stooped, elderly, with wisps of grey hair, carrying a market-basket . . .

Where eyes should be, a glint of red.

'Enas Yorl?' she whispered.

'That same.' With a dry chuckle. 'Inasmuch as I can ever make the statement . . . Are you content?'

'I – I guess I'm not.' Jarveena turned away and began to follow the drift of the crowd. 'I ought to be! I begged the privilege of writing the authorization for his execution in my own hand, and I thought I might include mention of my parents, my friends, the villagers he slaughtered or enslaved, but my formal Rankene isn't good enough, so I had to make do copying a draft by Melilot!' She tossed her head. 'And I hoped to stand up in open court, swear to what he did, watch the faces of the people change as they realized what a filthy villain came hither disguised as an imperial officer . . . They said there was no need for any other evidence after Aye-Gophlan's and Melilot's and the prince's.'

'To speak after princes is a dangerous habit,' opined the wizard. 'But at all events, it appears to have dawned on you that revenge is never what you hope for. Take my own case. He who did to me what you know of was so determined to wreak his vengeance that he created one spell more than he could handle. To each he was obliged to cede a certain portion of his will; for as I told you, spells have no aim or purpose of their own. He thereby deprived himself of ordinary sense, and to his death sat blubbering and moaning like an infant.'

'Why do you tell me this?' cried Jarveena. 'I want to make the most of my moment of satisfaction, even if it can't be as rich and memorable as I dreamed.'

'Because,' said the wizard, taking her arm by fingers whose touch evoked extraordinary thrills all over her, 'you paid a fair and honest price for the service I undertook. I shall not forget you. Scarred and branded you may be without; within you are beautiful.'

'Me?' said Jarveena with genuine astonishment. 'As well call a toad beautiful, or a mud wall!'

'As you like,' Enas Yorl answered with a shrug. The movement revealed that he was no longer quite what he had been earlier. 'At all events, there is a second reason.'

46

'What?'

'You read the writing on the scroll, and previously I had described it to you. Nonetheless you're acting as though you have forgotten something.'

For a brief moment she failed to take his point. Then her hand flew to her open mouth.

'Two deaths,' she whispered.

'Yes, indeed. And I scarcely need to tell you to whom a traitor in the imperial court would apply for a spell powerful enough to drag me into the matter willy-nilly. I could make the paper legible. I could not evade the consequences of undoing a colleague's work.'

'Whose death? *Mine?*'

'It would be politic to minimize the danger, as for instance by taking employment with a seafarer. Many merchant-captains would be glad of a skilful clerk, and after your apprenticeship with Melilot you're well equipped for such a post. Moreover, your present master is inclined to jealousy. You are half his age, yet already he regards you as a rival.'

'He dissembles well,' muttered Jarveena, 'but now and then he's acted in a fashion that makes me believe you.'

'He might regard you more kindly were you to become a sort of foreign agent for him. I'm sure you could contrive – for a reasonable fee – to supply him with commercially valuable information. He would scarcely object to adding other strings to his bow: trading in spices, for instance.'

For a while Jarveena had seemed enlivened by his discourse. Now she fell back into gloom.

'Why should I want to make myself rich, let alone him? Ever since I can remember I've had a purpose in life. It's gone – carried to the sky with the stench of Nizharu!'

'It takes a very rich person to commission a spell.'

'What would I want with magic?' she said contemptuously.

A second later, and it was as though fire coursed all over her body, outlining every mark that defaced her, every whiplash, every burn, every cut and scratch. She had forgotten until now, but sometime during that extraordinary night when she had lain with him, he had taken the trouble to trace her whole violent life-story from the map of her skin.

Now she also remembered thinking that it must be for some private magical reason. Could she have been wrong? Could it have been simpler than that – could it just have been that he sympathized with one whom life had scarred in another way?

'You might wish,' he was saying calmly, 'to cleanse your body of the past as I think you have now begun to cleanse your mind.'

'Even . . .?' She could not complete the question save by raising her hand to the right side of her chest.

'In time. You are young. Nothing is impossible. But one thing is much too possible. We've spoken of it. Now, act!'

They were almost at the gate, and the crowd was pressing and jostling; people were setting their hands to their money-belts and pouches, for these were prime conditions for theft.

'I take it you'd not have spoken up unless you had a new employer in mind for me?' Jarveena said at length.

'You're most perceptive.'

'And if there were not some long-term advantage in it for yourself?'

Enas Yorl sighed. 'There is a long-term purpose to everything. If there were not, spells would be impossible.'

'So there was a purpose behind Nizharu's dropping of the scroll?'

'Dropping . . . ?'

'Oh! Why didn't I think of that?'

'In time, I'm sure you would have done. But you came to Sanctuary so recently, you could scarcely be expected to know that in his boyhood Aye-Gophlan was counted among the smartest dips and cutpurses in the city. How else do you think he managed to buy himself a commission in the guards? Does he talk as though he came from a wealthy background?'

They were at the gate, and being squeezed through. Clutching her writing-case tightly with one hand, keeping the other folded over the silver pin which fastened her cloak in a roll around her waist, Jarveena thought long and long.

And came to a decision.

Even though her main purpose in life up to now had vanished there was no reason why she should not find another and maybe better ambition. If that were so, there were good reasons to try and prolong her life by quitting Sanctuary.

Although . . .

She glanced around in alarm for the magician, thinking them separated in the throng, and with relief was able to catch him by the arm.

'Will distance make any difference? I mean, if the doom is on me, can I flee from it?'

'Oh, it's not on you. It's merely that there were two deaths in the charm, and only one has happened. Any day of any year, scores of hundreds die in any city of this size. It's probable that the spell will work itself out locally; when there's a thunderstorm, the lightning strikes beneath it, not a hundred leagues away. Not inconceivably the other death may be that of someone who was as guilty as Nizharu in the sack of Forgotten Holt. He had soldiers with him, did he not?'

'Yes, they were all soldiers, whom I long mistook for bandits . . . ! Oh, what a pass this land has come to! You're quite right! I'm going away, as far as I can, whether or not it means I can outrun my death!'

She caught his hand, gave it a squeeze, and leaned close. 'Name the ship that I must look for!'

The day the ship sailed it was unsafe for Enas Yorl to venture on the street; occasionally the changes working in him cycled into forms that nobody, not with the kindest will in the world, could mistake for human. He was therefore obliged to watch the tiring way, making use of a scrying-glass, but he was determined to make certain that nothing had gone wrong with his scheme.

All turned out well. He tracked the ship, with Jarveena at her stern, until sea-mists obscured her, and then leaned back in what, for the time being, could not exactly be a chair as most people thought of chairs.

'And with you no longer around to attract it,' he murmured to the air, 'perhaps luck may lead that second death-sentence to be passed on one who wearies beyond measure of mad existence, sport of a hundred mindless spells, this miserable, this pitiable Enas Yorl.'

Yet some hope glimmered, like the red pits he had to wear for eyes, in the knowledge that at least one person in the world thought more kindly of him than he did himself. At length, with a snorting laugh, he covered the scrying-glass and settled down resignedly to wait out the implacable transformation, a little comforted by knowing that so far he had never been the same shape twice.

THE FACE OF CHAOS

Lynn Abbey

The cards lay face down in a wide crescent on the black-velvet-covered table Illyra used for her fortune-telling. Closing her eyes, she touched one at random with her index finger, then overturned it. The face of Chaos, portrait of man and woman seen in a broken mirror. She had done a card-reading for herself; an attempt to penetrate the atmosphere of foreboding that had hung over the ramshackle cloth-and-wood structure she and Dubro, the bazaar smith, called home. Instead it had only brought more anxiety.

She went to another small table to apply a thick coating of kohl to her eyelids. No one would visit a young, pretty S'danzo to have their fortune told, and no stranger could enter her home for any other reason. The kohl and the formless S'danzo costume concealed her age in the dimly lit room, but if some love-deluded soldier or merchant moved too close, there was always Dubro under the canopy a few steps away. One sight of the brawny, sweating giant with his heavy mallet ended any crisis.

'Sweetmeats! Sweetmeats! Always the best in the bazaar. Always the best in Sanctuary!'

The voice of Haakon, the vendor, reached through the cloth-hung doorway. Illyra finished her toilette quickly. Dark masses of curly hair were secured with one pin under a purple silk scarf which contrasted garishly with each of the skirts, the shawl, and the blouse she wore. She reached deep within those skirts for her purse and removed a copper coin.

It was still early enough in the day that she might venture outside their home. Everyone in the bazaar knew she was scarce more than a girl, and there would be no city-folk wandering about for another hour, at least.

'Haakon! Over here!' She called from under the canopy where Dubro kept his tools. 'Two ... no, three, please.'

He lifted three of the sticky treats on to a shell that she held out for them, accepting her copper coin with a smile. In an hour's time, Haakon would want five of the same coin for such a purchase, but the bazaar-folk sold the best to each other for less.

She ate one, but offered the other two to Dubro. She would have kissed him, but the smith shrank back from public affection, preferring privacy for all things which pass between a man and woman. He smiled and accepted them wordlessly. The big man seldom spoke; words came slowly to him. He mended the metal wares of the bazaar-folk, improving many as he did so. He had protected Illyra since she'd been an orphaned child wandering the stalls, turned out by her own people for the irredeemable crime of being a half-caste. Bright-eyed, quick-tongued Illyra spoke for him now whenever anything needed to be said, and in turn, he still took care of her.

The sweetmeats gone, Dubro returned to the fire, lifting up a barrel hoop he had left there to heat. Illyra watched with never-sated interest as he laid it on the anvil to pound it back into a true circle for Jofan, the wine-seller. The mallet fell, but instead of the clear, ringing sound of metal on metal, there was a hollow clang. The horn of the anvil fell into the dirt.

Even Haakon was wide-eyed with silent surprise. Dubro's anvil had been in the bazaar since ... since Dubro's grandfather for certain, and perhaps longer – no one could remember before that. The smith's face darkened to the colour of the cooling iron. Illyra placed her hands over his.

'We'll get it fixed. We'll take it up to the Court of Arms this afternoon. I'll borrow Moonflower's ass-and-cart ...'

'No!' Dubro exploded with one tortured word, shook loose her hands, and stared at the broken piece of his livelihood.

'Can't fix an anvil that's broken like that one,' Haakon explained softly to her. 'It'll only be as strong as the seam.'

'Then we'll get a new one,' she responded, mindful of Dubro's bleak face and her own certain knowledge that no one else in the bazaar possessed an anvil to sell.

'There hasn't been a new anvil in Sanctuary since before Ranke closed down the sea-trade with Ilsig. You'd need four camels and a year to get a mountain-cast anvil like that one into the bazaar – if you had the gold.'

A single tear smeared through the kohl. She and Dubro were well off by the standards of the bazaar. They had ample copper coins for Haakon's sweetmeats and fresh fish three times a week, but a pitifully small hoard of gold with which to convince the caravan merchants to bring an anvil from distant Ranke.

'We've got to have an anvil!' She exclaimed to the unlistening gods, since Dubro and Haakon were already aware of the problem.

Dubro kicked dirt over his fire and strode away from the small forge.

'Watch him for me, Haakon. He's never been like this.'

'I'll watch him – but it will be your problem tonight when he comes home.'

A few of the city-folk were already milling in the aisles of the bazaar; it was high time to hide in her room. Never before in her five years of working the S'danzo trade within the bazaar had she faced a day when Dubro did not lend his calm presence to the stream of patrons. He controlled their coming and going. Without him, she did not know who was waiting, or how to discourage a patron who had questions – but no money. She sat in the incense-heavy darkness waiting and brooding.

Moonflower. She would go to Moonflower, not for the old woman's broken-down cart, but for advice. The old woman had never shunned her the way the other S'danzo had. But Moonflower wouldn't know about fixing anvils, and what could she add to the message so clearly conveyed by the Face of Chaos? Besides, Moonflower's richest patrons arrived early in the day to catch her best 'vibrations'. The old woman would not appreciate a poor relation taking up her patrons' valuable time.

No patrons of her own yet, either. Perhaps the weather had turned bad. Perhaps, seeing the forge empty, they assumed that the inner chamber was empty also. Illyra dared not step outside to find out.

She shuffled and handled the deck of fortune-telling cards,

acquiring a measure of self-control from their worn surfaces. Palming the bottom card, Illyra laid it face-up on the black velvet.

'Five of Ships,' she whispered.

The card was a stylized scene of five small fishing boats, each with its net cast into the water. Tradition said that the answer to her question was in the card. Her gift would let her find it – if she could sort out the many questions floating in her thoughts.

'Illyra, the fortune-teller?'

Illyra's reverie was interrupted by her first patron before she had gained a satisfactory focus in the card. This first woman had problems with her many lovers, but her reading was spoiled by another patron stepping through the door at the wrong time. This second patron's reading was disrupted by the fish-smoker looking for Dubro. The day was everything the Face of Chaos had promised.

The few readings which were not disrupted reflected her own despair more than the patron's. Dubro had not returned, and she was startled by any sound from the outside canopy. Her patrons sensed the confusion and were unsatisfied with her performance. Some refused to pay. An older, more experienced S'danzo would know how to handle these things, but Illyra only shrank back in frustration. She tied a frayed rope across the entrance to her fortune-telling room to discourage anyone from seeking her advice.

'Madame Illyra?'

An unfamiliar woman's voice called from outside, undaunted by the rope.

'I'm not seeing anyone this afternoon. Come back tomorrow.'

'I can't wait until tomorrow.'

They all say that, Illyra thought. Everyone else always knows that they are the most important person I see and that their questions are the most complex. But they are all very much the same. Let the woman come back.

The stranger could be heard hesitating beyond the rope. Illyra heard the sound of rustling cloth – possibly silk – as the woman finally turned away. The sound jarred the S'danzo to alertness. Silken skirts meant wealth. A flash of vision illuminated Illyra's mind – this was a patron she could not let go elsewhere.

'If you can't wait, I'll see you now,' she yelled.

'You will?'

Illyra untied the rope and lifted the hanging cloth to let the woman enter. She had surrounded herself with a shapeless, plain shawl; her face was veiled and shadowed by a corner of the shawl wound around her head. The stranger was certainly not someone who came to the S'danzo of the bazaar often. Illyra retied the rope after seating her patron on one side of the velvet-covered table.

A woman of means who wishes to be mysterious. That shawl might be plain, but it is too good for someone as poor as she pretends to be. She wears silk beneath it, and smells of roses, though she has tried to remove perfumes. No doubt she has gold, not silver or copper.

'Would you not be more comfortable removing your shawl? It is quite warm in here,' Illyra said, after studying the woman.

'I'd prefer not to.'

A difficult one, Illyra thought.

The woman's hand emerged from the shawl to drop three old Ilsig gold coins on to the velvet. The hand was white, smooth, and youthful. The Ilsig coins were rare now that the Rankan empire controlled Sanctuary. The woman and her questions were a welcome relief from Illyra's own thoughts.

'Well, then, what is your name?'

'I'd prefer not to say.'

'I must have some information if I'm to help you,' Illyra said as she scooped the coins into a worn piece of silk, taking care not to let her fingers touch the gold.

'My ser ... There are those who tell me that you alone of the S'danzo can see the near future. I must know what will happen to me tomorrow night.'

The question did not fulfil Illyra's curiosity or the promise of mystery, but she reached for her deck of cards.

'You are familiar with these?' she asked the woman.

'Somewhat.'

'Then divide them into three piles and choose one card from each pile – that will show me your future.'

'For tomorrow night?'

'Assuredly. The answer is contained within the moment of the question. Take the cards.'

The veiled woman handled the cards fearfully. Her hands shook so badly that the three piles were simply unsquared heaps. The woman was visibly reluctant to touch the cards again and gingerly overturned the top card of each rather than handle them again.

Lance of Flames.

The Archway.

Five of Ships, reversed.

Illyra drew her hands back from the velvet in alarm. The Five of Ships – the card had been in her own hands not moments before. She did not remember replacing it in the deck. With a quivering foreknowledge that she would see a part of her own fate in the cards, Illyra opened her mind to receive the answer. And closed it almost at once.

Falling stones, curses, murder, a journey without return. None of the cards was particularly auspicious, but together they created an image of malice and death that was normally hidden from the living. The S'danzo never foretold death when they saw it, and though she was but half-S'danzo and shunned by them, Illyra abided by their codes and superstitions.

'It would be best to remain at home, especially tomorrow night. Stand back from walls which might have loose stones in them. Safety lies within yourself. Do not seek other advice – especially from the priests of the temples.'

Her visitor's reserve crumbled. She gasped, sobbed, and shook with unmistakable terror. But before Illyra could speak the words to calm her, the black-clad woman dashed away, pulling the frayed rope from its anchorage.

'Come back!' Illyra called.

The woman turned while still under the canopy. Her shawl fell back to reveal a fair-skinned blonde woman of a youthful and delicate beauty. A victim of a spurned lover? Or a jealous wife?

'If you had already seen your fate – then you should have asked a different question, such as whether it can be changed,' she chided softly, guiding the woman back into the incense-filled chamber.

56

'I thought if you saw differently . . . But Molin Torchholder will have his way. Even you have seen it.'

Molin Torchholder. Illyra recognized the name. He was the priestly temple-builder within the Rankan prince's entourage. She had another friend and patron living within his household. Was this the woman of Cappen Varra's idylls? Had the minstrel finally overstepped himself?

'Why would the Rankan have his way with you?' she asked, prying gently.

'They have sought to build a temple for their gods.'

'But you are not a goddess, nor even Rankan. Such things should not concern you.'

Illyra spoke lightly, but she knew, from the cards, that the priests sought her as part of some ritual – not in personal interest.

'My father is rich – proud and powerful among those of Sanctuary who have never accepted the fall of the Ilsig kingdom and will never accept the empire. Molin has singled my father out. He has demanded our lands for his temple. When we refused, he forced the weaker men not to trade with us. But my father would not give in. He believes the gods of Ilsig are stronger, but Molin has vowed revenge rather than admit failure.'

'Perhaps your family will have to leave Sanctuary to escape this foreign priest, and your home be torn down to build their temple. But though the city may be all you know, the world is large, and this place but a poor part of it.'

Illyra spoke with far more authority than she actually commanded. Since the death of her mother, she had left the bazaar itself only a handful of times and had never left the city. The words were part of the S'danzo oratory Moonflower had taught her.

'My father and the others must leave, but not me. I'm to be part of Molin Torchholder's revenge. His men came once to my father's house. The Rankan offered us my full bride-price, though he is married. Father refused the "honour". Molin's men beat him senseless and carried me screaming from the house.

'I fought with him when he came to me that night. He will not want another woman for some time. But my father could not believe I had not been dishonoured. And Molin said that if I would not yield to him, then no living man should have me.'

'Such are ever the words of scorned men,' Illyra added gently.

'No. It was a curse. *I* know this for certain. Their gods are strong enough to answer when they call.

'Last night two of their Hell Hounds appeared at our estate to offer new terms to my father. A fair price for our land, safe conduct to Ilsig – but I am to remain behind. Tomorrow night they will consecrate the cornerstone of their new temple with a virgin's death. I am to be under that stone when they lay it.'

Though Illyra was not specifically a truth-seer, the tale tied all the horrific visions into a whole. It would take the gods to save this woman from the fate Molin Torchholder had waiting for her. It was no secret that the empire sought to conquer the Ilsig gods as they had conquered their armies. If the Rankan priest could curse a woman with unbreachable virginity, Illyra didn't think there was much she could do.

The woman was still sobbing. There was no future in her patronage, but Illyra felt sorry for her. She opened a little cabinet and shook a good-sized pinch of white powder into a small liquid-filled vial.

'Tonight, before you retire, take this with a glass of wine.'

The woman clutched it tightly, though the fear did fade from her eyes.

'Do I owe you more for this?' she asked.

'No, it is the least I could do for you.'

There was enough of the cylantha powder to keep the woman asleep for three days. Perhaps Molin Torchholder would not want a sleeping virgin in his rite. If he did not mind, the woman would not awaken to find out.

'I can give you much gold. I could bring you to Ilsig.'

Illyra shook her head.

'There is but one thing I wish – and you do not have it,' she whispered, surprised by the sudden impulsiveness of her words. 'Nor all the gold in Sanctuary will find another anvil for Dubro.'

'I do not know this Dubro, but there is an anvil in my father's stables. It will not return to Ilsig. It can be yours, if I'm alive to tell my father to give it to you.'

58

The impulsiveness cleared from Illyra's mind. There were reasons now to soothe the young woman's fears.

'It is a generous offer,' she replied. 'I shall see you then, three days hence at your father's home – if you will tell me where it is.'

And if you do, she added to herself, then it will not matter if you survive or not.

'It is the estate called "Land's End", behind the temple of Ils, Himself.'

'Whom shall I ask for?'

'Marilla.'

They stared at each other for a few moments, then the blonde woman made her way into the afternoon-crowded bazaar. Illyra knotted the rope across the entrance to her chambers with distracted intensity.

How many years – five at least – she had been answering the banal questions of city-folk who could not see anything for themselves. Never, in all that time, had she asked a question of a patron, or seen such a death, or one of her own cards in a reading. And in all the years of memory within the S'danzo community within the bazaar, never had any of them crossed fates with the gods.

No, I have nothing to do with gods. I do not notice them, and they do not see me. My gift is S'danzo. I am S'danzo. We live by fate. We do not touch the affairs of gods.

But Illyra could not convince herself. The thought circled in her mind that she had wandered beyond the realms of her people and gifts. She lit the incense of gentle-forgetting, inhaling it deeply, but the sound of Dubro's anvil breaking and the images of the three cards remained ungentle in her thoughts. As the afternoon waned, she convinced herself again to approach Moonflower for advice.

The obese S'danzo woman's three children squalled at each other in the dust while her dark-eyed husband sat in the shade holding his hands over his eyes and ears. It was not an auspicious moment to seek the older woman's counsel. The throngs of people were leaving the bazaar, making it safe for Illyra to wander among the stalls looking for Dubro.

'Illyra!'

She had expected Dubro's voice, but this one was familiar also. She looked closely into the crowd at the wine-seller's.

'Cappen Varra?'

'The same.' He answered, greeting her with a smile. 'There was a rope across your gate today, and Dubro was not busy at his fire – otherwise I should have stopped to see you.'

'You have a question?'

'No, my life could not be better. I have a song for you.'

'Today is not a day for songs. Have you seen Dubro?'

'No. I'm here to get wine for a special dinner tomorrow night. Thanks to you, I know where the best wine in Sanctuary is still to be found.'

'A new love?'

'The same. She grows more radiant with each day. Tomorrow the master of the house will be busy with his priestly functions. The household will be quiet.'

'The household of Molin Torchholder must agree with you then. It is good to be in the grace of the conquerors of Ilsig.'

'I'm discreet. So is Molin. It is a trait which seems to have been lost among the natives of Sanctuary – S'danzo excepted, of course. I'm most comfortable within his house.'

The seller handed him two freshly washed bottles of wine, and with brief farewells, Illyra saw him on his way. The wine-seller had seen Dubro earlier in the day. He offered that the smith was visiting every wine-seller in the bazaar and not a few of the taverns outside it. Similar stories waited for her at the other wine-sellers. She returned to the forge-home in the gathering twilight and fog.

Ten candles and the oil stove could not cut through the dark emptiness in the chamber. Illyra pulled her shawls tightly around her and tried to nap until Dubro returned. She would not let herself think that he would not return.

'You have been waiting for me.'

Illyra jumped at the sound. Only two of the candles remained lit; she had no idea how long she had slept, only that her home quivered with shadows and a man, as tall as Dubro but of cadaverous thinness, stood within the knotted rope.

'Who are you? What do you want?' She flattened against the back of the chair.

'Since you do not recognize me, then say, I have been looking for you.'

The man gestured. The candles and stove rekindled and Illyra found herself staring at the blue-starred face of the magician Lythande.

'I have done nothing to cross you,' she said, rising slowly from her chair.

'And I did not say that you had. I thought you were seeking me. Many of us have heard you calling today.'

He held up the three cards Marilla had overturned and the Face of Chaos.

'I – I had not known my problems could disturb your studies.'

'I was reflecting on the legend of the Five Ships – it was comparatively easy for you to touch me. I have taken it to myself to learn things for you.

'The girl Marilla appealed first to her own gods. They sent her to you since for them to act on her fate would rouse the ire of Sabellia and Savankala. They have tied your fates together. You will not solve your own troubles unless you can relieve hers.'

'She is a dead woman, Lythande. If the gods of Ilsig wish to help her, they will need all their strength – and if that isn't enough, then there is nothing I can do for her.'

'That is not a wise position to take, Illyra,' the magician said with a smile.

'That is what I *saw*. S'danzo do not cross fates with the gods.'

'And you, Illyra, are not S'danzo.'

She gripped the back of the chair, angered by the reminder but unable to counter it.

'They have passed the obligation to you,' he said.

'I do not know how to break through Marilla's fate,' Illyra said simply. 'I *see*, they must *change*.'

Lythande laughed. 'Perhaps there *is* no way, child. Maybe it will take two sacrifices to consecrate the temple Molin Torchholder builds. *You* had best hope there is a way through Marilla's fate.'

A cold breeze accompanied his laughter. The candles flickered a moment, and the magician was gone. Illyra stared at the undisturbed rope.

Let Lythande and the others help her if it's so important. I want only the anvil, and that I can have regardless of her fate.

The cold air clung to the room. Already her imagination was embroidering upon the consequences of enraging any of the powerful deities of Sanctuary. She left to search for Dubro in the fog-shrouded bazaar.

Fog tendrils obscured the familiar stalls and shacks of the day-time bazaar. A few fires could be glimpsed through cracked door-ways, but the area itself had gone to sleep early, leaving Illyra to roam through the moist night alone.

Nearing the main entrance she saw the bobbing torch of a running man. The torch and runner fell with an aborted shout. She heard lighter footsteps running off into the unlit fog. Cautiously, fearfully, Illyra crept towards the fallen man.

It was not Dubro, but a shorter man wearing a blue hawk-mask. A dagger protruded from the side of his neck. Illyra felt no sorrow at the death of one of Jubal's bully-boys, only relief that it had not been Dubro. Jubal was worse than the Rankans. Perhaps the crimes of the man behind the mask had finally caught up with him. More likely someone had risked venting a grudge against the seldom-seen former gladiator. Anyone who dealt with Jubal had more enemies than friends.

As if in silent response to her thoughts, another group of men appeared out of the fog. Illyra hid among the crates and boxes while five men without masks studied the dead man. Then, without warning, one of them threw aside his torch and fell on the warm corpse, striking it again and again with his knife. When he had had his fill of death, the others took their turns.

The bloody hawk-mask rolled to within a hand-span of Illyra's foot. She held her breath and did not move, her eyes riveted in horror on the unrecognizable body in front of her. She wandered away from the scene blind to everything but her own disbelieving shock. The atrocity seemed to be the final, senseless gesture of the Face of Chaos in a day which had unravelled her existence.

She leaned against a canopy-post fighting waves of nausea, but Haakon's sweetmeats had been the only food she had eaten all day. The dry heaving of her stomach brought no relief.

'Lyra!'

A familiar voice roared behind her and an arm thrown protectively around her shoulder broke the spell. She clung to Dubro with clenched fingers, burying her convulsive sobs in his leather vest. He reeked of wine and the salty fog. She savoured every breath of him.

'Lyra, what are you doing out here?' He paused, but she did not reply. 'Did you begin to think I'd not come back to you?'

He held her tightly, swaying restlessly back and forth. The story of the hawk-masked man's death fell from her in racked gasps. It took Dubro only a moment to decide that his beloved Illyra had suffered too much in his absence and to repent that he had gotten drunk or sought work outside the bazaar. He lifted her gently and carried her back to their home, muttering softly to himself as he walked.

Not even Dubro's comforting arms could protect Illyra from the nightmare visions that stalked her sleep once they had returned to their home. He shook off his drunkenness to watch over her as she tossed and fretted on the sleeping linens. Each time he thought she had settled into a calm sleep, the dreams would start again. Illyra would awaken sweating and incoherent from fear. She would not describe her dreams to him when he asked. He began to suspect that something worse than the murder had taken place in his absence, though their home showed no sign of attack or struggle.

Illyra did try to voice her fears to him at each waking interlude, but the mixture of visions and emotions found no expression in her voice. Within her mind, each re-dreaming of the nightmare brought her closer to a single image which both collected her problems and eliminated them. The first rays of a feeble dawn had broken through the fog when she had the final synthetic experience of the dream.

She saw herself at a place the dream-spirit said was the estate called Land's End. The estate had been long abandoned, with only an anvil chained to a pedestal in the centre of a starlit courtyard to show that it had been inhabited. Illyra broke the chain easily and lifted the anvil as if it had been paper. Clouds rushed in as she walked away and a moaning wind began to blow dust-devils around her. She hurried towards the doorway where Dubro waited for his gift.

The steel cracked before she had travelled half the distance, and the anvil crumbled completely as she transferred it to him. Rain began to fall, washing away Dubro's face to reveal Lythande's cruel, mocking smile. The magician struck her with the card marked with the Face of Chaos. And she died, only to find herself captive within her body which was being carried by unseen hands to a vast pit. The dissonant music of priestly chants and cymbals surrounded her. Within the dream, Illyra opened her dead eyes to see a large block of stone descending into the pit over her.

'I'm already dead!' She screamed, struggling to free her arms and legs from invisible bindings. 'I can't be sacrificed – I'm already dead!'

Her arms came free. She flailed wildly. The walls of the pit were glassy and without hand-holds. The lowered stone touched her head. She shrieked as the life left her body for a second time. Her body released her spirit, and she rose up through the stone, waking as she did.

'It was a dream,' Illyra said before Dubro could ask.

The solution was safe in her mind now. The dream would not return. But it was like a reading with the cards. In order to understand what the dream-spirit had given her, she would have to meditate upon it.

'You said something of death and sacrifice,' Dubro said, unmollified by her suddenly calmed face.

'It was a dream.'

'What sort of dream? Are you afraid that I will leave you or the bazaar now that I have no work to do?'

'No,' she said quickly, masking the fresh anxiety his words produced. 'Besides, I have found an anvil for us.'

'In your dream with the death and sacrifice?'

'Death and sacrifice are keys the dream-spirit gave me. Now I must take the time to understand them.'

Dubro stepped back from her. He was not S'danzo, and though bazaar-folk, he was not comfortable around their traditions or their gifts. When Illyra spoke of 'seeing' or 'knowing', he would draw away from her. He sat, quiet and sullen, in a chair pulled into the corner most distant from her S'danzo paraphernalia.

She stared at the black-velvet covering of her table until well past the dawn and the start of a gentle rain. Dubro placed a shell with a sweetmeat in it before her. She nodded, smiled, and ate it, but did not say anything. The smith had already turned away two patrons when Illyra finished her meditation.

'Are you finished, now, Lyra?' he asked, his distrust of S'danzo ways not overshadowing his concern for her.

'I think so.'

'No more death and sacrifice?'

She nodded and began to relate the tale of the previous day's events. Dubro listened quietly until she reached the part about Lythande.

'In my home? Within these walls?' he demanded.

'I saw him, but I don't know how he got in here. The rope was untouched.'

'No!' Dubro exclaimed, beginning to pace like a caged animal. 'No, I want none of this. I will not have magicians and sorcerors in my home!'

'You weren't here, and I did not invite him in.' Illyra's dark eyes flashed at him as she spoke. 'And he'll come back again if I don't do these things, so hear me out.'

'No, just tell me what we must do to keep him away.'

Illyra dug her fingernails into the palm of one hand hidden in the folds of her skirts.

'We will have to – to stop the consecration of the cornerstone of the new temple for the Rankan gods.'

'"Gods", Lyra, you would not meddle with the gods? Is this the meaning you found in "death and sacrifice"?'

'It is also the reason Lythande was here last night.'

'But, Lyra . . .'

She shook her head, and he was quiet.

'He won't ask me what I plan to do', she thought as he tied the rope across the door and followed her towards the city. 'As long as everything is in my head, I'm certain everything is possible and that I will succeed. But if I spoke of it to anyone – even him – I would hear how little hope I have of stopping Molin Torchholder or of changing Marilla's fate.'

In the dream, her already dead body had been offered to

Sabellia and Savankala. Her morning's introspection had convinced her that she was to introduce a corpse into Molin Torchholder's ceremonies. They passed the scene of the murder, but Jubal's men had reclaimed their comrade. The only other source of dead men she knew of was the governor's palace where executions were becoming a daily occurrence under the tightening grip of the Hell Hounds.

They passed by the huge charnel-house just beyond the bazaar gates. The rain held the death smells close by the half-timbered building. Could Sabellia and Savankala be appeased with the mangled bones and fat of a butchered cow? Hesitantly she mounted the raised wooden walk over the red-brown effluvia of the building.

'What do the Rankan gods want from this place?' Dubro asked before setting foot on the walkway.

'A substitute for the one already chosen.'

A man emerged from a side door pushing a sloshing barrel which he dumped into the slow-moving stream. Shapeless red lumps flowed under the walkway between the two bazaar-folk. Illyra swayed on her feet.

'Even the gods of Ranke would not be fooled by these.' Dubro lowered his head towards the now-ebbing stream. 'At least offer them the death of an honest man of Ilsig.'

He held out a hand to steady her as she stepped back on the street, then led the way past the Serpentine to the governor's palace. Three men hung limply from the gallows in the rain, their crimes and names inscribed on placards tied around their necks. Neither Illyra nor Dubro had mastered the arcane mysteries of script.

'Which one is most like the one you need?' Dubro asked.

'She should be my size, but blonde.' Illyra explained while looking at the two strapping men and one grandfatherly figure hanging in front of them.

Dubro shrugged and approached the stern-faced Hell Hound standing guard at the foot of the gallows.

'Father,' he grunted, pointing at the elderly corpse.

'It's the law – to be hung by the neck until sundown. You'll have to come back then.'

'Long walk home. He's dead now – why wait?'

'There is *law* in Sanctuary now, peon, Rankan law. It will be respected without exception.'

Dubro stared at the ground, fumbling with his hands in evident distress.

'In the rain I cannot see the sun – how shall I know when to return?'

Guard and smith stared at the steely-grey sky, both knowing it would not clear before nightfall. Then, with a loud sigh, the Hell Hound walked to the ropes, selected and untied one, which dropped Dubro's 'father' into the mud.

'Take him and begone!'

Dubro shouldered the dead man, walking to Illyra who waited at the edge of the execution grounds.

'He's – he's –' she gasped in growing hysteria.

'Dead since sunrise.'

'He's covered with filth. He reeks. His face ...'

'You wanted another for the sacrifice.'

'But not like that!'

'It is the way of men who have been hung.'

They walked back towards the charnel-house where Sanctuary's undertakers and embalmers held sway. There, for five copper coins, they found a man to prepare the body. For another coin he would have rented them a cart and his son as a digger to take the unfortunate ex-thief to the common field outside the Gate of Triumph for proper burial. Illyra and Dubro made a great show of grief, however, and insisted that they would bury their father with their own hands. Wrapped in a nearly clean shroud, the old man was bound to a plank. Illyra held the foot-end, Dubro the other. They made their way back to the bazaar.

'Do we take the body to the temple for the exchange?' he asked as they pushed aside their chairs to make room for the plank.

Illyra stared at him, not realizing at first that his faith in her had made the question sincere.

'During the night the Rankan priests will leave the governor's palace for the estate called Land's End. They will bear Marilla with them. We will have to stop them and replace Marilla with our corpse, without their knowledge.'

The smith's eyes widened with disillusion. 'Lyra, it is not the same as stealing fruit from Blind Jakob! The girl will be alive. He is dead. Surely the priests will see.'

She shook her head clinging desperately to the image she had found in meditation. 'It rains. There will be no moonlight, and their torches will give more smoke than light. I gave the girl cylantha. They will have to carry her as if she were dead.'

'Will she take the drug?'

'Yes!'

But Illyra wasn't sure – couldn't be sure – until they actually saw the procession. So many questions: if Marilla had taken the drug, if the procession were small, unguarded and slowed by their burden, if the ritual were like the one in her dream. The cold panic she had felt as the stone descended on her returned. The Face of Chaos loomed, laughing, in her mind's eye.

'Yes! She took the drug last night,' she said firmly, dispelling the Face by force of will.

'How do you know this?' Dubro asked incredulously.

'I *know*.'

There was no more discussion as Illyra threw herself into the preparation of a macabre feast that they ate on a table spread over their dead guest. The vague point of sundown passed, leaving Sanctuary in a dark rainy night, as Illyra had foreseen. The continuing rain bolstered her confidence as they moved slowly through the bazaar and out of the Common Gate.

They faced a long, but not difficult, walk beyond the walls of the city. As Dubro pointed out, the demoiselles of the Street of Red Lanterns had to follow their path each night on their way to the Promise of Heaven. The ladies giggled behind their shawls at the sight of the two bearing what was so obviously a corpse. But they did nothing to hinder them, and it was far too early for the more raucous traffic returning from the Promise.

Huge piles of stone in a sea of muddy craters marked the site of the new temple. A water-laden canopy covered sputtering braziers and torches; otherwise the area was quiet and deserted.

It is the night of the Ten-Slaying. Cappen Varra told me the priests would be busy. Rain will not stop the dedication. Gods do not feel rain! Illyra thought, but again did not *know* and sat with her back to Dubro quivering more from doubt and fear than from the cold water dripping down her back.

While she sat, the rain slowed to a misty drizzle and gave promise of stopping altogether. She left the inadequate shelter of the rock pile to venture nearer the canopy and braziers. A platform had been built above the mud at the edge of a pit with ropes dangling on one side that might be used to lower a body into the pit. A great stone was poised on logs opposite, ready to crush anything below. At least they were not too late – no sacrifice had taken place. Before Illyra had returned to Dubro's side, six torches appeared in the mist-obscured distance.

'They are coming,' Dubro whispered as she neared him.

'I see them. We have only a few moments now.'

From around her waist she unwound two coils of rope taken from the bazaar forge. She had devised her own plan for the actual exchange, as neither the dream-spirit nor her meditations had offered solid insight or inspiration.

'They will most likely follow the same path we did, since they are carrying a body also,' she explained as she laid the ropes across the mud, burying them slightly. 'We will trip them here.'

'And I will switch our corpse for the girl?'

'Yes.'

They said nothing more as each crouched in a mud-hole waiting, hoping, that the procession would pass between them.

The luck promised in her dream held. Molin Torchholder led the small procession, bearing a large brass and wood torch from Sabellia's temple in Ranke itself. Behind him were three chanting acolytes bearing both incense and torches. The last two torches were affixed to a bier carried on the shoulders of the last pair of priests. Torchholder and the other three trod over the ropes without noticing them. When the first pallbearer was between the ropes Illyra snapped them taut.

The burdened priests heard the smack as the ropes lifted from the mud, but were tripped before they could react. Marilla and the torches fell towards Dubro, the priests towards Illyra. In the dark commotion, Illyra got safely to a nearby pile of building stones, but without being able to see if Dubro had accomplished the exchange.

'What's wrong?' Torchholder demanded, hurrying back with his torch to light the scene.

'The damned workmen left the hauling ropes strewn about,' a mud-splattered priest exclaimed as he scrambled out of the knee-deep mud-hole.

'And the girl?' Molin continued.

'Thrown over there, from the look of it.'

Lifting his robes in one hand, Molin Torchholder led the acolytes and priests to the indicated mud-pit. Illyra heard sounds she prayed were Dubro making his own way to the safe shadows.

'A hand here.'

'Damned Ilsig mud. She weighs ten times as much now.'

'Easy. A little more mud, a little sooner won't affect the temple, but it's an ill thought to rouse the Others.' Torchholder's calm voice quieted the others.

The torches were re-lit. From her hideout, Illyra could see a mud-covered shroud on the bier. Dubro had succeeded somehow: she did not allow herself to think anything else.

The procession continued on towards the canopy. The rain had stopped completely. A sliver of moonlight showed through the dispersing clouds. Torchholder loudly hailed the break in the clouds as an omen of the forgiving, sanctifying, presence of Vashanka and began the ritual. In due time the acolytes emptied braziers of oil on to the shroud, setting it and the corpse on fire. They lowered the flaming bier into the pit. The acolytes threw symbolic armloads of stone after it. Then they cut the ropes that held the cornerstone in its place at the edge. It slid from sight with a loud, sucking sound.

Almost at once, Torchholder and the other two priests left the platform to head back towards the palace, leaving only the acolytes to perform a night-long vigil over the new grave. When the priests were out of sight Illyra scrambled back to the mud-holes and whispered Dubro's name.

'Here,' he hissed back.

She needed only one glance at his moon-shadowed face to know something had gone wrong.

70

'What happened?' she asked quickly, unmindful of the sound of her voice. 'Marilla? Did they bury Marilla?'

There were tears in Dubro's eyes as he shook his head. 'Look at her!' he said, his voice barely under control.

A mud-covered shroud lay some paces away. Dubro would neither face it nor venture near it. Illyra approached warily.

Dubro had left the face covered. Holding her breath, Illyra reached down to peel back the damp, dirty linen.

For a heartbeat, she saw Marilla's sleeping face. Then it became her own. After a second of self-recognition, the face underwent a bewildering series of changes to portraits of people from her childhood and others whom she did not recognize. It froze for a moment in the shattered image of the Face of Chaos, then was still with pearly-white skin where there should have been eyes, nose, and mouth.

Illyra's fingers stiffened. She opened her mouth to scream, but her lungs and throat were paralysed with fright. The linen fell from her unfeeling hands, but did not cover the hideous thing that lay before her.

Get away! Get away from this place!

The primitive imperative rose in her mind and would not be appeased by anything less than headlong flight. She pushed Dubro aside. The acolytes heard her as she blundered through the mud, but she ignored them. There were buildings ahead – solid stone buildings outlined in the moonlight.

It was a manor house of an estate long since abandoned. Illyra recognized it from her dream, but her panic and terror had been sated in the headlong run from the faceless corpse. An interior door hung open on rusty hinges that creaked when she pushed the door. She was unsurprised to see an anvil sitting on a plain wooden box in the centre of a courtyard that her instincts told her was not entirely deserted.

'I'm only prolonging it now. The anvil, and the rest; they are there for me.'

She stepped into the courtyard. Nothing happened. The anvil was solid and far too heavy for her to lift.

'You've come to collect your reward?' a voice called.

'Lythande?' she whispered, waiting for the cadaverous magician to appear.

'Lythande is elsewhere.'

A hooded man stepped into the moonlight.

'What has happened? Where is Marilla? Her family?'

The man gestured to his right. Illyra followed his movement and saw the tumbledown headstones of an old graveyard.

'But . . . ?'

'The priests of Ils seek to provoke the new gods. They created the homunculus, disguising it to appear as a young woman to an untrained observer. Had it been interred in the foundation of the new temple, it would have created a disruptive weakness. The anger of Savankala and Sabellia would reach across the desert. That is, of course, exactly what the priests of Ils wanted.

'We magicians – and even you gifted S'danzo – do not welcome the meddling feuds of gods and their priests. They tamper with the delicate balances of fate. Our work is more important than the appeasement of deities, so this time, as in the past, we have intervened.'

'But the temple? They should have buried a virgin, then?'

'A forged person would arouse the Rankan gods, but not an imperfect virgin. When the temple of Ils was erected, the old priests sought a royal soul to inter beneath the altar. They wanted the youngest, and most loved, of the royal princes. The queen was a sorceress of some skill herself. She disguised an old slave, and his bones still rest beneath the altar.'

'So the gods of Ilsig and Ranke are equal?'

The hooded man laughed. 'We have seen to it that all gods within Sanctuary are equally handicapped, my child.'

'And what of me? Lythande warned me not to fail.'

'Did I not just say that our purpose – and therefore your purpose – was accomplished? You did not fail, and we repay, as Marilla promised, with a black-steel anvil. It is yours.'

He laid a hand on the anvil and disappeared in a wisp of smoke.

'Lyra, are you all right? I heard you speaking with someone. I buried that girl before I came looking for you.'

'Here is the anvil.'

'I do not want such an ill-gotten thing.'

Dubro took her arm and tried to lead her out of the court-yard.

'I have paid too much already!' she shouted at him, wresting away from his grasp. 'Take it back to the bazaar – then we will forget all this ever happened. Never speak of it to anyone. But don't leave the anvil here, or it's all worth nothing!'

'I can never forget your face on that dead girl . . . thing.'

Illyra remained silently staring at the still-muddy ground. Dubro went to the anvil and brushed the water and dirt from its surface.

'Someone has carved a symbol in it. It reminds me of one of your cards. Tell me what it means before I take it back to the bazaar with us.'

She stood by his side. A smiling Face of Chaos had been freshly etched into the worn surface of the metal.

'It is an old S'danzo sign of good luck.'

Dubro did not seem to hear the note of bitterness and deceit in her voice. His faith in Illyra had been tried but not shattered. The anvil was heavy, an ungainly bundle in his arms.

'Well, it won't get home by itself, will it?' He stared at her as she started walking.

She touched the pedestal and thought briefly of the questions still whirling in her head. Dubro called again from outside the courtyard. The entire length of Sanctuary lay between them and the bazaar, and it was not yet midnight. Without glancing back, she followed him out of the courtyard.

THE GATE OF
THE FLYING KNIVES

Poul Anderson

Again penniless, houseless, and ladyless, Cappen Varra made a brave sight just the same as he wove his way amidst the bazaar throng. After all, until today he had for some weeks been in, if not quite of, the household of Molin Torchholder, as much as he could contrive. Besides the dear presence of ancilla Danlis, he had received generous reward from the priest-engineer whenever he sang a song or composed a poem. That situation had changed with suddenness and terror, but he still wore a bright green tunic, scarlet cloak, canary hose, soft half-boots trimmed in silver, and plumed beret. Though naturally heartsick at what had happened, full of dread for his darling, he saw no reason to sell the garb yet. He could raise enough money in various ways to live on while he searched for her. If need be, as often before, he could pawn the harp that a goldsmith was presently redecorating.

If his quest had not succeeded by the time he was reduced to rags, then he would have to suppose Danlis and the Lady Rosanda were forever lost. But he had never been one to grieve over future sorrows.

Beneath a westering sun, the bazaar surged and clamoured. Merchants, artisans, porters, servants, slaves, wives, nomads, courtesans, entertainers, beggars, thieves, gamblers, magicians, acolytes, soldiers, and who knew what else mingled, chattered, chaffered, quarrelled, plotted, sang, played games, drank, ate, and who knew what else. Horsemen, camel-drivers, waggoners pushed through, raising waves of curses. Music tinkled and tweedled from wine-shops. Vendors proclaimed the wonders of their wares from booths, neighbours shouted at each other, and devotees chanted from flat rooftops. Smells thickened the air, of flesh, sweat, roast meat and nuts, aromatic drinks, leather, wool, dung, smoke, oils, cheap perfume.

Ordinarily, Cappen Varra enjoyed this shabby-colourful spectacle. Now he single-mindedly hunted through it. He kept full awareness, of course, as everybody must in Sanctuary. When light fingers brushed him, he knew. But whereas aforetime he would have chuckled and told the pickpurse, 'I'm sorry, friend; I was hoping I might lift somewhat off *you*,' at this hour he clapped his sword in such forbidding wise that the fellow recoiled against a fat woman and made her drop a brass tray full of flowers. She screamed and started beating him over the head with it.

Cappen didn't stay to watch.

On the eastern edge of the market-place he found what he wanted. Once more Illyra was in the bad graces of her colleagues and had moved her trade to a stall available elsewhere. Black curtains framed it, against a mud-brick wall. Reek from a nearby tannery well-nigh drowned the incense she burned in a curious holder, and would surely overwhelm any of her herbs. She herself also lacked awesomeness, such as most seeresses, mages, conjurers, scryers, and the like affected. She was too young; she would have looked almost wistful in her flowing, gaudy S'danzo garments, had she not been so beautiful.

Cappen gave her a bow in the manner of Caronne. 'Good-day, Illyra the lovely,' he said.

She smiled from the cushion whereon she sat. 'Good-day to you, Cappen Varra.' They had had a number of talks, usually in jest, and he had sung for her entertainment. He had hankered to do more than that, but she seemed to keep all men at a certain distance, and a hulk of a blacksmith who evidently adored her saw to it that they respected her wish.

'Nobody in these parts has met you for a fair while,' she remarked. 'What fortune was great enough to make you forget old friends?'

'My fortune was mingled, inasmuch as it left me without time to come down here and behold you, my sweet,' he answered out of habit.

Lightness departed from Illyra. In the olive countenance, under the chestnut mane, large eyes focused hard on her visitor. 'You find time when you need help in disaster,' she said.

He had not patronized her before, or indeed any fortune-teller of thaumaturge in Sanctuary. In Caronne, where he grew up, most folk had no use for magic. In his later wanderings he had encountered sufficient strangeness to temper his native scepticism. As shaken as he already was, he felt a chill go along his spine. 'Do you read my fate without even casting a spell?'

She smiled afresh, but bleakly. 'Oh, no. It's simple reason. Word did filter back to the Maze that you were residing in the Jewellers' Quarter and a frequent guest at the mansion of Molin Torchholder. When you appear on the heels of a new word – that last night his wife was reaved from him – plain to see is that you've been affected yourself.'

He nodded. 'Yes, and sore afflicted. I have lost –' He hesitated, unsure whether it would be quite wise to say 'my love' to this girl whose charms he had rather extravagantly praised.

'– your position and income,' Illyra snapped. 'The high priest cannot be in any mood for minstrelsy. I'd guess his wife favoured you most, anyhow. I need not guess you spent your earnings as fast as they fell to you, or faster, were behind in your rent, and were accordingly kicked out of your choice apartment as soon as rumour reached the landlord. You've returned to the Maze because you've no place else to go, and to me in hopes you can wheedle me into giving you a clue – for if you're instrumental in recovering the lady, you'll likewise recover your fortune, and more.'

'No, no, no,' he protested. 'You wrong me.'

'The high priest will appeal only to his Rankan gods,' Illyra said, her tone changing from exasperated to thoughtful. She stroked her chin. 'He, kinsman of the Emperor, here to direct the building of a temple which will overtop that of Ils, can hardly beg aid from the old gods of Sanctuary, let alone from our wizards, witches, and seers. But you, who belong to no part of the empire, who drifted hither from a kingdom far in the West ... you may seek anywhere. The idea is your own; else he would furtively have slipped you some gold, and you have engaged a diviner with more reputation than is mine.'

Cappen spread his hands. 'You reason eerily well, dear lass,' he conceded. 'Only about the motives are you mistaken. Oh, yes, I'd be glad to stand high in Molin's esteem, be richly rewarded, and so forth. Yet I feel for him; beneath that sternness of his, he's not a bad sort, and he bleeds. Still more do I feel for his lady, who was indeed kind to me and who's been snatched away to an unknown place. But before all else –' He grew quite earnest. 'The Lady Rosanda was not seized by herself. Her ancilla has also vanished, Danlis. And – Danlis is she whom I love, Illyra, she whom I meant to wed.'

The maiden's look probed him further. She saw a young man of medium height, slender but tough and agile. (That was due to the life he had had to lead; by nature he was indolent, except in bed.) His features were thin and regular on a long skull, clean-shaven, eyes bright blue, black hair banged and falling to the shoulders. His voice gave the language a melodious accent, as if to bespeak white cities, green fields and woods, quicksilver lakes, blue sea, of the homeland he left in search of his fortune.

'Well, you have charm, Cappen Varra,' she murmured, 'and how you do know it.' Alert: 'But coin you lack. How do you propose to pay me?'

'I fear you must work on speculation, as I do myself,' he said. 'If our joint efforts lead to a rescue, why, then we'll share whatever material reward may come. Your part might buy you a home on the Path of Money.' She frowned. 'True,' he went on, 'I'll get more than my share of the immediate bounty that Molin bestows. I will have my beloved back. I'll also regain the priest's favour, which is moderately lucrative. Yet consider. You need but practise your art. Thereafter any effort and risk will be mine.'

'What makes you suppose a humble fortune-teller can learn more than the Prince-Governor's investigator guardsmen?' she demanded.

'The matter does not seem to lie within their jurisdiction,' he replied.

She leaned forward, tense beneath the layers of clothing. Cappen bent towards her. It was as if the babble of the market-place receded, leaving these two alone with their wariness.

'I was not there,' he said low, 'but I arrived early this morning after the thing had happened. What's gone through the city has been rumour, leakage that cannot be caulked, household servants blabbing to friends outside and they blabbing onward. Molin's locked away most of the facts till he can discover what they mean, if ever he can. I, however, I came on the scene while chaos still prevailed. Nobody kept me from talking to folk, before the lord himself saw me and told me to begone. Thus I know about as much as anyone, little though that be.'

'And –?' she prompted.

'And it doesn't seem to have been a worldly sort of capture, for a worldly end like ransom. See you, the mansion's well guarded, and neither Molin nor his wife have ever gone from it without escort. His mission here is less than popular, you recall. Those troopers are from Ranke and not subornable. The house stands in a garden, inside a high wall whose top is patrolled. Three leopards run loose in the grounds after dark.

'Molin had business with his kinsman the Prince, and spent the night at the palace. His wife, the Lady Rosanda, stayed home, retired, later came out and complained she could not sleep. She therefore had Danlis wakened. Danlis is no chambermaid; there are plenty of those. She's amanuensis, adviser, confidante, collector of information, ofttimes guide or interpreter – oh, she earns her pay, does my Danlis. Despite she and I having a dawntide engagement, which is why I arrived then, she must now out of bed at Rosanda's whim, to hold milady's hand or take dictation of milady's letters or read to milady from a soothing book – but I'm a spendthrift of words. Suffice to say that they two sought an upper chamber which is furnished as both solarium and office. A single staircase leads thither, and it is the single room at the top. There is a balcony, yes; and, the night being warm, the door to it stood open, as well as the windows. But I inspected the façade beneath. That's sheer marble, undecorated save for varying colours, devoid of ivy or of anything that any climber might cling to, save he were a fly.

'Nevertheless ... just before the east grew pale, shrieks were heard, the watch pelted to the stair and up it. They must break down the inner door, which was bolted. I suppose that was merely against chance interruptions, for nobody had felt threatened. The solarium was in disarray; vases and things were broken; shreds torn off a robe and slight traces of blood lay about. Aye, Danlis, at least, would have resisted. But she and her mistress were gone.

'A couple of sentries on the garden wall reported hearing a loud sound as of wings. The night was cloudy-dark and they saw nothing for certain. Perhaps they imagined the noise. Suggestive is that the leopards were found cowering in a corner and welcomed their keeper when he would take them back to their cages.

'And this is the whole of anyone's knowledge, Illyra,' Cappen ended. 'Help me. I pray you, help me get back my love!'

She was long quiet. Finally she said, in a near whisper, 'It could be a worse matter than I'd care to peer into, let alone enter.'

'Or it could not,' Cappen urged.

She gave him a quasi-defiant stare. 'My mother's people reckon it unlucky to do any service for a Shavakh – a person not of their tribe – without recompense. Pledges don't count.'

Cappen scowled. 'Well, I could go to a pawnshop and – But no, time may be worth more than rubies. From the depths of unhappiness, his grin broke forth. 'Poems also are valuable, right? You S'danzo have your ballads and love ditties. Let me indite a poem, Illyra, that shall be yours alone.'

Her expression quickened. 'Truly?'

'Truly. Let me think ... Aye, we'll begin thus.' And, venturing to take her hands in his, Cappen murmured:

> 'My lady comes to me like break of day.
> I dream in darkness if it chance she tarries,
> Until the banner of her brightness harries
> The hosts of Shadowland from off the way –'

She jerked free and cried, 'No! You scoundrel, that has to be something you did for Danlis – or for some earlier woman you wanted in your bed –'

'But it isn't finished,' he argued. 'I'll complete it for you, Illyra.'

79

Anger left her. She shook her head, clicked her tongue, and sighed. 'No matter. You're incurably yourself. And I ... am only half S'danzo. I'll attempt your spell.'

'By every love goddess I ever heard of,' he promised unsteadily, 'you shall indeed have your own poem after this is over.'

'Be still,' she ordered. 'Fend off anybody who comes near.'

He faced about and drew his sword. The slim, straight blade was hardly needed, for no other enterprise had site within several yards of hers, and as wide a stretch of paving lay between him and the fringes of the crowd. Still, to grasp the hilt gave him a sense of finally making progress. He had felt helpless for the first hours, hopeless, as if his dear had actually died instead of – of what? Behind him he heard cards riffled, dice cast, words softly wailed.

All at once Illyra strangled a shriek. He whirled about and saw how the blood had left her olive countenance, turning it grey. She hugged herself and shuddered.

'What's wrong?' he blurted in fresh terror.

She did not look at him. 'Go away,' she said in a thin voice. 'Forget you ever knew that woman.'

'But – but what –'

'Go away, I told you! Leave me alone!'

Then somehow she relented enough to let forth: 'I don't know. I dare not know. I'm just a little half-breed girl who has a few cantrips and a tricksy second sight, and – and I saw that this business goes outside of space and time, and a power beyond any magic is there – Enas Yorl could tell more, but he himself –' Her courage broke. 'Go away!' she screamed. 'Before I shout for Dubro and his hammer!'

'I beg your pardon,' Cappen Varra said, and made haste to obey.

He retreated into the twisting streets of the Maze. They were narrow; most of the mean buildings around him were high; gloom already filled the quarter. It was as if he had stumbled into the same night where Danlis had gone ... Danlis, creature of sun and horizons ... If she lived, did she remember their last time together as he remembered it, a dream dreamed centuries ago?

Having the day free, she had wanted to explore the countryside

80

north of town. Cappen had objected on three counts. The first he did not mention; that it would require a good deal of effort, and he would get dusty and sweaty and saddle-sore. She despised men who were not at least as vigorous as she was, unless they compensated by being venerable and learned.

The second he hinted at. Sleazy though most of Sanctuary was, he knew places within it where a man and a woman could enjoy themselves, comfortably, privately – his apartment, for instance. She smiled her negation. Her family belonged to the old aristocracy of Ranke, not the newly rich, and she had been raised in its austere tradition. Albeit her father had fallen on evil times and she had been forced to take service, she kept her pride, and proudly would she yield her maidenhead to her bridegroom. Thus far she had answered Cappen's ardent declarations with the admission that she liked him and enjoyed his company and wished he would change the subject. (Buxom Lady Rosanda seemed as if she might be more approachable, but there he was careful to maintain a cheerful correctness.) He did believe she was getting beyond simple enjoyment, for her patrician reserve seemed less each time they saw each other. Yet she could not altogether have forgotten that he was merely the bastard of a minor nobleman in a remote country, himself disinherited and a footloose minstrel.

His third objection he dared say forth. While the hinterland was comparatively safe, Molin Torchholder would be furious did he learn that a woman of his household had gone escorted by a single armed man, and he no professional fighter. Molin would probably have been justified, too. Danlis smiled again and said, 'I could ask a guardsman off duty to come along. But you have interesting friends, Cappen. Perhaps a warrior is among them?'

As a matter of fact, he knew any number, but doubted she would care to meet them – with a single exception. Luckily, Jamie the Red had no prior commitment, and agreed to join the party. Cappen told the kitchen staff to pack a picnic hamper for four.

Jamie's girls stayed behind; this was not their sort of outing, and sun might harm their complexions. Cappen thought it a bit ungracious of the Northerner never to share them. That put him, Cappen, to considerable expense in the Street of Red Lanterns, since he could scarcely keep a paramour of his own while wooing

Danlis. Otherwise he was fond of Jamie. They had met after Rosanda, chancing to hear the minstrel sing, had invited him to perform at the mansion, and then invited him back, and presently Cappen was living in the Jeweller's Quarter. Jamie had an apartment near by.

Three horses and a pack mule clopped out of Sanctuary in the new-born morning, to a jingle of harness bells. That merriment found no echo in Cappen's head; he had been drinking past midnight, and in no case enjoyed rising before noon. Passive, he listened to Jamie:

'– Aye, milady, they're mountaineers where I hail from, poor folk but free folk. Some might call us barbarians, but that might be unwise in our hearing. For we've tales, songs, laws, ways, gods as old as any in the world, and as good. We lack much of your Southern lore, but how much of ours do you ken? Not that I boast, please understand. I've seen wonders in my wanderings. But I do say we've a few wonders of our own at home.'

'I'd like to hear of them,' Danlis responded. 'We know almost nothing about your country in the Empire – hardly more than mentions in the chronicles of Venafer and Mattathan, or the *Natural History* of Kahayavesh. How do you happen to come here?'

'Oh–ah, I'm a younger son of our king, and I thought I'd see a bit of the world before settling down. Not that I packed any wealth along to speak of. But what with one thing and another, hiring out hither and yon for this or that, I get by.' Jamie paused. 'You, uh, you've far more to tell, milady. You're from the crown city of the Empire, and you've got book learning, and at the same time you come out to see for yourself what land and rocks and plants and animals are like.'

Cappen decided he had better get into the conversation. Not that Jamie would undercut a friend, nor Danlis be unduly attracted by a wild highlander. Neverthless –

Jamie wasn't bad-looking in his fashion. He was huge, topping Cappen by a head and disproportionately wide in the shoulders. His loose-jointed appearance was deceptive, as the bard had learned when they sported in a public gymnasium; those were heavy bones and oak-hard muscles. A spectacular red mane drew attention from boyish face, mild blue eyes, and slightly diffident manner. Today he was plainly clad, in tunic and cross-gaitered breeks; but the knife at his belt and the axe at his saddlebow stood out.

As for Danlis, well, what could a poet do but struggle for words which might embody a ghost of her glory? She was tall and slender, her features almost cold in their straight-lined perfection and alabaster hue – till you observed the big grey eyes, golden hair piled on high, curve of lips whence came that husky voice. (How often he had lain awake yearning for her lips! He would console himself by remembering the strong, delicately blue-veined hand that she did let him kiss.) Despite waxing warmth and dust puffed up from the horses' hoofs, her cowled riding habit remained immaculate and no least dew of sweat was on her skin.

By the time Cappen got his wits out of the blankets wherein they had still been snoring, talk had turned to gods. Danlis was curious about those of Jamie's country, as she was about most things. (She did shun a few subjects as being unwholesome.) Jamie in his turn was eager to have her explain what was going on in Sanctuary. 'I've heard but the one side of the matter, and Cappen's indifferent to it,' he said. 'Folk grumble about your master – Molin, is that his name –?'

'He is not my master,' Danlis made clear. 'I am a free woman who assists his wife. He himself is a high priest in Ranke, also an engineer.'

'Why is the Emperor angering Sanctuary? Most places I've been, colonial governments know better. They leave the local gods be.'

Danlis grew pensive. 'Where shall I start? Doubtless you know that Sanctuary was originally a city of the kingdom of Ilsig. Hence it has built temples to the gods of Ilsig – notably Ils, Lord of Lords, and his queen Shipri the All-Mother, but likewise others – Anen of the Harvests, Thufir the tutelary of pilgrims –'

'But none to Shalpa, patron of thieves,' Cappen put in, 'though these days he has the most devotees of any.'

Danlis ignored his jape. 'Ranke was quite a different country, under quite different gods,' she continued. 'Chief of these are

Savankala the Thunderer, his consort Sabellia, Lady of Stars, their son Vashanka the Ten-Slayer, and his sister and consort Azyuna – gods of storm and war. According to Venafer, it was they who made Ranke supreme at last. Mattathan is more prosaic and opines that the martial spirit they inculcated was responsible for the Rankan Empire finally taking Ilsig into itself.'

'Yes, milady, yes, I've heard this,' Jamie said, while Cappen reflected that if his beloved had a fault, it was her tendency to lecture.

'Sanctuary has changed from of yore,' she proceeded. 'It has become polyglot, turbulent, corrupt, a canker on the body politic. Among its most vicious elements are the proliferating alien cults, not to speak of necromancers, witches, charlatans, and similar predators on the people. The time is overpast to restore law here. Nothing less than the Imperium can do that. A necessary preliminary is the establishment of the Imperial deities, the gods of Ranke, for everyone to see: symbol, rallying point, and actual presence.'

'But they *have* their temples,' Jamie argued.

'Small, dingy, to accommodate Rankans, few of whom stay in the city for long,' Danlis retorted. 'What reverence does that inspire, for the pantheon and the state? No, the Emperor has decided that Savankala and Sabellia must have the greatest fane, the most richly endowed, in this entire province. Molin Torchholder will build and consecrate it. Then can the degenerates and warlocks be scourged out of Sanctuary. Afterwards the Prince-Governor can handle common felons.'

Cappen didn't expect matters would be that simple. He got no chance to say so, for Jamie asked at once, 'Is this wise, milady? True, many a soul hereabouts worships foreign gods, or none. But many still adore the old gods of Ilsig. They look on your, uh, Savankala as an intruder. I intend no offence, but they do. They're outraged that he's to have a bigger and grander house than Ils of the Thousand Eyes. Some fear what Ils may do about it.'

'I know,' Danlis said. 'I regret any distress caused, and I'm sure Lord Molin does too. Still, we must overcome the agents of darkness, before the disease that they are spreads throughout the Empire.'

'Oh, no,' Cappen managed to insert, 'I've lived here awhile, mostly down in the Maze. I've had to do with a good many so-called magicians, of either sex or in between. They aren't that bad. Most I'd call pitiful. They just use their little deceptions to scrabble out what living they can, in this crumbly town where life has trapped them.'

Danlis gave him a sharp glance. 'You've told me people think ill of sorcery in Caronne,' she said.

'They do,' he admitted. 'But that's because we incline to be rationalists, who consider nearly all magic a bag of tricks. Which is true. Why, I've learned a few sleights myself.'

'You have?' Jamie rumbled in surprise.

'For amusement,' Cappen said hastily, before Danlis could disapprove. 'Some are quite elegant, virtual exercises in three-dimensional geometry.' Seeing interest kindle in her, he added, 'I studied mathematics in boyhood; my father, before he died, wanted me to have a gentleman's education. The main part has rusted away in me, but I remember useful or picturesque details.'

'Well, give us a show, come luncheon time,' Jamie proposed.

Cappen did, when they halted. That was on a hillside above the White Foal River. It wound gleaming through farmlands whose intense green denied that desert lurked on the rim of sight. The noonday sun baked strong odours out of the earth: humus, resin, juice of wild plants. A solitary plane tree graciously gave shade. Bees hummed.

After the meal, and after Danlis had scrambled off to get a closer look at a kind of lizard new to her, Cappen demonstrated his skill. She was especially taken – enchanted – by his geometric artifices. Like any Rankan lady, she carried a sewing kit in her gear; and being herself, she had writing materials along. Thus he could apply scissors and thread to paper. He showed how a single ring may be cut to produce two that are interlocked, and how a strip may be twisted to have but one surface and one edge, and whatever else he knew. Jamie watched with pleasure, if with less enthusiasm.

Observing how delight made her glow, Cappen was inspired to carry on the latest poem he was composing for her. It had been slower work than usual. He had the conceit, the motif, a comparison of her to the dawn, but hitherto only the first few lines had emerged, and no proper structure. In this moment –

> – the banner of her brightness harries
> The hosts of Shadowland from off the way
> That she now wills to tread – for what can stay
> . The triumph of that radiance she carries?

Yes, it was clearly going to be a rondel. Therefore the next two lines were:

> My lady comes to me like break of day.
> I dream in darkness if it chance she tarries.

He had gotten that far when abruptly she said: 'Cappen, this is such a fine excursion, such splendid scenery. I'd like to watch sunrise over the river tomorrow. Will you escort me?'

Sunrise? But she was telling Jamie, 'We need not trouble you about that. I had in mind a walk out of town to the bridge. If we choose the proper route, it's well guarded everywhere, perfectly safe.'

And scant traffic moved at that hour; besides, the monumental statues along the bridge stood in front of bays which they screened from passers-by – 'Oh, yes, indeed, Danlis, I'd love to,' Cappen said. For such an opportunity, he could get up before cockcrow.

– When he reached the mansion, she had not been there.

Exhausted after his encounter with Illyra, Cappen hied him to the Vulgar Unicorn and related his woes to One-Thumb. The big man had come on shift at the inn early, for a fellow boniface had not yet recovered from the effects of a dispute with a patron. (Shortly thereafter, the patron was found floating face down under a pier. Nobody questioned One-Thumb about this; his regulars knew that he preferred the establishment safe, if not always orderly.) He offered taciturn sympathy and the loan of a bed upstairs. Cappen scarcely noticed the insects that shared it.

Waking about sunset, he found water and a washcloth, and felt much refreshed – hungry and thirsty, too. He made his way to the taproom below. Dusk was blue in windows and open door, black under the rafters. Candles smeared weak light along counter and main board and on lesser tables at the walls. The air had grown cool, which allayed the stenches of the Maze. Thus Cappen was acutely aware of the smells of beer – old in the rushes underfoot, fresh where a trio of men had settled down to guzzle – and of spitted meat, wafting from the kitchen.

One-Thumb approached, a shadowy hulk save for highlights on his bald pate. 'Sit,' he grunted. 'Eat. Drink.' He carried a great tankard and a plate bearing a slab of roast beef on bread. These he put on a corner table, and himself on a chair.

Cappen sat also and attacked the meal. 'You're very kind,' he said between bites and draughts.

'You'll pay when you get coin, or if you don't, then in songs and magic stunts. They're good for trade.' One-Thumb fell silent and peered at his guest.

When Cappen was done, the innkeeper said, 'While you slept, I sent out a couple of fellows to ask around. Maybe somebody saw something that might be helpful. Don't worry – I didn't mention you, and it's natural I'd be interested to know what really happened.'

The minstrel stared. 'You've gone to a deal of trouble on my account.'

'I told you, I want to know for my own sake. If deviltry's afoot, where could it strike next?' One-Thumb rubbed a finger across the toothless part of his gums. 'Of course, if you should luck out – I don't expect it, but in case you do – remember who gave you a boost.' A figure appeared in the door and he went to render service.

After a bit of muttered talk, he led the newcomer to Cappen's place. When the minstrel recognized the lean youth, his pulse leaped. One-Thumb would not have brought him and Hanse together without cause; bard and thief found each other insufferable. They nodded coldly but did not speak until the tapster returned with a round of ale.

When the three were seated, One-Thumb said, 'Well spit it out, boy. You claim you've got news.'

'For him?' Hanse flared, gesturing at Cappen.

'Never mind who. Just talk.'

Hanse scowled. 'I don't talk for a single lousy mugful.'

'You do if you want to keep on coming in here.'

Hanse bit his lip. The Vulgar Unicorn was a rendezvous virtually indispensable to one in his trade.

Cappen thought it best to sweeten the pill: 'I'm known to Molin Torchholder. If I can serve him in this matter, he won't be stingy. Nor will I. Shall we say – hm – ten gold royals to you?'

The sum was not princely, but on that account plausible. 'Awright, awright,' Hanse replied. 'I'd been casing a job I might do in the Jewellers' Quarter. A squad of the watch came by towards morning and I figured I'd better go home, not by the way I came, either. So I went along the Avenue of Temples, as I might be wanting to stop in and pay my respects to some god or other. It was a dark night, overcast, the reason I'd been out where I was. But you know how several of the temples keep lights going. There was enough to see by, even upwards a ways. Nobody else was in sight. Suddenly I heard a kind of whistling, flapping noise aloft. I looked and –'

He broke off.

'And what?' Cappen blurted. One-Thumb sat impassive.

Hanse swallowed. 'I don't swear to this,' he said. 'It was still dim, you realize. I've wondered since if I didn't see wrong.'

'What was it?' Cappen gripped the table edge till his fingernails whitened.

Hanse wet his throat and said in a rush: 'What it *seemed* like was a huge black thing, almost like a snake, but bat-winged. It came streaking from, oh, more or less the direction of Molin's, I'd guess now that I think back. And it was aimed more or less towards the temple of Ils. There was something that dangled below, as it might be a human body or two. I didn't stay to watch, I ducked into the nearest alley and waited. When I came out, it was gone.'

He knocked back his ale and rose. 'That's all,' he snapped. 'I don't want to remember the sight any longer, and if anybody ever asks, I was never here tonight.'

'Your story's worth a couple more drinks,' One-Thumb invited.

'Another evening,' Hanse demurred. 'Right now I need a whore. Don't forget those ten royals, singer.' He left, stiff-legged.

'Well,' said the innkeeper after a silence, 'what do you make of this latest?'

Cappen suppressed a shiver. His palms were cold. 'I don't know, save that what we confront is not of our kind.'

'You told me once you've got a charm against magic.'

Cappen fingered the little silver amulet, in the form of a coiled snake, he wore around his neck. 'I'm not sure. A wizard I'd done a favour for gave me this, years ago. He claimed it'd protect me against spells and supernatural beings of less than godly rank. But to make it work, I have to utter three truths about the spellcaster or the creature. I've done that in two or three scrapes, and come out of them intact, but I can't prove the talisman was responsible.'

More customers entered, and One-Thumb must go to serve them. Cappen nursed his ale. He yearned to get drunk and belike the landlord would stand him what was needful, but he didn't dare. He had already learned more than he thought the opposition would approve of – whoever or whatever the opposition was. They might have means of discovering this.

His candle flickered. He glanced up and saw a beardless fat man in an ornate formal robe, scarcely normal dress for a visit to the Vulgar Unicorn. 'Greetings,' the person said. His voice was like a child's.

Cappen squinted through the gloom. 'I don't believe I know you,' he replied.

'No, but you will come to believe it, oh, yes, you will.' The fat man sat down. One-Thumb came over and took an order for red wine – 'a decent wine, mine host, a Zhanuvend or Baladach.' Coin gleamed forth.

Cappen's heart thumped. 'Enas Yorl?' he breathed.

The other nodded. 'In the flesh, the all too mutable flesh. I do hope my curse strikes again soon. Almost any shape would be better than this. I hate being overweight. I'm a eunuch, too. The times I've been a woman were better than this.'

'I'm sorry, sir,' Cappen took care to say. Though he could not rid himself of the spell laid on him, Enas Yorl was a powerful thaumaturge, no mere prestidigitator.

'At least I've not been arbitrarily displaced. You can't imagine how annoying it is, suddenly to find oneself elsewhere, perhaps

89

miles away. I was able to come here in proper wise, in my litter. Faugh, how can anyone voluntarily set shoes to these open sewers they call streets in the Maze?' The wine arrived. 'Best we speak fast and to the point, young man, that we may finish and I get home before the next contretemps.'

Enas Yorl sipped and made a face. 'I've been swindled,' he whined. 'This is barely drinkable, if that.'

'Maybe your present palate is at fault, sir,' Cappen suggested. He did not add that the tongue definitely had a bad case of logorrhea. It was an almost physical torture to sit stalled, but he had better humour the mage.

'Yes, quite probably. Nothing has tasted good since – Well. To business. On hearing that One-Thumb was inquiring about last night's incident, I sent forth certain investigators of my own. You will understand that I've been trying to find out as much as I can.' Enas Yorl drew a sign in the air. 'Purely precautionary. I have no desire whatsoever to cross the Powers concerned in this.'

A wintry tingle went through Cappen. 'You know who they are, what it's about?' His tone wavered.

Enas Yorl wagged a finger. 'Not so hasty, boy, not so hasty. My latest information was of a seemingly unsuccessful interview you had with Illyra the seeress. I also learned you were now in this hostel and close to its landlord. Obviously you are involved. I must know why, how, how much – everything.'

'Then you'll help – sir?'

A headshake made chin and jowls wobble. 'Absolutely not. I told you I want no part of this. But in exchange for whatever data you possess, I am willing to explicate as far as I am able, and to advise you. Be warned: my advice will doubtless be that you drop the matter and perhaps leave town.'

And doubtless he would be right, Cappen thought. It simply happened to be counsel that was impossible for a lover to follow ... unless – O kindly gods of Caronne, no, no! – unless Danlis was dead.

The whole story spilled out of him, quickened and deepened by keen questions. At the end, he sat breathless while Enas Yorl nodded.

90

'Yes, that appears to confirm what I suspected,' the mage said most softly. He stared past the minstrel, into shadows that loomed and flickered. Buzz of talk, clink of drinking ware, occasional gust of laughter among customers seemed remoter than the moon.

'What was it?' broke from Cappen.

'A sikkintair, a Flying Knife. It can have been nothing else.'

'A – what?'

Enas focused on his companion. 'The monster that took the women,' he explained. 'Sikkintairs are an attribute of Ils. A pair of sculptures on the grand stairway of his temple represent them.'

'Oh, yes, I've seen those, but never thought –'

'No, you're not a votary of any gods they have here. Myself, when I got word of the abduction, I sent my familiars scuttling about and cast spells of inquiry. I received indications ... I can't describe them to you, who lack arcane lore. I established that the very fabric of space had been troubled. Vibrations had not quite damped out as yet, and were centred on the temple of Ils. You may, if you wish a crude analogy, visualize a water surface and the waves, fading to ripples and finally to naught, when a diver has passed through.'

Enas Yorl drank more in a gulp than was his wont. 'Civilization was old in Ilsig when Ranke was still a barbarian village,' he said, as though to himself; his gaze had drifted away again, towards darkness. 'Its myths depicted the home of the gods as being outside the world – not above, not below, but outside. Philosophers of a later, more rationalistic era elaborated this into a theory of parallel universes. My own researches – you will understand that my condition has made me especially interested in the theory of dimensions, the subtler aspects of geometry – my own researches have demonstrated the possibility of transference between these different spaces.

'As another analogy, consider a pack of cards. One is inhabited by a king, one by a knight, one by a deuce, et cetera. Ordinarily none of the figures can leave the plane on which it exists. If, however, a very thin piece of absorbent material soaked in a unique kind of solvent were laid between two cards, the dyes that form them could pass through: retaining their configuration,

91

I trust. Actually, of course, this is a less than ideal comparison, for the transference is accomplished through a particular contortion of the continuum –'

Cappen could endure no more pedantry. He crashed his tankard down on the table and shouted, 'By all the hells of all the cults, will you get to the point?'

Men stared from adjacent seats, decided no fight was about to erupt, and went back to their interests. These included negotiations with street-walkers who, lanterns in hand, had come in looking for trade.

Enas Yorl smiled. 'I forgive your outburst, under the circumstances,' he said. 'I too am occasionally young.

'Very well. Given the foregoing data, including yours, the infrastructure of events seems reasonably evident. You are aware of the conflict over a proposed new temple, which is to outdo that of Ils and Shipri. I do not maintain that the god has taken a direct hand. I certainly hope he feels that would be beneath his dignity; a theomachy would not be good for us, to understate the case a trifle. But he may have inspired a few of his more fanatical priests to action. He may have revealed to them, in dreams or vision, the means whereby they could cross to the next world and there make the sikkintairs do their bidding. I hypothesize that the Lady Rosanda – and, to be sure, her coadjutrix, your inamorata – are incarcerated in that world. The temple is too full of priests, deacons, acolytes, and lay people for hiding the wife of a magnate. However, the gate need not be recognizable as such.'

Cappen controlled himself with an inward shudder and made his trained voice casual: 'What might it look like, sir?'

'Oh, probably a scroll, taken from a coffer where it had long lain forgotten, and now unrolled – yes, I should think in the sanctum, to draw power from the sacred objects and to be seen by as few persons as possible who are not in the conspiracy –'
Enas Yorl came out of his abstraction. 'Beware! I deduce your thought. Choke it before it kills you.'

Cappen ran sandy tongue over leathery lips. 'What ... should we ... expect to happen, sir?'

'That is an interesting question,' Enas Yorl said. 'I can but conjecture. Yet I am well acquainted with the temple hierarchy and – I don't think the Archpriest is privy to the matter. He's too aged and weak. On the other hand, this is quite in the style of Hazroah, the High Flamen. Moreover, of late he has in effect taken over the governance of the temple from his nominal superior. He's bold, ruthless – should have been a soldier – Well, putting myself in his skin, I'll predict that he'll let Molin stew a while, then cautiously open negotiations – a hint at first, and always a claim that this is the will of Ils.

'None but the Emperor can cancel an undertaking for the Imperial deities. Persuading him will take much time and pressure. Molin is a Rankan aristocrat of the old school; he will be torn between his duty to his gods, his state, and his wife. But I suspect that eventually he can be worn down to the point where he agrees that it is, in truth, bad policy to exalt Savankala and Sabellia in a city whose tutelaries they have never been. He in his turn can influence the Emperor as desired.'

'How long would this take, do you think?' Cappen whispered. 'Till the women are released?'

Enas Yorl shrugged. 'Years, possibly. Hazroah may try to hasten the process by demonstrating that the Lady Rosanda is subject to punishment. Yes, I should imagine that the remains of an ancilla who had been tortured to death, delivered on Molin's doorstep, would be a rather strong argument.'

His look grew intense on the appalled countenance across from him. 'I know,' he said. 'You're breeding fever-dreams of a heroic rescue. It cannot be done. Even supposing that somehow you won through the gate and brought her back, the gate would remain. I doubt Ils would personally seek revenge; besides being petty, that could provoke open strife with Savankala and his retinue, who're formidable characters themselves. But Ils would not stay the hand of the Flamen Hazroah, who is a most vengeful sort. If you escaped his assassins, a sikkintair would come after you, and nowhere in the world could you and she hide. Your talisman would be of no avail. The sikkintair is not supernatural, unless you give that designation to the force which enables so huge a mass to fly; and *it* is from no magician, but from the god.

'So forget the girl. The town is full of them.' He fished in his purse and spilled a handful of coins on the table. 'Go to a good whorehouse, enjoy yourself, and raise one for poor old Enas Yorl.'

He got up and waddled off. Cappen sat staring at the coins. They made a generous sum, he realized vaguely: silver lunars, to the number of thirty.

One-Thumb came over. 'What'd he say?' the taverner asked.

'I should abandon hope,' Cappen muttered. His eyes stung; his vision blurred. Angrily, he wiped them.

'I've a notion I might not be smart to hear more.' One-Thumb laid his mutilated hand on Cappen's shoulder. 'Care to get drunk? On the house. I'll have to take your money or the rest will want free booze too, but I'll return it tomorrow.'

'No, I – I thank you, but – but you're busy, and I need someone I can talk to. Just lend me a lantern, if you will.'

'That might attract a robber, fellow, what with those fine clothes of yours.'

Cappen gripped swordhilt. 'He'd be very welcome, the short while he lasted,' he said in bitterness.

He climbed to his feet. His fingers remembered to gather the coins.

Jamie let him in. The Northerner had hastily thrown a robe over his massive frame; he carried the stone lamp that was a night light. 'Sh,' he said. 'The lassies are asleep.' He nodded towards a closed door at the far end of this main room. Bringing the lamp higher, he got a clear view of Cappen's face. His own registered shock. 'Hey-o, lad, what ails you? I've seen men pole-axed who looked happier.'

Cappen stumbled across the threshold and collapsed in an arm-chair. Jamie barred the outer door, touched a stick of punk to the lamp flame and lit candles, filled wine goblets. Drawing a seat opposite, he sat down, laid red-furred right shank across left knee, and said gently, 'Tell me.'

When it had spilled from Cappen, he was a long span quiet. On the walls shimmered his weapons, among pretty pictures that his housemates had selected. At last he asked low, 'Have you quit?'

94

'I don't know, I don't know,' Cappen groaned.

'I think you can go on aways, whether or no things are as the witchmaster supposes. We hold where I come from that no man can flee his weird, so he may as well meet it in a way that'll leave a good story. Besides, this may not be our death-day; and I doubt yon dragons are unkillable, but it could be fun finding out; and chiefly, I was much taken with your girl. Not many like her, my friend. They also say in my homeland, "Waste not, want not".'

Cappen lifted his glance, astounded. 'You mean I should try to free her?' he exclaimed.

'No, I mean *we* should.' Jamie chuckled. 'Life's gotten a wee bit dull for me of late – aside from Butterfly and Light-of-Pearl, of course. Besides, I could use a share of reward money.'

'I . . . I want to,' Cappen stammered. 'How I want to! But the odds against us –'

'She's your girl, and it's your decision. I'll not blame you if you hold back. Belike, then, in your country, they don't believe a man's first troth is to his woman and kids. Anyway, for you that was no more than a hope.'

A surge went through the minstrel. He sprang up and paced, back and forth, back and forth. 'But what could we *do*?'

'Well, we could scout the temple and see what's what,' Jamie proposed. 'I've been there once in a while, reckoning 'twould do no hurt to give those gods their honour. Maybe we'll find that indeed naught can be done in aid. Or maybe we won't, and go ahead and do it.'

Danlis –

Fire blossomed in Cappen Varra. He was young. He drew his sword and swung it whistling on high. 'Yes! We will!'

A small grammarian part of him noted the confusion of tenses and moods in the conversation.

The sole traffic on the Avenue of Temples was a night breeze, cold and sibilant. Stars, as icy to behold, looked down on its broad emptiness, on darkened buildings and weather-worn idols and rustling gardens. Here and there flames cast restless light, from porticoes or gables or ledges, out of glass lanterns or iron pots or pierced stone jars. At the foot of the grand staircase leading to the fane of Ils and Shipri, fire formed haloes on the enormous figures, male and female in robes of antiquity, that flanked it.

Beyond, the god-house itself loomed, porticoed front, great bronze doors, granite walls rising sheer above to a gilt dome from which light also gleamed; the highest point in Sanctuary.

Cappen started up. 'Halt' said Jamie, and plucked at his cloak. 'We can't walk straight in. They keep guards in the vestibule, you know.'

'I want a close view of those sikkintairs,' the bard explained.

'Um, well, maybe not a bad idea, but let's be quick. If a squad of the watch comes by, we're in trouble.' They could not claim they simply wished to perform their devotions, for a civilian was not allowed to bear more arms in this district than a knife. Cappen and Jamie each had that, but no illuminant like honest men. In addition, Cappen carried his rapier, Jamie a claymore, a visored conical helmet, and a knee-length byrnie. He had, moreover, furnished spears for both.

Cappen nodded and bounded aloft. Half-way, he stopped and gazed. The statue was a daunting sight. Of obsidian polished glassy smooth, it might have measured thirty feet were the tail not coiled under the narrow body. The two legs which supported the front ended in talons the length of Jamie's dirk. An upreared, serpentine neck bore a wickedly lanceolate head, jaws parted to show fangs that the sculptor had rendered in diamond. From the back sprang wings, bat-like save for their sharp-pointed curvatures, which if unfolded might well have covered another ten yards.

'Aye,' Jamie murmured, 'such a brute could bear off two women like an eagle a brace of leverets. Must take a lot of food to power it. I wonder what quarry they hunt at home.'

'We may find out,' Cappen said, and wished he hadn't.

'Come.' Jamie led the way back, and around to the left side of the temple. It occupied almost its entire ground, leaving but a narrow strip of flagstones. Next to that, a wall enclosed the flower-fragrant sanctum of Eshi, the love goddess. Thus the space between was gratifyingly dark; the intruders could not now be spied from the avenue. Yet enough light filtered in that they saw what they were doing. Cappen wondered if this meant she smiled on their venture. After all, it was for love, mainly. Besides, he had always been an enthusiastic worshipper of hers, or at any rate of her counterparts in foreign pantheons; oftener than most men had he rendered her favourite sacrifice.

Jamie had pointed out that the building must have lesser doors for utilitarian purposes. He soon found one, bolted for the night and between windows that were hardly more than slits, impossible to crawl through. He could have hewn the wood panels asunder, but the noise might be heard. Cappen had a better idea. He got his partner down on hands and knees. Standing on the broad back, he poked his spear through a window and worked it along the inside of the door. After some fumbling and whispered obscenities, he caught the latch with the head and drew the bolt.

'Hoosh, you missed your trade, I'm thinking,' said the Northerner as he rose and opened the way.

'No, burglary's too risky for my taste,' Cappen replied in feeble jest. The fact was that he had never stolen or cheated unless somebody deserved such treatment.

'Even burgling the house of a god?' Jamie's grin was wider than necessary.

Cappen shivered. 'Don't remind me.'

They entered a storeroom, shut the door, and groped through murk to the exit. Beyond was a hall. Widely spaced lamps gave bare visibility. Otherwise the intruders saw emptiness and heard silence. The vestibule and nave of the temple were never closed; the guards watched over a priest always prepared to accept offerings. But elsewhere hierarchy and staff were asleep. Or so the two hoped.

Jamie had known that the holy of holies was in the dome, Ils being a sky god. Now he let Cappen take the lead, as having more familiarity with interiors and ability to reason out a route. The minstrel used half his mind for that and scarcely noticed the splendours through which he passed. The second half was busy recollecting legends of heroes who incurred the anger of a god, especially a major god, but won to happiness in the end because they had the blessing of another. He decided that future attempts to propitiate Ils would only draw the attention of that august personage; however, Savankala would be pleased, and, yes, as for native deities, he would by all means fervently cultivate Eshi.

A few times, which felt ghastly long, he took a wrong turning and must retrace his steps after he had discovered that. Presently, though, he found a staircase which seemed to zig-zag over the inside of an exterior wall. Landing after landing passed by –

The last was enclosed in a very small room, a booth, albeit richly ornamented –

He opened the door and stepped out –

Wind searched between the pillars that upheld the dome, through his clothes and in towards his bones. He saw stars. They were the brightest in heaven, for the entry booth was the pedestal of a gigantic lantern. Across a floor tiled in symbols unknown to him, he observed something large at each cardinal point – an altar, two statues, and the famous Thunderstone, he guessed; they were shrouded in cloth of gold. Before the eastern object was stretched a band, the far side of which seemed to be aglow.

He gathered his courage and approached. The thing was a parchment, about eight feet long and four wide, hung by cords from the upper corners to a supporting member of the dome. The cords appeared to be glued fast, as if to avoid making holes in the surface. The lower edge of the scroll, two feet above the floor, was likewise secured; but to a pair of anvils surely brought here for the purpose. Nevertheless the parchment flapped and rattled a bit in the wind. It was covered with cabalistic signs.

Cappen stepped around to the other side, and whistled low. That held a picture, within a narrow border. Past the edge of what might be a pergola, the scene went to a meadowland made stately by oak trees standing at random intervals. About a mile away – the perspective was marvellously executed – stood a building of manorial size in a style he had never seen before, twistily colonaded, extravagantly sweeping of roof and eaves, blood-red. A formal garden surrounded it, whose paths and topiaries were of equally alien outline; fountains sprang in intricate patterns. Beyond the house, terrain rolled higher, and snow-peaks thrust above the horizon. The sky was deep blue.

'What the pox!' exploded from Jamie. 'Sunshine's coming out of that painting. I *feel* it.'

98

Cappen rallied his wits and paid heed. Yes, warmth as well as light, and ... and odours? And were those fountains not actually at play?

An eerie thrilling took him. 'I ... believe ... we've ... found the gate,' he said.

He poked his spear cautiously at the scroll. The point met no resistance; it simply moved on. Jamie went behind. 'You've not pierced it,' he reported. 'Nothing sticks out on this side – which, by the way, is quite solid.'

'No,' Cappen answered faintly, 'the spear-head's in the next world.'

He drew the weapon back. He and Jamie stared at each other.

'Well?' said the Northerner.

'We'll never get a better chance,' Cappen's throat responded for him. 'It'd be blind foolishness to retreat now, unless we decide to give up the whole venture.'

'We, uh, we could go tell Molin, no, the Prince what we've found.'

'And be cast into a madhouse? If the Prince *did* send investigators anyway, the plotters need merely take this thing down and hide it till the squad has left. No.' Cappen squared his shoulders. 'Do what you like, Jamie, but I am going through.'

Underneath, he heartily wished he had less self-respect, or at least that he weren't in love with Danlis.

Jamie scowled and sighed. 'Aye, right you are, I suppose. I'd not looked for matters to take so headlong a course. I awaited that we'd simply scout around. Had I foreseen this, I'd have roused the lassies to bid them, well, good night.' He hefted his spear and drew his sword. Abruptly he laughed. 'Whatever comes, 'twill not be dull!'

Stepping high over the threshold, Cappen went forward.

It felt like walking through any door, save that he entered a mild summer's day. After Jamie had followed, he saw that the vista in the parchment was that on which he had just turned his back: a veiled mass, a pillar, stars above a nighted city. He checked the opposite side of the strip, and met the same designs as had been painted on its mate.

No, he thought, not its mate. If he had understood Enas Yorl aright, and rightly remembered what his tutor in mathematics had told him about esoteric geometry, there could be but a single scroll. One side of it gave on this universe, the other side on his, and a spell had twisted dimensions until matter could pass straight between.

Here too the parchment was suspended by cords, though in a pergola of yellow marble, whose circular stairs led down to the meadow. He imagined a sikkintair would find the passage tricky, especially if it was burdened with two women in its claws. The monster had probably hugged them close to it, come in at high speed, folded its wings, and glided between the pillars of the dome and the margins of the gate. On the outbound trip, it must have crawled through into Sanctuary.

All this Cappen did and thought in half a dozen heartbeats. A shout yanked his attention back. Three men who had been idling on the stairs had noticed the advent and were on their way up. Large and hard-featured, they bore the shaven visages, high-crested morions, gilt cuirasses, black tunics and boots, short-swords, and halberds of temple guards. 'Who in the Unholy's name are you?' called the first. 'What're you doing here?'

Jamie's qualms vanished under a tide of boyish glee. 'I doubt they'll believe any words of ours,' he said. 'We'll have to convince them a different way. If you can handle him on our left, I'll take his feres.'

Cappen felt less confident. But he lacked time to be afraid; shuddering would have to be done in a more convenient hour. Besides, he was quite a good fencer. He dashed across the floor and down the stair.

The trouble was, he had no experience with spears. He jabbed. The halberdier held his weapon, both hands close together, near the middle of the shaft. He snapped it against Cappen's, deflected the thrust, and nearly tore the minstrel's out of his grasp. The watchman's return would have skewered his enemy, had the minstrel not flopped straight to the marble.

The guard guffawed, braced his legs wide, swung the halberd back for an axe-head blow. As it descended, his hands shifted towards the end of the helve.

Chips flew. Cappen had rolled downstairs. He twirled the whole

100

way to the ground and sprang erect. He still clutched his spear, which had bruised him whenever he crossed above it. The sentry bellowed and hopped in pursuit. Cappen ran.

Behind them, a second guard sprawled and flopped, diminuendo, in what seemed an impossibly copious and bright amount of blood. Jamie had hurled his own spear as he charged and taken the man in the neck. The third was giving the Northerner a brisk fight, halberd against claymore. He had longer reach, but the redhead had more brawn. Thump and clatter rang across the daisies.

Cappen's adversary was bigger than he was. This had the drawback that the former could not change speed or direction as readily. When the guard was pounding along at his best clip, ten or twelve feet in the rear, Cappen stopped within a coin's breadth, whirled about, and threw his shaft. He did not do that as his comrade had done. He pitched it between the guard's legs. The man crashed to the grass. Cappen plunged in. He didn't risk trying for a stab. That would let the armoured combatant grapple him. He wrenched the halberd loose and skipped off.

The sentinel rose. Cappen reached an oak and tossed the halberd. It lodged among boughs. He drew blade. His foe did the same.

Shortsword versus rapier – *much* better, though Cappen must have a care. The torso opposing him was protected. Still, the human anatomy has more vulnerable points than that. 'Shall we dance?' Cappen asked.

As he and Jamie approached the house, a shadow slid across them. They glanced aloft and saw the gaunt black form of a sikkintair. For an instant, they nerved themselves for the worst. However, the Flying Knife simply caught an updraught, planed high, and hovered in sinister magnificence. 'Belike they don't hunt men unless commanded to,' the Northerner speculated. 'Bear and buffalo are meatier.'

Cappen frowned at the scarlet walls before him. 'The next question,' he said, 'is why nobody has come out against us.'

'Um, I'd deem those wights we left scattered around were the only fighting men here. What task was theirs? Why, to keep the ladies from escaping, if those are allowed to walk outdoors by day. As for yon manse, while it's plenty big, I suspect it's on loan from its owner. Naught but a few servants need be on hand – and the women, let's hope. I don't suppose anybody happened to see our little brawl.'

The thought that they might effect the rescue – soon, safely, easily – went through Cappen in a wave of dizziness. Afterwards – he and Jamie had discussed that. If the temple hierophants, from Hazroah on down, were put under immediate arrest, that ought to dispose of the vengeance problem.

Gravel scrunched underfoot. Rose, jasmine, honeysuckle sweetened the air. Fountains leaped and chimed. The partners reached the main door. It was oaken, with many glass eyes inset; the knocker had the shape of a sikkintair.

Jamie leaned his spear, unsheathed his sword, turned the knob left-handed, and swung the door open. A maroon sumptuousness of carpet, hangings, upholstery brooded beyond. He and Cappen entered. Inside were quietness and an odour like that just before a thunderstorm.

A man in a deacon's black robe came through an archway, his tonsure agleam in the dimness. 'Did I hear – Oh!' he gasped, and scuttled backwards.

Jamie made a long arm and collared him. 'Not so fast, friend,' the warrior said genially. 'We've a request, and if you oblige, we won't get stains on this pretty rug. Where are your guests?'

'What, what, what,' the deacon gobbled.

Jamie shook him, in leisured wise lest he quite dislocate the shoulder. 'Lady Rosanda, wife to Molin Torchholder, and her assistant Danlis. Take us to them. Oh, and we'd liefer not meet folk along the way. It might get messy if we did.'

The deacon fainted.

'Ah, well,' Jamie said. 'I hate the idea of cutting down unarmed men, but chances are they won't be foolhardy.' He filled his lungs. *'Rosanda!'* he bawled. *'Danlis! Jamie and Cappen Varra are here! Come on home!'*

The volume almost bowled his companion over. 'Are you mad?' the minstrel exclaimed. 'You'll warn the whole staff –' A flash lit his mind: if they had seen no further guards, surely there were none, and nothing corporeal remained to fear. Yet every minute's delay heightened the danger of something else going wrong. Somebody might find signs of invasion back in the temple; the gods alone knew what lurked in this realm ... Yes, Jamie's judgement might prove mistaken, but it was the best he could have made.

Servitors appeared, and recoiled from naked steel. And then, and then –

Through a doorway strode Danlis. She led by the hand, or dragged, a half-hysterical Rosanda. Both were decently attired and neither looked abused, but pallor in cheeks and smudges under eyes bespoke what they must have suffered.

Cappen came nigh dropping his spear. 'Beloved!' he cried. 'Are you hale?'

'We've not been ill-treated in the flesh, aside from the snatching itself,' she answered efficiently. 'The threats, should Hazroah not get his way, have been cruel. Can we leave now?'

'Aye, the soonest, the best,' Jamie growled. 'Lead them on ahead, Cappen.' His sword covered the rear. On his way out, he retrieved the spear he had left.

They started back over the garden paths. Danlis and Cappen between them must help Rosanda along. That woman's plump prettiness was lost in tears, moans, whimpers, and occasional screams. He paid scant attention. His gaze kept seeking the clear profile of his darling. When her grey eyes turned towards him, his heart became a lyre.

She parted her lips. He waited for her to ask in dazzlement, 'How did you ever do this, you unbelievable, wonderful men?'

'What have we ahead of us?' she wanted to know.

Well, it was an intelligent query. Cappen swallowed disappointment and sketched the immediate past. Now, he said, they'd return via the gate to the dome and make their stealthy way from the temple, thence to Molin's dwelling for a joyous reunion. But then they must act promptly – yes, roust the Prince out of bed for authorization – and occupy the temple and arrest everybody in sight before new trouble got fetched from this world.

Rosanda gained some self-control as he talked. 'Oh, my, oh, my,' she wheezed, 'you unbelievable, wonderful men.'

An ear-piercing trill slashed across her voice. The escapers looked behind them. At the entrance to the house stood a thickset middle-aged person in the scarlet robe of a ranking priest of Ils. He held a pipe to his mouth and blew.

'Hazroah!' Rosanda shrilled. 'The ringleader!'

'The High Flamen –' Danlis began.

A rush in the air interrupted. Cappen flung his vision skyward and knew the nightmare was true. The sikkintair was descending. Hazroah had summoned it.

'Why, you son of a bitch!' Jamie roared. Still well behind the rest, he lifted his spear, brought it back, flung it with his whole strength and weight. The point went home in Hazroah's breast. Ribs did not stop it. He spouted blood, crumpled, and spouted no more. The shaft quivered above his body.

But the sikkintair's vast wings eclipsed the sun. Jamie rejoined his band and plucked the second spear from Cappen's fingers. 'Hurry on, lad,' he ordered. 'Get them to safety.'

'Leave you? No!' protested his comrade.

Jamie spat an oath. 'Do you want the whole faring to've gone for naught? Hurry, I said!'

Danlis tugged at Cappen's sleeve. 'He's right. The state requires our testimony.'

Cappen stumbled onward. From time to time he glanced back.

In the shadow of the wings, Jamie's hair blazed. He stood four-square, spear grasped as a huntsman does. Agape, the Flying Knife rushed down upon him. Jamie thrust straight between those jaws, and twisted.

The monster let out a sawtoothed shriek. Its wings threshed, made thundercrack, it swooped by, a foot raked. Jamie had his claymore out. He parried the blow.

The sikkintair rose. The shaft waggled from its throat. It spread great ebon membranes, looped, and came back earthward. Its claws were before it. Air whirred behind.

Jamie stood his ground, sword in right hand, knife in left. As the talons smote, he fended them off with the dirk. Blood sprang from his thigh, but his byrnie took most of the edged sweep. And his sword hewed.

The sikkintair ululated again. It tried to ascend, and couldn't.

Jamie had crippled its left wing. It landed – Cappen felt the impact through soles and bones – and hitched itself towards him. From around the spear came a geyser hiss.

Jamie held fast where he was. As fangs struck at him, he side-stepped, sprang back, and threw his shoulders against the shaft. Leverage swung jaws aside. He glided by the neck towards the forequarters. Both of his blades attacked the spine.

Cappen and the women hastened on.

They were almost at the pergola when footfalls drew his eyes rearwards. Jamie loped at an overtaking pace. Behind him, the sikkintair lay in a heap.

The redhead pulled alongside. 'Hai, what a fight!' he panted. 'Thanks for this journey, friend! A drinking bout's worth of thanks!'

They mounted the death-defiled stairs. Cappen peered across miles. Wings beat in heaven, from the direction of the mountains. Horror stabbed his guts. 'Look!' He could barely croak.

Jamie squinted. 'More of them,' he said. 'A score, maybe. We can't cope with so many. An army couldn't.'

'That whistle was heard farther away than mortals would hear,' Danlis added starkly.

'What do we linger for?' Rosanda wailed. 'Come, take us home!'

'And the sikkintairs follow?' Jamie retorted. 'No. I've my lassies, and kinfolk, and –' He moved to stand before the parchment. Edged metal dripped in his hands; red lay splashed across helm, ringmail, clothing, face. His grin broke forth, wry. 'A spaewife once told me I'd die on the far side of strangeness. I'll wager she didn't know her own strength.'

'You assume that the mission of the beasts is to destroy us, and when that is done they will return to their lairs.' The tone Danlis used might have served for a remark about the weather.

'Aye, what else? The harm they'd wreak would be in a hunt for us. But put to such trouble, they could grow furious and harry our whole world. That's the more likely when Hazroah lies skewered. Who else can control them?'

'None that I know of, and he talked quite frankly to us.' She nodded. 'Yes, it behoves us to die where we are.' Rosanda sank down and blubbered. Danlis showed irritation. 'Up!' she commanded her mistress. 'Up and meet your fate like a Rankan matron!'

Cappen goggled hopelessly at her. She gave him a smile. 'Have no regrets, dear,' she said. 'You did well. The conspiracy against the state has been checked.'

The far side of strangeness – check – chessboard – that version of chess where you pretend the right and left sides of the board are identical on a cylinder – tumbled through Cappen. The Flying Knives drew closer fast. *Curious aspects of geometry –*

Lightning-smitten, he knew ... or guessed he did ... 'No, Jamie, we go!' he yelled.

'To no avail save reaping of innocents?' The big man hunched his shoulders. 'Never.'

'Jamie, let us by! I can close the gate. I swear I can – I swear by – by Eshi –'

The Northerner locked eyes with Cappen for a span that grew. At last: 'You are my brother in arms.' He stood aside. 'Go on.'

The sikkintairs were so near that the noise of their speed reached Cappen. He urged Danlis towards the scroll. She lifted her skirt a trifle, revealing a dainty ankle, and stepped through. He hauled on Rosanda's wrist. The woman wavered to her feet but seemed unable to find her direction. Cappen took an arm and passed it into the next world for Danlis to pull. Himself, he gave a mighty shove on milady's buttocks. She crossed over.

He did. And Jamie.

Beneath the temple dome, Cappen's rapier reached high and slashed. Louder came the racket of cloven air. Cappen severed the upper cords. The parchment fell, wrinkling, crackling. He dropped his weapon, a-clang, squatted, and stretched his arms wide. The free corners he seized. He pulled them to the corners that were still secured, to make a closed band of the scroll.

From it sounded monstrous thumps and scrapes. The sikkintairs were crawling into the pergola. For them the portal must hang unchanged, open for their hunting.

Cappen gave that which he held a half-twist and brought the edges back together.

Thus he created a surface which had but a single side and a single edge. Thus he obliterated the gate.

He had not been sure what would follow. He had fleetingly supposed he would smuggle the scroll out, held in its paradoxical form, and eventually glue it – unless he could burn it. But upon the instant that he completed the twist and juncture, the parchment was gone. Enas Yorl told him afterwards that he had made it impossible for the thing to exist.

Air rushed in where the gate had been, crack and hiss. Cappen heard that sound as it were an alien word of incantation: '*Mö*bius-s-s.'

Having stolen out of the temple and some distance thence, the party stopped for a few minutes of recovery before they proceeded to Molin's house.

This was in a blind alley off the avenue, a brick-paved recess where flowers grew in planters, shared by the fanes of two small and gentle gods. Wind had died away, stars glimmered bright, a half moon stood above easterly roofs and cast wan argence. Afar, a tomcat serenaded his intended.

Rosanda had gotten back a measure of equilibrium. She cast herself against Jamie's breast. 'Oh, hero, hero,' she crooned, 'you shall have reward, yes, treasure, ennoblement, everything!' She snuggled. 'But nothing greater than my unbounded thanks . . .'

The Northerner cocked an eyebrow at Cappen. The bard shook his head a little. Jamie nodded in understanding, and disengaged. 'Uh, have a care, milady,' he said. 'Pressing against ringmail, all bloody and sweaty too, can't be good for a complexion.'

Even if one rescues them, it is not wise to trifle with the wives of magnates.

Cappen had been busy himself. For the first time, he kissed Danlis on her lovely mouth; then for the second time; then for the third. She responded decorously.

Thereafter she likewise withdrew. Moonlight made a mystery out of her classic beauty. 'Cappen,' she said, 'before we go on, we had better have a talk.'

He gaped. 'What?'

She bridged her fingers. 'Urgent matters first,' she continued crisply. 'Once we get to the mansion and wake the high priest, it will be chaos at first, conference later, and I – as a woman –

107

excluded from serious discussion. Therefore best I give my counsel now, for you to relay. Not that Molin or the Prince are fools; the measures to take are for the most part obvious. However, swift action is desirable, and they will have been caught by surprise.'

She ticked her points off. 'First, as you have indicated, the Hell Hounds' – her nostrils pinched in distaste at the nickname – 'the Imperial elite guard should mount an immediate raid on the temple of Ils and arrest all personnel for interrogation, except the Arch-priest. He's probably innocent, and in any event it would be inept politics. Hazroah's death may have removed the danger, but this should not be taken for granted. Even if it has, his co-conspirators ought to be identified and made examples of.

'Yet, second, wisdom should temper justice. No lasting harm was done, unless we count those persons who are trapped in the parallel universe; and they doubtless deserve to be.'

They seemed entirely males, Cappen recalled. He grimaced in compassion. Of course, the sikkintairs might eat them.

Danlis was talking on: '– humane governance and the art of compromise. A grand temple dedicated to the Rankan gods is cer-tainly required, but it need be no larger than that of Ils. Your counsel will have much weight, dear. Give it wisely. I will advise you.'

'Uh?' Cappen said.

Danlis smiled and laid her hands over his. 'Why, you can have unlimited preferment, after what you did,' she told him. 'I'll show you how to apply for it.'

'But – but I'm no blooming statesman!' Cappen stuttered.

She stepped back and considered him. 'True,' she agreed. 'You're valiant, yes, but you're also flighty and lazy and – Well, don't despair. I will mould you.'

Cappen gulped and shuffled aside. 'Jamie,' he said, 'uh, Jamie, I feel wrung dry, dead on my feet. I'd be worse than no use – I'd be a drogue on things just when they have to move fast. Better I find me a doss, and you take the ladies home. Come over here and I'll tell you how to convey the story in fewest words. Excuse us, ladies. Some of those words you oughtn't to hear.'

*

A week thence, Cappen Varra sat drinking in the Vulgar Unicorn. It was mid-afternoon and none else were present but the associate tapster, his wound knitted.

A man filled the doorway and came in, to Cappen's table. 'Been casting about everywhere for you,' the Northerner grumbled. 'Where've you been?'

'Lying low,' Cappen replied. 'I've taken a place here in the Maze which'll do till I've dropped back into obscurity, or decide to drift elsewhere altogether.' He sipped his wine. Sunbeams slanted through windows; dust motes danced golden in their warmth; a cat lay on a sill and purred. 'Trouble is, my purse is flat.'

'We're free of such woes for a goodly while.' Jamie flung his length into a chair and signalled the attendant. 'Beer!' he thundered.

'You collected a reward, then?' the minstrel asked eagerly.

Jamie nodded. 'Aye. In the way you whispered I should, before you left us. I'm baffled why and it went sore against the grain. But I did give Molin the notion that the rescue was my idea and you naught but a hanger-on whom I'd slip a few royals. He filled a box with gold and silver money, and said he wished he could afford ten times that. He offered to get me Rankan citizenship and a title as well, and make a bureaucrat of me, but I said no, thanks. We share, you and I, half and half. But right this now, drinks are on me.'

'What about the plotters?' Cappen inquired.

'Ah, those. The matter's been kept quiet, as you'd await. Still, while the temple of Ils can't be abolished, seemingly it's been tamed.' Jamie's regard sought across the table and sharpened. 'After you disappeared, Danlis agreed to let me claim the whole honour. She knew better – Rosanda never noticed – but Danlis wanted a man of the hour to carry her redes to the prince, and none remained save me. She supposed you were simply worn out. When last I saw her, though, she ... um-m ... she "expressed disappointment".' He cocked his ruddy head. 'Yon's quite a girl. I thought you loved her.'

Cappen Varra took a fresh draught of wine. Old summers glowed along his tongue. 'I did,' he confessed. 'I do. My heart is broken, and in part I drink to numb the pain.'

Jamie raised his brows. 'What? Makes no sense.'

'Oh, it makes very basic sense,' Cappen answered. 'Broken hearts tend to heal rather soon. Meanwhile, if I may recite from a rondel I completed before you found me –

> 'Each sword of sorrow that would maim or slay,
> My lady of the morning deftly parries.
> Yet gods forbid I be the one she marries!
> I rise from bed the latest hour I may.
> My lady comes to me like break of day;
> I dream in darkness if it chance she tarries.'

A FEW REMARKS BY
FURTWAN COINPINCH,
MERCHANT

The first thing I noticed about him, just that first impression you understand, was that he couldn't be a poor man. Or boy, or youth, or whatever he was then. Not with all those weapons on him. From the shagreen belt he was wearing over a scarlet sash – a violently scarlet sash! – swung a curved dagger on his left hip and on the right one of those Ilbarsi 'knives' long as your arm. Not a proper sword, no. Not a military man, then. That isn't all, though. Some few of us know that his left buskin is equipped with a sheath; the slim thing and knife-hilt appear to be only a decoration. Gift from a woman, I heard him tell Old Thumpfoot one afternoon in the bazaar. I doubt it.

(I've been told he has another sticker strapped less than comfortably to his inner thigh, probably the right. Maybe that's part of the reason he walks the way he does. Cat-supple and yet sort of stiff of leg all at once. A tumbler's gait – or a punk's swagger. Don't tell him I said!)

Anyhow, about the weapons and my first impression that he couldn't be poor. There's a throwing knife in that leather and copper armlet on his right upper arm, and another in the long bracer of black leather on that same arm. Both are short. The stickers I mean, not the bracers or the arms either.

All that armament would be enough to scare anybody on a dark night, or even a moonbright one. Imagine being in the Maze or some place like that and out of the shadows comes this young bravo, swaggering, wearing all that sharp metal! Right at you out of the shadows that spawned him. Enough to chill even one of those Hell Hounds. Even one of you-know-who's boys in the blue hawk-masks might step aside.

That was my impression. Shadowspawn. About as pleasant as gout or dropsy.

SHADOWSPAWN

Andrew Offutt

His mop of hair was blacker than black and his eyes nearly so, under brows that just missed meeting above a nose not quite falcate. His walk reminded some of one of those red-and-black gamecocks brought over from Mrsevada They called him Shadow spawn. No compliment was intended, and he objected until Cudget told him it was good to have a nickname – although he wished his own weren't Cudget Swearoath. Besides, *Shadowspawn* had a romantic and rather sinister sound, and that appealed to his ego, which was the largest thing about him. His height was almost average and he was rangy, wiry; swiftly wiry, with those bulgy rocks in his biceps and calves that other males wished they had.

Shadowspawn. It was descriptive enough. No one knew where he'd been spawned, which was shadowy, and he worked among shadows. Perhaps it was down in the shadows of the 'streets' of Downwind and maybe it was over in Syr that he'd been birthed. It didn't matter. He belonged to Sanctuary and wished it belonged to him. He acted as if it did. If he knew or suspected that he'd come out of Downwind, he was sure he had risen above it. He just didn't have time for those street-gangs of which surely he'd have been chieftain.

He was no more sure of his age than anyone else. He might have lived a score of years. It might have been fewer. Had a creditable moustache before he was fifteen.

The raven-wing hair, tending to an indecisive curl, covered his ears without reaching his shoulders. He'd an earring under that hair, on the left. Few knew it. Had it done at fourteen, to impress her who took his virginity that year. (She was twoscore-

113

and-two then, married to a man like a building stone with a belly. She's a hag with a belly out to here, now.)

'The lashes under those thick glossy brows of his are so black and thick they look almost kohled, like a woman's or a priest over in Yenized,' a man called Weasel told Cusharlain, in the Vulgar Unicorn. 'Some fool made that remark once, in his presence. The fellow wears the scar still and knows he's lucky to be wearing tongue and life. Should have known that a bravo who wears two throwing knives on his right arm is dangerous, and left-handed. And with a name like Shadowspawn . . .!'

His name was not Shadowspawn, of course. True, many did not know or no longer remembered his name. It was Hanse. Just Hanse. Not Hanse Shadowspawn; people called him the one or the other or nothing at all.

He seemed to wear a cloak about him at all times, a thoughtful S'danzo told Cusharlain. Not a cloak of fabric; this one concealed his features, his mind. Eyes hooded like a cobra's, some said. They weren't, really. They just did not seem directed outward, those glittering black onyxes he had for eyes. Perhaps their gaze was fixed on the plank-sized chips on his shoulders. Mighty easily knocked off.

By night he did not swagger, save when he entered a public place. Night of course was Hanse's time, as it had been Cudget's. By night . . . 'Hanse walks like a hungry cat,' some said, and they might shiver a bit. In truth he did not. He *glided*. His buskins' soft soles lifting only a finger's breadth with each step. They came down on the balls of the feet, not the heels. Some made fun of that – not to Hanse – because it made for a sinuous glide strange in appearance. The better-born watched him with an aesthetic fascination. And some horripilation. Among females, highborn or otherwise, the fascination was often layered with interest, however unwilling. Most then said the predictable: a distasteful, rather sexy animal; that Hanse, that Shadowspawn.

It had been suggested to him that a bit of committed practice could make him a real sword-slinger: he was a natural. Employment, a uniform . . . Hanse was not interested. Indeed he sneered at soldiers, at uniforms. And now he hated them, with a sort of un-reasoning reason.

These things Cusharlain learned, and he began to know him called Shadowspawn. And to dislike him. Hanse sounded the sort of too-competent young snot you step aside for – and hate yourself for doing it.

'Hanse is a bastard!' This from Shive the Changer, with a thump of his fist on the broad table on which he dealt with such as Hanse, changing loot into coin.

'Ah.' Cusharlain looked innocently at him. 'You mean by nature.'

'Probably by birth too. A bastard by birth and by nature! Better that all such cocky snotty stealthy arrogant bravos were stillborn!'

'He's bitten you then, Shive?'

'A bravo and a lowborn punk he is, and that's all.'

'Punk?'

'Well ... perhaps a cut above punk.' Shive touched his moustachioes, which he kept curled like the horns of a mountain goat. 'Cudget was a damned good thief. The sort of fellow who made the trade honourable. An art form. A pleasure doing business with. And Hanse was his apprentice, or nearly, sort of ... and he has the potential of being an even better thief. Not man – thief.' Shive wagged a finger made shiny by wax. 'The potential, mind you. He'll never realize it.' The finger paused on its way back to stroke one moustachio.

'You think not,' Cusharlain said, drawing Shive out, pulling words from a man who knew how to keep his mouth shut and was alive and wealthy because he did.

'I think not. He'll absorb a foot or so of sharp metal long before. Or dance on the air.'

'As, I remind you, Cudget did,' Cusharlain said, noting that within the trade no one said 'hanged'.

Shive took umbrage. 'After a long career! And Cudget was respected! He's respected still.'

'Umm. Pity you admire the master but not the apprentice. He could use you, surely. And you him. If he's a successful thief, there'll be profit for the fence he chooses to –'

'Fence? Fence?'

'Sorry, Shive. The Changer he chooses to exchange his ... goods with, for Rankan coin. There's always a profit to –'

'He cheated me!'

So. At last Shive admitted it. That's how he'd been bitten by this Hanse. Fat and fifty and the second most experienced Changer in Sanctuary, Shive had been cheated by a cocky youngster. 'Oh,' Cusharlain said. He rose, showing Shive a satirical little smile. 'You know, Shive ... you shouldn't admit that. You are after all a man with some twenty years' experience ... and he has only that many years of life, if not less.'

Shive stared after the customs inspector. An Aurveshan raised in Sanctuary and now employed by their mutual conqueror, Ranke. As well as by an informal league of Changers and Sanctuary's foremost thieves; those so successful they employed other thieves. With a distinct curl of his lip – a cultivated artificial manoeuvre – and a brush of his double-curled left moustachio, Shive returned his attention to the prying of a nice ruby from its entirely too recognizable setting.

Just now Cusharlain's prowling the Maze was in service of still another employer, for he was an ambitious and ever-hungry man. An amenable man, to opportunities for profit and new contracts. Today he was merely collecting information about the former apprentice of Cudget Swearoath, who had been swung shortly after the new Prince-Governor came out from Ranke to 'whip this Thieves' World of a town into shape'. Above bribery, beyond threat, the (very) young ass actually meant to govern Sanctuary! To clean it up! Young Kadakithis, whom they called Kittycat!

So far he had angered the priesthood and every thief and Changer in Sanctuary. And a good three-fifths of the taverners. And even a number of the garrison soldiers, with those baby-clean, revolting competent Hell Hounds of his. Some of the old villa-dwellers thought he was just wonderful.

Probably wets his bed, Cusharlain thought with a jerk of his head – at the same time as he expertly twitched his robe's hem away from the touch of a legless beggar. Cusharlain knew very well that the fellow's legs were single-strapped up under his long, long, tattered coat. Well, and well. So one boy of nineteen or twenty, a thief, hated another, a half-brother of the Emperor sent out here because it was the anus of the Empire, good and far from the Rankan imperial seat! This the customs inspector had learned today, while gathering information for his secretive and clandestine employer. Hanse, Hanse. In all his life this Hanse had held regard for one person other than his cocky self: Cudget Swearoath. Respected senior thief. And Cudget had been arrested, which certainly would not have happened in the old days. The days BDP, Cusharlain thought; Before this Damned Prince! Far more incredibly, if there could be grades of incredibility, Cudget had been hanged!

Prince Stupid!

'Ah, the lad knows he can't hope to do injury on the prince,' someone had told the night proprietor of the Golden Lizard, who had told Cusharlain's old friend Gelicia, proprietor of the popular House of Mermaids. 'He schemes to steal from the very Prince-Governor, and make a quick *large* profit in the doing.'

Cusharlain stared at her. 'This young gamecock means to try to rob the very palace?' he said, feeling stupid instantly; so she'd said, yes.

'Don't scoff, Cusher,' Gelicia said, waving a doughy hand well leavened with rings. This noon she was wearing apple-green and purple and lavender and mauve and orange, all in a way that exposed a large portion of her unrivalled bosom, which resembled two white cushions for a large divan and which Cusharlain was singularly uninterested in viewing.

'If it can be done, Shadowspawn'll do it,' she said. 'Oh, go ahead, tip yourself some more wine. Did you hear about the ring he tugged from under Corlas's pillow – while Corlas's head was on it, sleeping? You know, Corlas the camel-dealer. Or've you heard tell of how our boy Hanse clumb up and stole the eagle off the roof of Barracks Three for a lark?'

'I wondered what had happened to that!'

She nodded wisely with a trembling of chin and a flashing wing of earrings whose diameter was the same as his wine-cup – which was of silver. Her wine-cup, that is; the one he was using. 'Shadowspawn,' she said, 'as Eshi is my witness. Had a prodigal offer from some richie up in Twand, too – and do you know Hanse wouldn't take it? Said he liked having the thing. Pisses on it every morning on rising, he says.'

Cusharlain smiled. 'And ... if it can't be done? Roaching the palace, I mean.'

Gelicia's shrug imparted to her bosom a quake of seismic proportions. 'Why then Sanctuary will be minus one more cockroach, and no one'll miss him. Oh, my Lycansha will moon for a while, but she'll soon be over it.'

'Lycansha? Who's Lycansha?'

Nine rings flashed on Gelicia's hands as she sketched a form in the air exactly as a man would have done. 'Ah, the sweetest little Cadite oral-submissive you ever laid eyes on, who fancies that leanness and those midnight eyes of his, Cusher. Like to ... meet her? She's at liberty just now.'

'I'm on business, Gelicia.' His sigh was carefully elaborate.

'Asking about our little Shadowspawn?' Gelicia's meaty face took on a businesslike expression, which some would have called crafty-furtive.

'Aye.'

'Well. Whoever you're reporting to, Cusher – you haven't talked to me!'

'Of course not, Gelicia! Don't be silly. I haven't talked with anyone with a name, or an address, or a face. I enjoy my ... relationship with some of you more enterprising citizens' – he paused for her mirthful snort – 'and have no wish to jeopardize it. Or to lose the physical attributes necessary to my availing myself of your dear girls from time to time.'

Her snickering laugh rose and went on up to whoops about the time he reached the street, assuring him that eventually the successful Gelicia had got his parting joke. Red Lanterns was a quiet neighbourhood this time of day, after the sweeping up of the dust and tracks of last night's customers. Now sheets were being washed. A few deliveries made. A couple of workmen were occupied with a broken door-hasp at a House down the street. Cusharlain squinted upwards. The Enemy, a horrid white ball in a horrid sky going the colour of turmeric powder laced with saffron, was high, nigh to passing noon. One-Thumb should be stirring himself about now. Cusharlain decided to go and have a talk with him, too, and maybe he could get his report made by sunset. His employer did not seem as long on patience as on funds. The customs inspector of a fading city whose chief business was theft and the disposal of its product had learned the former, and was ever at work on increasing his share of the latter.

'Did what?' the startlingly good-looking woman said. 'Roaching? What's roaching mean?'

Her companion, who was only a little older than her seventeen or eighteen years, stiffened his neck to keep from looking anxiously around. 'Sh – not so loud. When do cockroaches come out?'

She blinked at the dark, so-intense young man. 'Why – at night.'

'So do thieves.'

'Oh!' She laughed, struck her hands together with a jangling of bangles – gold, definitely – and touched his arm. 'Oh, Hanse, I know so little! You know just about everything, don't you.' Her face changed. 'My, these hairs are soft.' And she left her hand on that arm with its dark, dark hairs.

'The streets are my home,' he told her. 'They birthed me and gave me suck. I know quite a bit, yes.'

He could hardly believe his luck, sitting here in a decent tavern out of the Maze with this genuinely beautiful Lirain who was ... by the Thousand Eyes and by Eshi, too, could it be? – one of the concubines the Prince-Governor had brought over from Ranke! And she's obviously fascinated with me, Hanse thought. He acted as if he sat here in the Golden Oasis every afternoon with such as she. What a coincidence, what great good fortune to have run into her in the bazaar that way! Run into her indeed! She had been hurrying and he'd been turning, glancing back at one of those child-affrighters of Jubal's, and they had slammed together and had to cling to each other to avoid falling. She had been so apologetic and in seeming need to make amends and – here they were, Hanse and a palace conky unguarded or watched, and a beauty at that – and *wearing* enough to support him for a year. He strove to be oh so cool.

'You certainly do like my gourds, don't you.'

'Wha –'

'Oh, don't dissemble. I'm not mad. Really, Hanse. If I didn't want 'em looked at I'd cover 'em in high-necked homespun.'

'Uh ... Lirain, I've seen one other pearl-sewn halter of silk in my life, and it didn't have those swirls of gold thread, or so many pearls. I wasn't this close, either.' *Damn*, he thought. *Should have complimented her, not let her know my interest is greed for the container!*

'Oh! Here I am, one of seven women for one man and bored, and I thought you were wanting to get into my bandeau, when what you really want is *it*. What's a poor girl to do, used to the flatteries of courtiers and servants, when she meets a real man who speaks his real thoughts?'

Hanse tried not to let his preening show. Nor did he know how to apologize, or to fancy-talk beyond the level of the Maze. Besides, he thought this pout-lipped beauty with her heart-shaped face and nice woman's belly was having some fun with him. She knew that pout was irresistible!

'Wear high-necked homespun,' he said, and while she laughed, 'and try not to look that way. This real man knows what you're used to, and that you can't be interested in Hanse the roach!'

Her expression became very serious. 'You must not have access to a mirror, Hanse. Why don't you try me?'

Hanse fought his astonishment and made swift recovery. With prickly armpits and outward confidence, he said, 'Would you like to take a walk, Lirain?'

'Is there a more private room at the end of it?'

Holding her gaze as she held his, he nodded.

'Yes,' she said, that quickly. Concubine of Prince Kadakithis! 'Could anything as good as this bandeau be bought in the bazaar?'

He was rising. 'Who'd buy it? No,' he said, puzzled at the question.

'Then you must buy me the best we can find after a *short* search.' She chuckled at the sight of his stricken face. The cocky creature thought she was a whore, to charge him some trifle like any girl! 'So that I can wear it back to the palace,' she said, and watched understanding brighten that frightening yet sensuous pair of onyxes he wore for eyes, all hard and cold and wary. She slid her hand into his, and they departed the Golden Oasis.

'Of *course* I'm sure, Bourne!' Lirain twitched off the blue-arabesqued bandeau of green silk Hanse had bought her, and hurled it at the man on the divan. He grinned so that his big brown beard writhed. 'He has such *needs*! He is never relaxed, and wants and needs so badly, and so wants to be and to do. He is *so* impressed with who or rather what I am, and yet he would deny under torture that I was anything but another nice tumble. You and I both well know about low-borns who hunger for far more than food! He is completely taken in and he'll be the perfect tool, Bourne. My agent assured me that he is a competent sneak-thief, and that he wants to rob and gain a leg on Prince Kittycat so badly he can taste it. I saw that, right enough. Look, it's perfect!'

'A thief. And competent, you say.' Bourne scratched his thigh under the tunic of his Hell Hound's uniform. He glanced around the apartment she occupied on nights when the prince might come – hours from now. 'And he has a valuable halter of you now, to sell. Perhaps to brag about and get you into trouble. That kind of trouble ends in death, Lirain.'

'You find it hard to admit that I – a *woman* – have accomplished this, love? Look here, that gourd-holster was stolen today in the market-place. Sliced through in back and snatched off, in a single act. Some child of about thirteen, a dirty girl who ran off with it like a racing dromedary. I did not tell anyone because I *so* hated its loss and am *so* mortified.'

'All right. Maybe. That's not bad – forget the part about its being sliced in back, lest it turn up whole. Hmm – I guess it won't. Likely perfectly good silk will be dumped while the pearls and gold thread are sold. And how *competent* was he at the couching, Lirain?'

Lirain looked to the heavens. 'O Sabellia, and we call Thee the Sharp-Tongued One! Men! Plague and drought, Bourne, can't you be more than a man? He was ... fair. That's all. I was on business. *We* are on business, love. Our assignment for those "certain interested nobles" back in Ranke – my hind leg, it's the Emperor himself, worried about his half-brother's pretty golden-haired magnetism! – is to embarrass His pretty golden-haired Highness Kadakithis! He's been doing that well enough all by himself! Trying to implement civilized law in this roach-nest of a town! Continuing to insist that temples to Savankala and Sabellia have to be mightier than the one to the Ils these people worship, and that Vashanka's must be equal to Ils's. Priests hate him and merchants hate him and thieves hate him – and thieves make this town go!'

Bourne nodded – and demonstrated his strength by drawing a fifteen-inch dagger to clean his nails.

Lirain tossed her girdle of silver links on to a pile of cushions and idly fingered her navel. 'Now we provide the finishing touch. There will never be a threat to the Emperor from this pretty boy's supporters again! We help Hanse the roach into the palace.'

'After which he is absolutely on his own,' he said, pointing with the dagger. 'We've got to be uncompromised.'

'Oh,' she said flaunting, '*I* shall be a-couching with His Highness! The while, Hanse steals his Rod of Authority: the Savankh of Ranke, given him personally by the Emperor as symbol of full authority here! Hanse will wish to negotiate a private, quiet trade with Kittycat. Rod for a fat ransom, and his safety. We will be busily seeing that word gets around. A thief broke into the palace and stole the Savankh! And the Prince-Governor is the laughing stock of the capital! He'll either rot here – or, worse still, be recalled in disgrace.'

The big man lounging so familiarly on her divan nodded slowly. 'I do have to point out that you may well rot here with him.'

'Oh, no. You and I are promised reprieve from this midden-heap town. And . . . Bourne . . . *particularly* if we heroically regain the Savankh for the honour of the Empire. After its theft is just terribly well known, of course.'

'Now, that's good!' Bourne's brows tipped up and his lips pursed, a rather obscene spectacle between the bushiness of brown moustache and beard. 'And how do we do that? You going to trade this Hanse another halter for it?'

She looked long at him. Coolly, brows arched above blue-lidded eyes. 'What's that in your hand, Guardian; Hell Hound so loyal to His Highness?'

Bourne regarded the dagger in his big hairy hand, looked at Lirain, and began to smile.

*

Though hardly beloved nor indeed particularly lovable, Hanse was a member of the community. Though a paid ally, the customs inspector was not. Hanse heard from three sources that Cusharlain had been asking after him, on behalf of someone else. After giving that thought, Hanse traded with a grimy little thief. First Hanse reminded him that he could easily take the five truly fine melons the boy had been so deft as to steal, all in an afternoon. The boy agreed to accept a longish, stiffish piece of braided gold thread, and Hanse gained four melons. With his hilt and then thumb, Hanse made a nice depression in the top of each. Into each he tucked a nice pearl; four of his thirty-four.

These he set before the hugely fat and grossly misnamed Moonflower, a S'danzo who liked food, melons, pearls, Hanse, and proving that she was more than a mere charlatan. Many others were. Few had the Gift. Even the cynical Hanse was convinced that Moonflower had.

She sat on a cushioned stool of extra width and sturdy legs. Her pile of red and yellow and green skirts overflowed it, while disguising the fact that so did her vast backside. Her back was against the east wall of the tired building wherein she and her man and seven of their brood of nine dwelt, and wherein her man sold ... things. Hanse sat cross-legged before her. Looking boyish without his arm-sheaths and in a dusty tunic the colour of an old camel. He watched a pearl disappear under Moonflower's shawl into what she called her treasure chest. He watched the melon disappear between her lavender-painted lips. Swiftly.

'You are such a good boy, Hanse.' When she talked, Moonflower was a kitten.

'Only when I want something, passionflower.'

She laughed and beamed and tousled his hair for he knew that such talk pleased her. Then he told her the story. Handed her, disguised in carefully smudged russet, a strip of silken cloth: two straps and two cupped circles bearing many thread-holes.

'Ah! You've been visiting a lady in the Path of Money! Nice of you to let Moonflower have four of the pearls you've laboriously sliced off this little sheath!'

'She gave it me for services rendered.' He waved a hand.

'Oh, of course. Hmm.' She folded it, unfolded it, fondled it, drew it through her dimple-backed hands, sniffed and tasted it with a dainty tongue-tip. A gross kitten at her divining. She closed her eyes and was very still. As Hanse was, waiting.

'She is indeed a c— what you said,' she told him, able to be discreet even though in something approaching a trance. 'Oh, Shadowspawn! You are involved in a plot beyond your dreaming. Odd – this must be the Emperor I see, watching from afar. And this big man with your – acquaintance. A big man with a big beard. In a uniform? I think so. Close to our ruler, both. Yet ... ahh ... they are his enemies. Yes. They plot. She is a serpent and he a lion of no little craft. They seek ... ah, I see. The Prince-Governor has become faceless. Yes. They seek to cost him face.' Her eyes opened to stare wide at him, two big garnets set amid a heavy layer of kohl. 'And you, Hanse my sweet, are their *tool*.'

They stared at each other for a moment. 'Best you vanish for a time, Shadowspawn. You know what becomes of tools once they are no longer needed.'

'Discarded,' he snarled, not even bemoaning the loss of Lirain's denuded bandeau, which Moonflower made vanish within a shawl-buried vaster one.

'Or,' she said, keeping him fixed by her gaze, 'hung up.'

Lirain and her (uniformed?) confederate were tools then, Hanse reasoned, prowling the streets. Prince Kadakithis was nice to look at, and charismatic. So his imperial half-brother had sent him way out here, to Sanctuary. Now he wanted him sorely embarrassed here. Hanse could see the wisdom of that, and knew that despite what any might say, the Emperor was no fool. So, then. They two plotted. Lirain gained enough knowledge of Hanse to employ Cusharlain to investigate him. She had found a way to effect their meeting. Yes; though it hurt his ego, he admitted to himself that she had made the approach and the decisions. So now he was their tool. A tool of tools!

Robbing Kadakithis, however, had been his goal before he met that cupidinous concubine. So long as she helped, he was quite willing to let her think he was her dupe. He wanted to be their tool, then – insofar as it aided him to gain easy entry to the palace. Forewarned and all that. There was definitely potential here for a clever man, and Hanse deemed himself twice as clever as he was, which was considerably. Finally, being made the tool of plotting tools was far too demeaning for the Hansean ego to accept.

Yes. He would gain the wand. Trade it to the Prince-Governor for gold – no, better make it the less intimidating silver – and freedom. From Suma or Mrsevada or some place, he'd send a message back, anonymously informing Kadakithis that Lirain was a traitor. Hanse smiled at that pleasant thought. Perhaps he'd just go up to Ranke and tell the Emperor what a pair of incompetent agents he had down in Sanctuary. Hanse saw himself richly rewarded, an intimate of the Emperor . . .

And so he and Lirain met again, and made their agreement and plan.

A gate was indeed left open. A guard did indeed quit his post before a door of the palace. It did indeed prove to be unlatched. Hanse locked it after him. Thus a rather thick-waisted Shadowspawn gained entry to the palatial home of the governor of Sanctuary. Dark corridors led him to the appointed chamber. As the prince was not in it, it was not specifically guarded. The ivory rod, carved to resemble rough-barked wood, was indeed there. So, unexpectedly enjoying the royal couch in its owner's absence, was Lirain's sister concubine. She proved not to have been drugged. She woke and opened her mouth to yell. Hanse reduced that to a squeak by punching her in the belly, which was shockingly convex and soft, considering her youth. He held a pillow over her face, sustaining a couple of scratches and a bruised shin. She became still. He made sure that she was limp but quite alive, and bound her with a gaiter off her own sandal. The other he pulled around so as to hold in place the silken garment he stuffed into her mouth, and tied behind her head. He removed the pendant from one ear. All in darkness. He hurried to wrap the rod of authority in the drape off a low table. Hitching up his tunic, he began drawing from around his waist the thirty feet of knotted rope he had deemed wise. Lirain had assured him that a sedative would be administered to the Hell Hounds' evening libation. Hanse had no way of knowing that to be the truth; that not only had one of those big burly five done the administering, he had drunk no less than the others. Bourne and company slept most soundly. The plan was that Hanse would leave the same way he had entered. Because he knew he was a tool and was suspicious unto caution, Hanse had decided to effect a different exit.

One end of the rope he secured to the table whose drape he'd stolen. The other he tossed out the window. Crosswise, the table would hold the rope without following him through the window.

It proved true. Hanse went out, and down. Slipping out westwards to wend his way among the brothels, he was aware of a number of scorpions scuttling up and down his back, tails poised. Evidently the bound occupant of His Highness's bed was not found. Dawn was still only a promise when Hanse reached his second-floor room in the Maze.

He was a long time wakeful. Admiring the symbol of Rankan authority, named for the god they claimed had given it them. Marvelling at its unimposing aspect. A twig-like wand not two feet long, of yellowing ivory. He had done it!

Shortly after noon next day, Hanse had a talk with babbly old Hakiem, who had lately done much babbling about what a fine fellow His handsome Highness was, and how he had even spoken with Hakiem, giving him two pieces of good silver as well! Today Hakiem listened to Hanse, and he swallowed often. What could he do save agree?

Carrying a pretty pendant off a woman's earring, Hakiem hied him to the palace. Gained the Presence by sending in one word to the Prince, with the pendant. Assured him he had nothing to do with the theft. Most privily Hakiem stated what he'd been told, and the thief's terms. Ransom.

The Prince-Governor had to pay, and knew it. If he could get the damned Savankh back, he'd never have to let out that it had been stolen in the first place. Taya, who had spent a night in his bed less comfortable than she had expected, had no notion what had been taken. Too, she seemed to believe his promise to stretch or excise various parts of her anatomy should she flap her mouth to anyone at all.

126

Meanwhile the concubine Lirain and Hell Hound Bourne were jubilant. Plotting. Grinning. Planning the Revelation that would destroy their employer. Indeed, they lost no time in dispatching a message to their other employers, back in Ranke. That was premature, unwise, and downright stupid.

Next came the coincidence, though it wasn't all that much one. Zalbar and Quag were sword-happy hotheads. Razkuli complained of fire in the gut and had the runs besides. That left only two Hell Hounds; whom else would the prince entrust with this mission? After a short testing conference, he chose Bourne to implement the transaction with the thief. Bourne's instructions were detailed and unequivocal: all was to be effected precisely as the thief, through Hakiem, had specified. Bourne would, of course, receive a nice bonus. He was made to understand that it was also to serve as a gag. Bourne agreed, promised, saluted, louted, departed.

Once the villa had commanded a fine view of the sea and naturally terraced landscape flowing a league along the coast to Sanctuary. Once a merchant had lived here with his family, a couple of concubines who counted themselves lucky, servants, and a small army or defence force. The merchant was wealthy. He was not liked and did not care that many did not care for the way he had achieved wealth and waxed richer. One day a pirate attack began. Two days later the gorge that marked the beginning of rough country disgorged barbarians. They also attacked. The merchant's small army proved too small. He and his armed force and servants and unlucky concubines and family were wiped out. The manse he had called Eaglenest was looted and burned. The pirates had not been pirates and the barbarians had not been barbarians – technically, at least: they were mercenaries. Thus, forty years ago, had some redistribution of wealth been achieved by that clandestine alliance of Sanctuarite nobles and merchants. Others had called Eaglenest 'Eaglebeak' then and still did, though now the tumbled ruins were occupied only by spiders, snakes, lizards, scorpions, and snails. As Eaglebeak was said to be haunted, it was avoided.

It was a fine plan for a night meeting and transfer of goods, and to Eaglebeak came Bourne, alone, on a good big prancing horse that swished its tail for the sheer joy and pride of it. The horse bore Bourne and a set of soft saddlebags, weighty and jingling.

Near the scrubby acacia specified, he drew rein and glanced about at a drear pile and scatter of building stones and their broken or crumbled pieces. His long cloak he doffed before he dismounted. Sliding off his horse, he stood clear while he unbuckled his big weapons belt. The belt, with sheathed sword and dagger, he hung on his saddle-horn. He removed the laden bags. Made them jingle. Laid them on the ground. Stepping clear of horse and ransom, he held his arms well out from his body while he turned, slowly.

He had shown the ransom and shown himself unarmed. Now a pebble flew from somewhere to whack a big chunk of granite and go skittering. At that signal, Bourne squatted and, on clear ground in the moonlight, emptied both saddlebags in a clinking, chiming, shimmering, glinting pile of silver coinage amid which gleamed a few gold disks. Laboriously and without happiness, Bourne clinked them all back into the pouches of soft leather, each the size of a nice cushion. He paced forward to lay them, clinking, atop a huge square stone against which leaned another. All as specified.

'Very good.' The voice, male and young, came out of the shadows somewhere; no valley floor was so jumbled with stones as this once-courtyard of Eaglebeak. 'Now get on your horse and ride back to Sanctuary.'

'I will not. You have something for me.'

'Walk over to the acacia tree, then, and look towards Sanctuary.'

'I will walk over to the tree and watch the saddlebags, thanks, thief. If you show up without that rod . . .'

Bourne did that, and the shadows seemed to cough up a man, young and lean and darkly dressed. The crescent moon was behind him so that Bourne could not see his face. The fellow pounced lithely atop a stone, and held high the stolen Savankh.

'I see it.'

'Good. Walk back to your horse, then. I will put this down when I pick up the bags.'

Bourne hesitated, shrugged, and began ambling towards his horse. Hanse, thinking that he was very clever indeed and wanting all that money in his hands, dropped from his granite dais and hurried to the bags. Sliding his right arm through the connecting strap, he laid down the rod he carried in his left. That was when Bourne turned around and charged. While he demonstrated how fast a big burly man in mail-coat could move, he also showed what a dishonest rascal he was. Down his back, inside his mail-shirt, on a thong attached to the camel-hair torque he wore, was a sheath. As he charged, he drew a dagger long as his forearm.

His quarry saw that the weight of the silver combined with Bourne's momentum made trying to run not only stupid, but suicidal. Still, he was young, and a thief: supple, clever, and fast. Bourne showed teeth, thinking this *boy* was frozen with shock and fear. Until Hanse moved, fast as the lizards scuttling among these great stones. The saddlebags slam-jingled into Bourne's right arm, and the knife flew away while he was knocked half around. Hanse managed to hang on to his own balance; he bashed the Hell Hound in the back with his ransom. Bourne fell sprawling. Hanse ran – for Bourne's horse. He knew Bourne could outrun him so long as he was laden with the bags, and he was not about to part with them. In a few bounds, he gained a great rock and from there pounced on to the horse's back, just as he'd seen others do. It was Hanse's first attempt to mount a horse. Inexperience and the weight of his ransom carried him right off the other side.

In odd silence, he rose, on the far side of the horse. Not cursing as anyone might expect. Here came Bourne, and his fist sprouted fifteen inches of sharp iron. Hanse drew Bourne's other dagger from the sheath on the saddle and threw the small flat knife from his buckskin. Bourne went low and left, and the knife clattered among the stumbled stones of Eaglebeak. Bourne kept moving in, attacking under the horse. Hanse struck at him with his own dagger. To avoid losing his face, Bourne had to fall. Under the horse. Hanse failed to check his swipe, and his dagger nicked the inside of the horse's left hind leg.

The animal squealed, bucked, kicked, tried to gallop. Ruins barred him, and he turned back just as Bourne rose. Hanse was moving away fast, hugging one saddlebag to him and half-dragging the other. Bourne and his horse ran into each other. One of them fell backwards and the other reared, neighed, pranced – and stood still, as if stricken with guilt. The other, downed painfully in mail for the second time in two minutes, cursed horse, Hanse, luck, gods, and himself. And began getting up.

However badly it had been handled, Bourne had horse, sword, and a few paces away, the rod of Rankan authority. Hanse had more silver than would comprise Bourne's retirement. Under its weight he could not hope to escape. He could drop it and run or be overtaken. Dragging sword from sheath, Bourne hoped the roach kept running. What fun to carve him for the next hour or so!

Hanse was working at a decision, too, but none of it fell out that way. Perhaps he should have done something about trying to buy off a god or two; perhaps he should have taken better note of the well, this afternoon, and not run that way tonight. He discovered it too late. He fell in.

He was far less aware of the fall than of utter disorientation – and of being banged in every part of his body, again and again, by the sides of the well, which were brick, and by the saddlebags. When his elbow struck the bricks, the bags were gone. Hanse didn't notice their splash; he was busy crashing into something that wasn't water. And he was hurting.

The well's old wooden platform of a cover and sawhorse affair had fallen down inside, or been so hurled by vandals or ghosts. They weren't afloat, those pieces of very old, damp wood; they were braced across the well, at a slant. Hanse hit, hurt, scrabbled, clung. His feet were in water, and his shins. The wood creaked. The well's former cover deflected the head-sized stone Bourne hurled down. The fist-sized one he next threw struck the well's wall, bounced to roll down Hanse's back, caught a moment at his belt, and dropped into the water. The delay in his hearing the splash led Bourne to misconstrue the well's depth. Hanse clung and dangled. The water was cold.

In the circle of dim light above, Hanse saw Bourne's helmeted head. Bourne, peering down into a well, saw nothing.

'If you happen to be alive, thief, keep the saddlebags! No one will ever find you or them – or the Savankh you stole! You treacherously tricked us all, you see, and fled with both ransom and Savankh. Doubtless I will be chastised severely by His pretty

Highness – and once I'm in Ranke again, I'll be rewarded! You have been a fool and a tool, boy, because I've friends back home in Ranke who will be delighted by the way *I* have brought embarrassment and shame on Prince Kittycat!'

Hanse, hurting and scared that the wood would yield, played dead. Strange how cold water could be, forty feet down in a brick-walled shaft!

Grinning, Bourne walked over and picked up the Savankh, which His stupid Highness would never see. He shoved it into his belt. Stuck his sword into the ground. And began wrestling a huge stone to drop, just in case, down the well. His horse whickered. Bourne, who had left his sword several feet away, froze. He straightened and turned to watch the approach of two helmeted men. They bore naked swords. One was a soldier. The other was – *the Prince-Governor?!*

'We thank you for letting us hear your confession, Bourne, traitor.'

Bourne moved. He gained his sword. No slouch and no fool, he slashed the more dangerous enemy. For an instant the soldier's mail held Bourne's blade. Then the man crumpled. The blade came free and Bourne spun, just in time to catch the prince's slash in the side. Never burly, Kadakithis had learned that he had to put everything he had behind his practice strokes just so that his opponents would notice. He did that now, so wildly and viciously that his blade tore several links of Bourne's mail-coat and relocated them in his flesh. Bourne made an awful noise. Horribly shocked and knowing he was *hurt*, he decided it were best to fly. He staggered as he ran, and the prince let him go.

Kadakithis picked up the fallen rod of authority and slapped it once against his leather-clad leg. His heart beat unconscionably rapidly as he knelt to help the trusted man he'd brought with him. That was not necessary. In falling, the poor wight had smashed his head open on a chunk of marble from a statue. Slain by a god. Kadakithis glanced after Bourne, who had vanished in darkness and the ruins.

The Prince-Governor stood thinking. At last he went to the well. He knelt and called down into blackness.

'I am Prince Kadakithis. I have the wand. Perhaps I speak

uselessly to one dead or dying. Perhaps not, in which case you may remain there and die slowly, or be drawn up to die under torture, or ... you can agree to help me in a little plan I have just devised. Well – speak up!'

No contemplation was required to convince Hanse that he would go along with anything that meant vacating the well and seeing his next birthday. Who'd have thought pretty Prince Kittycat would come out here, and helmeted, too! He wondered at the noises he had heard. And made reply. The wood creaked.

'You need promise only this,' Kadakithis called down. 'Be silent until you are under torture. Suffer a little, then tell all.'

'Suffer? ... Torture?'

'Come, come, you deserve both. You'll suffer only a little of what you have coming. Don't, and betray these words, roach, and you will die out of hand. No, make that slowly. Nor will anyone believe you, anyhow.'

Hanse knew that he was in over his head, both literally and figuratively. Hanging on to creaky old wood that was definitely rotting away by the second, he agreed.

'I'll need help,' the prince called. 'Hang on.'

Hanse rolled his eyes and made an ugly face. He hung on. He waited. Daring not to pull himself up on to the wood. His shoulders burned. The water seemed to grow colder, and the cold rose up in his legs. He hung on. Sanctuary was only about a league away. He hoped Kitty – the prince – galloped. He hung on. Though the sun never came up and the moon's position changed only a little, Hanse was sure that a week or two passed. Cold, dark, and sore, those weeks. Riches! Wealth! Cudget had *told* him that revenge was a stupid luxury the poor couldn't afford!

Then His clever Highness was back, with several men of the night watch and a lot of rope. While they hauled up a bedraggled, bruised Shadowspawn, the prince mentioned a call of nature and strolled away amid the clutter of big stones. He did not lift his tunic. He *did* pause on the other side of a pile of rubble. He gazed earthwards, upon a dead traitor, and slowly he smiled in satisfaction. His first kill! Then Kadakithis began puking.

*

Pitchy torches flickered to create weird, dancing shadows on stone walls grim as death. The walls framed a large room strewn with tables, chains, needles, pincers, gyves, ropes, nails, shackles, hammers, wooden wedges and blocks and splinters, pliers, fascinating gags, mouth- and tongue-stretchers, heating irons, wheels, two braziers, pulleys. Much of this charming paraphernalia was stained dark here and there. On one of the tables lay Hanse. He was bruised, cut, contused – and being stretched, all in no more than his breechclout. Also present, were Prince Kadakithis, his bright-eyed consort, two severe Hell Hounds, his oddly attired old adviser, and three Sanctuarite nobles from the council. And the palace smith. Massively constructed and black-nailed, he was an imposing substitute for the torturer, who was ill.

He took up a sledgehammer and regarded it thoughtfully. Milady Consort's eyes brightened still more. So did those of Zalbar the Hell Hound. Hanse discovered that in his present posture a gulp turned his Adam's apple into a blade that threatened to cut his throat from the inside.

The smith put down the hammer and took up a pair of long-handled pincers.

'Does he have to keep that there rag on his jewels, Yer Highness?'

'No need to torture him there,' Kadakithis said equably. He glanced at his wife, who'd gone all trembly. '*Yet*. Try a few less horrific measures. *First*.'

'Surely he isn't tall enough,' Zalbar said hopefully. He stood about six inches from the crank of the rack on which Hanse lay, taut.

'Well do *something* to him!' Milady snapped.

The smith surprised everyone. The movement was swift and the crack loud. He drew back his whip from a white stripe across Hanse's stomach. It went pink, then darker, and began to rise. The smith raised his brows as if impressed with himself. Struck again, across the captive's chest. The whip cracked like a slack sail caught in a gust. Chains rattled and Hanse's eyes and mouth went wide. A new welt began to rise. The smith added one across the tops of his thighs. An inch from the jewels, that. Milady Consort breathed through a mouth gone open.

'I don't like whippin' a man,' the smith said. 'Nor thisun either. Think I'll just ease this arm out of its socket and turn it around t'other way.'

'You needn't walk all the way around to this side,' Zalbar rumbled. 'I'll turn the crank.'

To the considerable disappointment of Zalbar and Sanctuary's first lady, Hanse began to talk. He told them about Bourne and Lirain. He could not tell them of Bourne's death, as he did not know of it.

'The Prince Governor of Sanctuary,' Kadakithis said, 'and representative of the Emperor of Ranke, is merciful to one who tells him of a plot. Release him and hold him here – without torture. Give him wine and food.'

'Damn!' Zalbar rumbled.

'Might I be getting back to my wife now, Highness? This job ain't no work for me, and I got all that anchor chain to work on tomorrow.'

Hanse, not caring who released or guarded or fed him, watched the exit of the royal party.

With Zalbar and Quag, the prince went to Lirain's apartment. 'Do you stay here,' he said, and took Quag's sword. Neither Hell Hound cared for that and Zalbar said so.

'Zalbar: I don't know if you had a big brother you hated or what, you're a mean hothead who really ought to be employed as royal wasp-killer. Now stand here and shut up and wait for me.'

Zalbar came to attention. He and Quag waited, board-stiff save for a rolling of dark eyes, while their charge entered the chamber of his treacherous concubine. And closed the door. Zalbar was sure that a week or two passed before the door opened and Kadakithis called them in. Quag's sword dripped in his hand.

The Hell Hounds hurried within and stopped short. Staring. Lirain lay not dead, but asleep, sprawled naked and *dégagée* on a rumpled couch, obviously a recent participant in love-making. Naked beside her lay Bourne, not alive, and freshly bloodied.

'I've knocked her unconscious,' the Prince said. 'Take her down to the less comfortable bed so recently vacated by that Hanse fellow, who is to be sent to my apartment. Here, Quag – oh.' The prince carefully wiped Quag's sword on Lirain's belly and thighs and handed it to his Hell Hound. Both guards, impressed and pleased, saluted. And bowed as well. They looked passing happy with their prince. Prince Kadakithis looked flagrantly happy with himself.

Attired in a soft tunic that proved a thief could be the size of a prince, Hanse sipped wine from a goblet he wished he could conceal and carry off with him. He rolled his eyes to glance around this royal chamber for audiences most private. For that reason the door was open. By it sat a deaf woman plucking a lute.

'Both of us are overdue for sleep, Hanse. The day presses on to mid-morning.'

'I am ... more accustomed to night work than y – than His Highness.'

The prince laughed. 'So you are, Shadowspawn! Amazing how many clever men turn to crime. Broke into the very palace! My very chamber! Enjoyed a royal concubine too, eh?' He sat gazing reflectively at the thief, very aware that they were nearly of an age. Peasant and prince; thief and governor. 'Well, soon Lirain will be babbling her head off, and all will know there was a plot – and from home at that! Also that she was dishonouring her royal master's bed with her co-conspirator.'

'And that His heroic Highness not only slew the son of a toad, but showed a true noble ruler's mercy by sparing a thief,' Hanse said hopefully.

'Yes, Hanse. That is being put into writing at this moment. Ah, and there were witnesses to everything! All of it!'

Hanse was overboldened to say, 'Except ... Bourne's death, my lord prince.'

'Hoho! Would you like to know about that, Hanse? You know so much already. We have holds each on the other, you and I. I killed Bourne up at Eaglenest. With one stroke,' Kadakithis added. After all, it had been his first.

Hanse stared.

'You do seem to be learning caution, Shadowspawn! I do hope

you will accept the employment I'll soon be offering you. You avoid mentioning that when you came out of that well you saw no corpse. No; he tried to flee and died a few feet away. The moment we returned here, I drugged Lirain. Drank it herself; thought she was drinking poison! She has lain with no one this night. *I* arranged her on the couch. One absolutely loyal man and I went back and fetched Bourne. My lady wife and I placed the corpse beside Lirain. Along with a bladder of the blood of a – appropriately! – pig. I thrust my sword into it before I called in Quag and Zalbar.'

Hanse continued to stare. This saffron-haired boy was clever enough to be a thief! Hanse bet he was dissembling still, too; doubtless a favoured rug merchant had aided in the bringing of Bourne's corpse into the palace!

The prince saw his stare, read it. 'Perhaps I'm not Prince Kitty-cat after all? I will shortly have high respect in Sanctuary, and wide knowledge of the plot is a weapon against my enemies at home. You are a hero – ah.' The prince nodded towards the doorway, beckoned. An oldish man entered to hand him a sheet of parchment. It soon bore the governor's signature and seal. The secretary left. Kadakithis handed the document to Hanse with a small flourish and a smile that Hanse saw was distinctly royal. Hanse glanced at it – very impressive – and looked again at the prince.

'Oh,' Kadakithis said, and no more; a prince did not apologize to a thief for forgetting his lack of education. 'It says that by my hand and in the name of the Emperor in Ranke, you are forgiven of all you may have done up to this day, Hanse. You aren't a quintuple murderer, are you?'

'I've never killed anyone, Highness.'

'I have! This very night – last night, rather!'

'Pardon, Highness, but killing's the business of them that rule, not thieves.'

Kadakithis looked long and thoughtfully at Hanse after that, and would likely quote Shadowspawn long hence. Hanse had twice to mention the ransom at the bottom of the well.

'Ah! Forgot that, didn't I. It's been a bit busy tonight – last night. I've things to do. Hanse. A busy day ahead on no sleep and much excitement. I fear I can't be bothered thinking about some coins someone may have lost down an old well. If you can get it out, do. And do return here to discuss employment with me.'

Hanse rose. He felt the kinship between them and was not comfortable with it. 'That ... will need some ... some thinking, Prince-Governor, sir. I mean ... *work*. And for you! Uh, yourself, that is – Your Highness. First I have to try to get used to the fact that I can't hate you any more.'

'Well, Hanse, maybe you can help a few others not to. I could use the help. Unless you take it ill of me to remind you that half of salvage *found* in this demesne is the property of the government.'

Hanse began to wonder about the possibility of transferring the few gold coins into one saddlebag. If he was able to get the bags out of the well. That would take time, and help. And that would require paying someone. Or cutting someone in ...

Hanse left the palace wearing a soft new tunic, eyes narrowed. Planning, calculating. Plotting.

THE PRICE OF
DOING BUSINESS

Robert Lynn Asprin

Jubal was more powerful than he appeared. Not that his form conveyed any softness or weakness. If anything, his shiny ebony skin stretched tight over lithe, firm muscles gave an immediate impression of quick strength, while his scarred, severe facial features indicated a mind which would not hesitate to use that strength to his own advantage.

Rather, it was his wealth and the shrewd mind that had accumulated it which gave Jubal power above and beyond his iron muscles and razor-edged sword. His money, and the fierce entourage of sell-swords it had bought him made him a formidable force in the social order of Sanctuary.

Blood had been the price of his freedom; great quantities of blood shed by his opponents in the gladiator pits of Ranke. Blood, too, had given him his start at wealth: seizing a poorly guarded slave caravan for later sale at a sinful profit.

Where others might be content with modest gains, Jubal continued to amass his fortune with fanatic intensity. He had learned a dear lesson while glaring through hate-slitted eyes at the crowds who cheered his gory pit victories: swords and those who wielded them were bought and sold, and thus accounted as nothing in the minds of Society. Money and Power, not skill and courage, were what determined one's standing in the social order of men. It was fear which determined who spat and who wiped in his world.

So Jubal stalked the world of merchants as he had stalked the pits, ruthlessly pouncing on each opportunity and vulnerability as he had pitilessly cut down crippled opponents in the past. To enter into a deal with Jubal was to match wits with a mind trained to equate failure with death.

With this attitude, Jubal's concerns prospered and flourished in Sanctuary. With the first of his profits, he purchased one of the old mansions to the west of town. There he resided like a bloated spider in a web, waiting for signs of new opportunities. His fangs were his sell-swords, who swaggered through the streets of Sanctuary, their features disguised by blue hawk-masks. His web was a network of informants, paid to pass the word of any incident, any business deal, or any shift in local politics, which might be of interest to their generous master.

Currently the network was humming with word of the cataclysm in town. The Rankan prince and his new ideas were shaking the very roots of Sanctuary's economic and social structure.

Jubal sat at the centre of his web and listened.

*

After a while, the status reports all began to run together, forming one boring monotone.

Jubal slouched in his throne-like chair staring vacantly at one of the room's massive incense burners, bought in an unsuccessful attempt to counter the stench carried from Sanctuary by the easterly winds. Still the reports droned on. Things had been different when he was just beginning. Then he had been able to personally manage the various facets of his growing enterprises. Now, he had to listen while others ... Something in the report caught his attention.

'Who did you kill?' he demanded.

'A blind,' Saliman repeated, blinking at the interruption. 'An informer who was not an informer. It was done to provide an example ... as you ordered.'

'Of course.' Jubal waved. 'Continue.'

He relied heavily on informants from the town for the data necessary to conduct his affairs. It was known that if one sold false information to Jubal, one was apt to be found with a slit throat and a copper piece clenched between the teeth. This was known because it happened ... frequently. What was not widely known was that if Jubal felt his informants needed an example to remind them of the penalty for selling fabrications, he would order his men to kill someone at random and leave the body with the marks of a false informer. His actual informers were not targets for these examples – good informants were hard to find. Instead, someone would be chosen who had n:ver dealt with Jubal. As his informants did not know each other's identities, the example would work.

'. . . was found this morning.' Saliman plodded on in his tireless recitation voice. 'The coin was stolen by the person discovering the body, so there will be no investigation. The thief will talk, though, so word will spread.'

'Yes, yes.' Jubal grimaced impatiently. 'Go on with another item.'

'There is some consternation along the Avenue of Temples over the new shrines being erected to Savankala and Sabellia –'

'Does it affect our operations?' Jubal interrupted.

'No,' Saliman admitted. 'But I thought you should know.'

'Now I know,' Jubal countered. 'Spare me the details. Next item.'

'Two of our men were refused service at the Vulgar Unicorn last night.'

'By who?' Jubal frowned.

'One-Thumb. He oversees the place evenings from –'

'I know who One-Thumb is!' Jubal snapped. 'I also know he's never refused service to any of my men as long as they had gold and their manners were good. If he moved against two of mine, it was because of their own actions, not because he has ill feelings towards me. Next item.'

Saliman hesitated to reorganize his thoughts, then continued.

'Increased pressure from the prince's Hell Hounds has closed the wharves to the smugglers. It is rumoured they will be forced to land their goods at the Swamp of Night Secrets as they did in the old days.'

'An inconvenience which will doubtless drive their prices up,' Jubal mused. 'How well guarded are their landings?'

'It is not known.'

'Look into it. If there's a chance we can intercept a few shipments in the Swamp, there'll be no reason to pay their inflated prices at the bazaar.'

'But if the smugglers lose shipments, they will raise their prices all the more to recover the loss.'

'Of course.' Jubal smiled. 'Which means when we sell the stolen goods, we will be able to charge higher prices and still undercut the smugglers.'

'We shall investigate the possibility. But –'

'But what?' Jubal inquired, studying his lieutenant's face. 'Out with it, man. Something's bothering you about my plan, and I want to know what it is.'

'I fear we might encounter difficulty with the Hell Hounds,' Saliman blurted. 'If they have also heard rumours of the new landing sites, they might plan an ambush of their own. Taking a shipment away from smugglers is one thing, but trying to take confiscated evidence away from the Hell Hounds ... I'm not sure the men are up to it.'

'My men? Afraid of guardsmen?' Jubal's expression darkened. 'I thought I was paying good gold to have the finest swords in Sanctuary at my disposal.'

'The Hell Hounds are not ordinary guardsmen,' Saliman protested. 'Nor are they from Sanctuary. Before they arrived, I would have said ours were the finest swords. Now ...'

'The Hell Hounds!' Jubal snarled. 'It seems all anyone can talk about is the Hell Hounds.'

'And you should listen.' Saliman bristled. 'Forgive me, Jubal, but you yourself admit the men you hire are no newcomers to battle. When they speak of a new force at large in Sanctuary, you should listen instead of decrying their judgement or abilities.'

For a moment, a spark of anger flared in Jubal's eyes. Then it died, and he leaned forward attentively in his chair.

'Very well, Saliman. I'm listening. Tell me about the Hell Hounds.'

'They ... they are unlike the guardsmen we see in Sanctuary, or even the average soldier of the Rankan army.' Saliman explained, groping for words. 'They were handpicked from the Royal Elite Guard especially for this assignment.'

'Five men to guard a royal prince.' Jubal murmured thoughtfully. 'Yes, they would have to be good.'

'That's right,' Saliman confirmed hurriedly. 'With the entire Rankan army to choose from, these five were selected for their skill at arms and unswerving loyalty to the empire. Since their

141

arrival in Sanctuary, every effort to bribe or assassinate them has ended in death for whoever attempted it.'

'You're right.' Jubal nodded. 'They could be a disruptive force. Still, they are only men, and all men have weaknesses.'

He lapsed into thoughtful silence for several moments.

'Withdraw a thousand gold pieces from the treasury,' he ordered at last. 'Distribute it to the men to spread around town, particularly to those working in the governor's palace. In exchange, I want information about the Hell Hounds, individually and collectively. Listen especially for word of dissent within their own ranks ... anything that could be used to turn them against each other.'

'It shall be done.' Saliman responded, bowing slightly. 'Do you also wish a magical investigation commissioned?'

Jubal hesitated. He had a warrior's dread of magicians and avoided them whenever possible. Still, if the Hell Hounds constituted a large enough threat ...

'Use the money for normal informants,' he decided. 'If it becomes necessary to hire a magician, then I will personally –'

A sudden commotion at the chamber's entry-way drew the attention of both men. Two blue-masked figures appeared, dragging a third between them. Despite their masks, Jubal recognized them as Mor-Am and Moria, a brother-and-sister team of sell-swords in his employment. Their apparent captive was an urchin, garbed in the dirty rags common to Sanctuary's street children. He couldn't have been more than ten years of age, but the sizzling vindictives he screeched as he struggled against his captors marked him as one knowledgeable beyond his years.

'We caught this gutter-rat on the grounds,' Mor-Am announced, ignoring the boy's protests.

'Probably out to steal something,' his sister added.

'I wasn't stealing!' the boy cried, wrenching himself free.

'A Sanctuary street-rat who doesn't steal?' Jubal raised an eyebrow.

'Of course I steal!' the urchin spat. 'Everyone does. But that's not why I came here.'

'Then why did you come?' Mor-Am demanded, cuffing the boy and sending him sprawling. 'To beg? To sell your body?'

142

'I have a message!' the boy bawled. 'For Jubal!'

'Enough, Mor-Am,' Jubal ordered, suddenly interested. 'Come here, boy.'

The urchin scrambled to his feet, pausing only to knuckle tears of anger from his eyes. He shot a glare of pure venom at Mor-Am and Moria, then approached Jubal.

'What is your name, boy?' Jubal prompted.

'I – am called Mungo,' the urchin stammered, suddenly shy. 'Are you Jubal?'

'I am,' Jubal nodded. 'Well, Mungo, where is this message you have for me?'

'It . . . it's not written down,' Mungo explained, casting a hasty glance at Mor-Am. 'I was to tell you the message.'

'Very well, tell me,' Jubal urged, growing impatient. 'And also tell me who is sending the message.'

'The message is from Hakiem,' the boy blurted. 'He bids me tell you that he has important information for sale.'

'Hakiem?' Jubal frowned.

The old storyteller! He had often been of service to Jubal when people forgot that he could listen as well as talk.

'Yes, Hakiem. He sells stories in the bazaar . . .'

'I know, I know,' Jubal snapped. For some reason, today everyone thought he knew nothing of the people in town. 'What information does he have for me, and why didn't he come himself?'

'I don't know what the information is. But it's important. So important that Hakiem is in hiding, afraid for his life. He paid me to fetch you to him, for he feels the information will be especially valuable to you.'

'Fetch me to him?' Jubal rumbled, his temper rising.

'One moment, boy,' Saliman interceded, speaking for the first time since his report was interrupted. 'You say Hakiem paid you? How much?'

'A silver coin,' the boy announced proudly.

'Show it to us!' Saliman ordered.

The boy's hand disappeared within his rags. Then he hesitated.

'You won't take it from me, will you?' he asked warily.

'Show the coin!' Jubal roared.

Cowed by the sudden outburst, Mungo extended his fist and opened it, revealing a silver coin nestled in his palm.

Jubal's eyes sought Saliman, who raised his eyebrows in silent surprise and speculation. The fact the boy actually had a silver coin indicated many things.

First: Mungo was probably telling the truth. Street-rats rarely had more than a few coppers, so a silver coin would have had to come from an outside benefactor. If the boy had stolen it, he would himself be in hiding, gloating over his ill-gotten wealth – not displaying it openly as he had just done.

Assuming the boy was telling the truth, then Hakiem's information must indeed be valuable and the danger to him real. Hakiem was not the sort to give away silver coins unless he were confident of recouping the loss and making a healthy profit besides. Even then, he would save the expense and bring the information himself, were he not truly afraid for his life.

All this flashed through Jubal's mind as he saw the coin, and Saliman's reactions confirmed his thoughts.

'Very well. We shall see what information Hakiem has. Saliman, take Mor-Am and Moria and go with Mungo to find the storyteller. Bring him here and –'

'No!' the boy cried, interrupting. 'Hakiem will only give the information to Jubal personally, and he is to come alone.'

'What?' Saliman exclaimed.

'This sounds like a trap!' Moria scowled.

Jubal waved them to silence as he stared down at the boy. It could be a trap. Then again, there could be another reason for Hakiem's request. The information might involve someone in Jubal's own force! An assassin . . . or worse, an informer! That could explain Hakiem's reluctance to come to the mansion in person.

'I will go,' Jubal said, rising and sweeping the room with his eyes. 'Alone, with Mungo. Saliman, I will require the use of your mask.'

'I want my knife back!' Mungo declared suddenly.

Jubal raised a questioning eyebrow at Mor-Am, who flushed and produced a short dagger from his belt.

'We took it from him when we caught him,' the sell-sword explained. 'A safety precaution. We had no intent to steal it.'

'Give it back,' Jubal laughed. 'I would not send my worst enemy into the streets of Sanctuary unarmed.'

'Jubal,' Saliman murmured as he surrendered his hawk-mask. 'If this should be a trap . . .'

Jubal dropped a hand to his sword hilt.

'If it is a trap,' he smiled, 'they'll not find me easy prey. I survived five-to-one odds and worse in the pits before I won my freedom.'

'But –'

'You are not to follow,' Jubal ordered sternly. 'Nor allow any other to follow. Anyone who disobeys will answer to me.'

Saliman drew a breath to answer, then saw the look in Jubal's eyes and nodded in silent acceptance.

Jubal studied his guide covertly as they left the mansion and headed towards the town. Though he had not shown it openly, he had been impressed with the boy's spirit during their brief encounter. Alone and unarmed in the midst of hostile swords . . . men twice Mungo's age had been known to tremble and grovel when visiting Jubal at his mansion.

In many ways, the boy reminded Jubal of himself as a youth. Fighting and rebellious, with no parents but his pride and stubbornness to guide him, he had been bought from the slave pens by a gladiator trainer with an eye for cold, spirited fighters. If he had instead been purchased by a gentle master . . . if someone interceded in the dubious path Fate had chosen for Mungo . . .

Jubal halted that line of thought with a grimace as he realized where it was leading. Adopt the boy into his household? Ridiculous! Saliman and the others would think he had gone soft in his old age. More important, his competitors would see it as a sign of weakness, an indication that Jubal could be reached by sentimentality . . . that he had a heart. He had risen above his own squalid beginnings; the boy would just have to do the same!

The sun was high and staggering in its heat as Jubal followed the boy's lead into town. Sweat trickled in annoying rivulets from beneath his blue hawk-mask, but he was loath to acknowledge his discomfort by wiping them away. The thought of removing the mask never entered his mind. The masks were necessary to disguise those in his employment who were wanted by the law; to complete the camouflage, all must wear them. To exempt himself from his own rule would be unthinkable.

In an effort to distract himself from his discomfort, Jubal began to peer cautiously at the people about him as they approached the bazaar. Since they had crossed the bridge and placed the hovels of the Downwinders behind them, there was a marked improvement in the quality of clothes and manners of the citizenry.

His eye fell on a magician, and he wondered about the star tattooed on the man's forehead. Then, too, he noted that the mage was engaged in a heated argument with a brightly garbed young bravo who displayed numerous knives, their hilts protruding from arm-sheath, sash, and boot top in ominous warning.

'That's Lythande,' Mungo informed him, noting his interest. 'He's a fraud. If you're looking for a magician, there are better to be had . . . cheaper.'

'You're sure he's a fraud?' Jubal asked, amused at the boy's analysis.

'If he were a true magician, he wouldn't have to carry a sword,' Mungo countered, pointing to the weapon slung at the magician's side.

'A point well taken,' Jubal acknowledged. 'And the man he's arguing with?'

'Shadowspawn,' the boy announced loftily. 'A thief. Used to work with Cudget Swearoath before the old fool got himself hung.'

'A magician and a thief,' Jubal murmured thoughtfully, glancing at the two again. 'An interesting combination of talents.'

'Unlikely!' Mungo scoffed. 'Whatever Shadowspawn's last venture was, it was profitable. He's been spending freely and often, so it's unlikely he'll be looking for more work. My guess would be they're arguing over a woman. They each fancy themselves to be a gift from the gods to womankind.'

'You seem to be well informed,' Jubal commented, impressed anew with the boy's knowledge.

'One hears much in the streets.' Mungo shrugged. 'The lower

146

one's standing is, the more important information is for survival ... and few are lower than my friends and I.'

Jubal pondered this as the boy led the way past Shambles Cross. Perhaps he had overlooked a valuable information source in the street children when he built his network of informers. They probably would not hear much, but there were so many of them. Together they might be enough to confirm or quash a rumour.

'Tell me, Mungo,' he called to his guide. 'You know I pay well for information, don't you?'

'Everyone knows that.' The urchin turned into the Maze and skipped lightly over a prone figure, not bothering to see if the man were asleep or dead.

'Then why is it that none of your friends come to me with their knowledge?'

Jubal stepped carefully over the obstacle and cast a wary glance about. Even in broad daylight, the Maze could be a dangerous place for a lone traveller.

'We street-rats are close,' Mungo explained over his shoulder. 'Even closer than the bazaar people or the S'danzo. Shared secrets lose their value, so we keep them for ourselves.'

Jubal recognized the wisdom in the urchin's policy, but it only heightened his resolve to recruit the children.

'Talk it over with your friends,' he urged. 'A full stomach can ... where are we going?'

They had left the dank Serpentine for an alley so narrow that Jubal had to edge sideways to follow.

'To meet Hakiem,' Mungo called, not slackening his pace.

'But where is he?' Jubal pressed. 'I do not know this rat run.'

'If you knew it, it would not make a good hiding place.' The boy laughed. 'it's just a little further.'

As he spoke, they emerged from the crawl-space into a small courtyard.

'We're here,' Mungo announced, coming to a halt in the centre of the yard.

'Where?' Jubal growled standing beside him. 'There are no doors or windows in these walls. Unless he is hiding in one of those refuse heaps ...'

He broke off his commentary as the details of their surroundings sank into his mind. No doors or windows! The only other way out of the courtyard was another crawl-space as small as that they had just traversed . . . except that it was blocked by a pile of wooden cartons. They were in a cul-de-sac!

A sudden crash sounded behind them, and Jubal spun to face it, his hand going reflexively to his sword. Several wooden boxes had fallen from the roof of one of the buildings, blocking the entrance.

'It's a trap!' he hissed, backing towards a corner, his eyes scanning the rooftops.

There was a sudden impact on his back. He staggered slightly, then lashed backwards with his sword, swinging blind. His blade encountered naught but air, and he turned to face his attacker.

Mungo danced lightly just out of sword range, his eyes bright with triumph and glee.

'Mungo?' Jubal asked, knowing the answer.

He had been wounded often enough to recognize the growing numbness in his upper back. A rasp of pain as he shifted his stance told the rest of the story. The boy had planted his dagger in Jubal's back, and there it remained. In his mind's eye, Jubal could see it protruding from his shoulder at an unnatural angle.

'I told you we were close,' Mungo taunted. 'Maybe the big folk are afraid of you, but we aren't. You shouldn't have ordered Gambi's death.'

'Gambi?' Jubal frowned, weaving slightly. 'Who is Gambi?'

For a moment, the boy froze in astonishment. Then his face contorted with rage and he spat.

'He was found this morning with his throat cut and a copper coin in his mouth. Your trademark! Don't you even know who you kill?'

The blind! Jubal cursed himself for not listening closer to Saliman's reports.

'Gambi never sold you *any* information,' Mungo shouted. 'He hated you for what your men did to his mother. You had no right to kill him as a false informer.'

'And Hakiem?' Jubal asked, stalling for time.

'We guessed right about that, didn't we – about Hakiem being one of your informers?' the boy crowed. 'He's on the big wharf sleeping off a drunk. We pooled our money for the silver coin that drew you out from behind your guards.'

For some reason, this last taunt stung Jubal more than had the dagger thrust. He drew himself erect, ignoring the warm liquid dripping down his back from the knife wound, and glared down at the boy.

'I need no guard against the likes of you!' he boomed. 'You think you know killing? A street-rat who stabs overhand with a knife? The next time you try to kill a man   if there is another time – thrust underhand. Go between the ribs, not through them! And bring friends – one of you isn't enough to kill a real man.'

'I brought friends!' Mungo laughed, pointing. 'Do you think they'll be enough?'

Jubal risked a glance over his shoulder. The gutter-rats of Sanctuary were descending on the courtyard. Scores of them! Scrabbling over the wooden cases or swarming down from the roofs like spiders. Children in rags – none of them even half Jubal's height, but with knives, rocks, and sharp sticks.

Another man might have broken before those hate-filled eyes. He might have tried to beg or bribe his way out of the trap, claiming ignorance of Gambi's murder. But this was Jubal, and his eyes were as cold as his sword as he faced his tormentors.

'You claim you're doing this to avenge one death,' he sneered. 'How many will die trying to pull me down?'

'You feel free to kill us one at a time, for no reason,' Mungo retorted, circling wide to join the pack. 'If some of us die killing you, then at least the rest will be safe.'

'Only if you kill me,' Jubal corrected. Without taking his eyes from the pack, he reached his left hand over his right shoulder, found the knife hilt, and wrenched it free. 'And for that, you'll need your knife back!'

Mungo saw the knife coming as Jubal whipped his left hand down and across his body, but he froze for a split second. In that split second, the knife took him full in the throat. The world blurred and he went down, not feeling the fall.

The pack surged forward, and Jubal went to meet them, his sword flashing in the sun as he desperately tried to win his way to the exit.

A few fell before his first rush – he didn't know how many – but the rest scattered and closed about him from all sides. Sticks jabbed at his face faster than he could parry them, and he felt the touch of knives as small forms darted from behind him to slash and duck away.

Realization came to him that the harassment would bring him down before he could clear the wooden cases; abandoning his charge, he paused, whirling and cutting, trying to clear a space around him. The urchins were sharp-toothed, elusive phantoms, disappearing from in front of him to worry him from behind. It flashed through his mind that he was going to die! The survivor of countless gladiator duels was going to meet his end at the hands of angry children!

The thought drove him to desperate action. With one last powerful cut, he broke off his efforts at defence and tried to sprint for the wall to get something solid at his back. A small girl grabbed his ankle and clung with all her strength. He stumbled, nearly falling, and cut downwards viciously without looking. His leg came free, but another urchin leapt on to his back, hammering at his head with a rock.

Jubal lurched sideways, scraping the child off along the wall, then turned to face the pack. A stick pierced his mask, opening a gash in his forehead which began to drip blood in his eyes. Temporarily blinded, he laid about him wildly with his sword, sometimes striking something solid, sometimes encountering air. A rock caromed off his head, but he was past feeling and continued his sightless, mindless slashing.

Slowly it crept into his fogged brain that there was a new note in the children's screams. At the same time, he realized that his sword had not struck a target for ten or fifteen swings now. Shaking his head to clear it, he focused anew on the scene before him.

The courtyard was littered with small bodies, their blood a bright contrast to their drab rags. The rest of the pack was in full flight, pursued over the rubble piles by . . .

Jubal sagged against the wall, fighting for breath and numb from

150

wounds too numerous to count. He watched as his rescuer strode to his side, sheathing a sword wet with fresh blood.

'Your ... your name?' he gasped.

'Zalbar,' the uniformed figure panted in return. 'Bodyguard to His Royal Highness, Prince Kadakithis. Your wounds ... are they ...?'

'I've survived worse.' Jubal shrugged, wincing at the pain the movement caused.

'Very well.' the man nodded. 'Then I shall be on my way.'

'A moment,' Jubal asked, holding up a restraining hand. 'You have saved my life ... a life I value quite highly. I owe you thanks and more, for you can't spend words. Name your reward.'

'That is not necessary,' Zalbar sniffed. 'It is my duty.'

'Duty or not,' Jubal argued, 'I know no other guardsman who would enter the Maze, much less risk his life to save ... Did you say a royal bodyguard: Are you ...'

'A Hell Hound,' Zalbar finished with a grim smile. 'Yes, I am. And I promise you, the day is not far off when we will not be the only guardsmen in the Maze.'

He turned to go, but Jubal stopped him again, removing the hawk-mask to mop the blood from his eyes.

'Wait!' he ordered. 'I have a proposal for you. I have need of men such as you. Whatever pay you receive from the Empire, I'll double it ... as well as adding a bonus for your work today. What say you?'

There was no answer. Jubal squinted to get the Hell Hound's face in focus, and found the man was staring at him in frozen recognition.

'You are Jubal!' Zalbar said in a tone that was more statement than question.

'I am,' Jubal nodded. 'If you know that, you must also know that there is none in Sanctuary who pays higher than I for services rendered.'

'I know your reputation,' the Hell Hound acknowledged coldly. 'Knowing what I do, I would not work for you at any price.'

The rebuff was obvious, but Jubal chose to ignore it. Instead, he attempted to make light of the comment.

'But you already have,' he pointed out. 'You saved my life.'

'I saved a citizen from a pack of street-rats,' Zalbar countered. 'As I said before, it's my duty to my prince.'

'But –' Jubal began.

'Had I known your identity sooner,' the Hell Hound continued, 'I might have been tempted to delay my rescue.'

This time, the slight could not be ignored. More puzzled than angry, Jubal studied his opponent.

'I sense you are trying to provoke a fight. Did you save me, then, to wreak some vengeance of your own?'

'In my position, I cannot and will not engage in petty brawls,' Zalbar growled. 'I fight only to defend myself or the citizens of the empire.'

'And I will not knowingly raise a sword against one who has saved my life ... save in self-defence,' Jubal retorted. 'It would seem, then, that we will not fight each other. Still, it seems you hold some grudge against me. May I ask what it is?'

'It is the grudge I hold against any man who reaps the benefits of Rankan citizenship while accepting none of the responsibility,' the Hell Hound sneered. 'Not only do you not serve the empire that shelters you, you undermine its strength by openly flaunting your disrespect for its laws in your business dealings.'

'What do you know of my business dealings that allows you to make such sweeping judgements?' Jubal challenged.

'I know you make your money in ways decent men would shun,' Zalbar retorted. 'You deal in slaves and drugs and other high-profit, low-moral commodities ... but most of all, you deal in death.'

'A professional soldier condemns me for dealing in death?' Jubal smiled.

The Hell Hound flushed red at the barb. 'Yes. I also deal in death. But a soldier such as myself fights for the good of the empire, not for selfish gain. I lost a brother and several friends in the mountain campaigns fighting for the empire ... for the freedoms you and your kind abuse.'

'Imagine that,' Jubal mused. 'The whole Rankan army defending us against a few scattered mountain tribes. Why, if you and your friends hadn't been there, the Highlanders certainly would have swept down out of the mountains they haven't left for generations and murdered us all in our sleep. How silly of me to think it was the empire trying to extend its influence into one more place it wasn't wanted. I should have realized it was only trying to defend itself from a ferocious attacker.'

Zalbar swayed forwards, his hand going to his sword hilt. Then he regained his composure and hardened his features.

'I am done talking to you. You can't understand the minds of decent men, much less their words.'

He turned to go, but somehow Jubal was in his path – on his feet now, though he swayed from the effort. Though the soldier was taller by a head, Jubal's anger increased his stature to where it was Zalbar who gave ground.

'If you're done talking, Hell Hound, then it's time I had my say,' he hissed. 'It's true I make money from distasteful merchandise. I wouldn't be able to do that if your "decent men" weren't willing to pay a hefty price for it. I don't sell my goods at sword point. They come to me – so many of them, I can't fill the demand through normal channels.'

He turned to gesture at the corpse-littered courtyard.

'It's also true I deal in death,' he snarled. 'Your benevolent Rankan masters taught me the trade in the gladiator pits of the capital. I dealt in death then for the cheers of those same "decent men" you admire so.

'Those "decent men" allowed me no place in their "decent" society after I won my freedom, so I came to Sanctuary. Now I still deal in death, for that is the price of doing business here – a price I almost paid today.'

For a fleeting moment, something akin to sympathy flashed in the Hell Hound's eyes as he shook his head.

'You're wrong, Jubal,' he said quietly. 'You've already paid the price for doing business in Sanctuary. It isn't your life, it's your soul ... your humanity. You've exchanged it for gold, and in my opinion, it was a poor bargain.'

Their eyes met, and it was Jubal who averted his gaze first, unsettled by the Hell Hound's words. Looking away, his glance fell on the body of Mungo – the boy he had admired and thought of bringing into his household – the boy whose life he had wanted to change.

When he turned again, the Hell Hound was gone.

BLOOD BROTHERS

Joe Haldeman

Smiling, bowing as the guests leave. A good luncheon, much re-
assuring talk from the gentry assembled: the economy of Sanctuary
is basically sound. Thank you, my new cook ... he's from Twand,
isn't he a marvel? *The host appears to be rather in need of a new*
diet than a new cook, though the heavy brocades he affects may make
him look stouter than he actually is. Good leave ... certainly, tomorrow. Tell your aunt I'm thinking of her.

You will stay, of course, Amar. *One departing guest raises an*
eyebrow slightly, our host a boy-lover? We do have business.

Enoir, you may release the servants until dawn. Give yourself
a free evening as well. We will be dining in the city.

And thank you for the excellent service. Here.

He laughs. Don't thank me. Just don't spend it all on one
woman. *As the servant-master leaves, our host's bluff expression*
fades to one of absolute neutrality. He listens to the servant-master's
progress down the stone steps, overhears him dismissing the servants.
Turns and gestures to the pile of cushions by the huge fireplace.
The smell of winter's ashes masked by incense fumes.

I have a good wine, Amar. Be seated while I fetch it.

Were you comfortable with our guests?

Merchants, indeed. But one does learn from other classes, don't
you agree?

He returns with two goblets of wine so purple it is almost black.
He sets both goblets in front of Amar: choose. Even closest friends
follow this ritual in Sanctuary, where poisoning is art, sport, profes-
sion. Yes, it was the colour that intrigued me. Good fortune.

No, it's from a grove in the mountains, east of Syr. Kalos or

something; I could never get my tongue around their barbaric ...
yes. A good dessert wine. Would you care for a pipe?

Enoir returns, jingling his bell as he walks up the steps.

That will be all for today, thank you ...

No, I don't want the hounds fed. Better sport Ilsday if they're
famished. We can live with their whimpering.

The heavy front door creaks shut behind the servant-master. You
don't? You would not be the only noble in attendance. Let your
beard grow a day or two, borrow some rag from a servant ...

Well, there are two schools of thinking. Hungry dogs are weaker
but fight with desperation. And if your dogs aren't fed for a week,
there's a week they can't be poisoned by the other teams.

Oh, it does happen – I think it happened to me once. Not a
killing poison, just one that makes them listless, uncompetitive.
Perhaps a spell. Poison's cheaper.

*He drinks deeply, then sets the goblet carefully on the floor. He
crosses the room and mounts a step and peers through a slot window
cut in the deep wall.*

I'm sure we're alone now. Drink up; I'll fetch the krrf. *He is
gone for less than a minute, and returns with a heavy brick wrapped
in soft leather.*

Caronne's finest, pure black, unadulterated. *He unfolds the
package: ebony block embossed all over its surface with a foreign
seal. Try some?*

He nods. 'A wise vintner who avoids his wares.' You have the gold?

He weighs the bag in his hand. This is not enough. Not by half.

He listens and hands back the gold. Be reasonable. If you feel
you can't trust my assay, take a small amount back to Ranke;
have anyone test it. Then bring me the price we established.

*The other man suddenly stands and claws at his falchion, but it
barely clears its sheath, then clatters on the marble floor. He falls
to his hands and knees, trembling, stutters a few words, and collapses.*

No, not a spell, though nearly as swift, don't you think? That's
the virtue of coadjutant poisons. The first ingredient you had along
with everyone else, in the sauce for the sweetmeats. Everyone but
me. The second part was in the wine, part of its sweetness.

He runs his thumbnail along the block, collecting a pinch of krrf,

156

which he rubs between thumb and forefinger and then sniffs. You really should try it. It makes you feel young and brave. But then you are young and brave, aren't you.

He carefully wraps the krrf up and retrieves the gold. Excuse me. I have to go change. *At the door he hesitates.* The poison is not fatal; it only leaves you paralysed for a while. Surgeons use it.

The man stares at the floor for a long time. He is conscious of drooling, and other loss of control.

When the host returns, he is barely recognizable. Instead of the gaudy robe, he wears a patched and stained houppelande with a rope for a belt. The pomaded white mane is gone; his bald scalp is creased with a webbed old scar from a swordstroke. His left thumb is missing from the second joint. He smiles, and shows almost as much gap as tooth.

I am going to treat you kindly. There are some who would pay well to use your helpless body, and they would kill you afterwards.

He undresses the limp man, clucking, and again compliments himself for his charity, and the man for his well-kept youth. He lifts the grate in the fireplace and drops the garment down the shaft that serves for disposal of ashes.

In another part of town, I'm known as One-Thumb; here, I cover the stump with a taxidermist's imitation. Convincing, isn't it? *He lifts the man easily and carries him through the main door.* No fault of yours, of course, but you're distantly related to the magistrate who had my thumb off. *The barking of the dogs grows louder as they descend the stairs.*

Here we are. *He pushes open the door to the kennels. The barking quiets to pleading whines. Ten fighting hounds, each in an individual run, up against its feeding trough, slavering politely, yawning grey sharp fangs.*

We have to feed them separately, of course. So they don't hurt each other.

At the far end of the room is a wooden slab at waist-level, with channels cut in its surface leading to hanging buckets. On the wall above it, a rack with knives, cleavers, and a saw.

He deposits the mute staring man on the slab and selects a heavy cleaver.

I'm sorry, Amar. I have to start with the feet. Otherwise it's a terrible mess.

There are philosophers who argue that there is no such thing as evil *qua* evil: that, discounting spells (which of course relieve an individual of responsibility), when a man commits an evil deed he is the victim himself, the slave of his progeniture and nurturing. Such philosophers might profit by studying Sanctuary.

Sanctuary is a seaport, and its name goes back to a time when it provided the only armed haven along an important caravan route. But the long war ended, the caravans abandoned that route for a shorter one, and Sanctuary declined in status – but not in population, because for every honest person who left to pursue a normal life elsewhere, a rogue drifted in to pursue *his* normal life.

Now, Sanctuary is still appropriately named, but as a haven for the lawless. Most of them, and the worst of them, are concentrated in that section of town known as the Maze, a labyrinth of streets and nameless alleys and no churches. There is communion, though, of a rough kind, and much of it goes on in a tavern named the Vulgar Unicorn, which features a sign in the shape of that animal improbably engaging itself, and is owned by the man who usually tends bar on the late shift, an ugly sort of fellow by the name of One-Thumb.

One-Thumb finished feeding the dogs, hosed the place down, and left his estate by way of a long tunnel, that led from his private rooms to the basement of the Lily Garden, a respectable whorehouse a few blocks from the Maze.

He climbed the long steps up from the basement and was greeted by a huge eunuch with a heavy glaive balanced insolently over his shoulder.

'Early today, One-Thumb.'

'Sometimes I like to check on the help at the Unicorn.'

'Surprise inspection?'

'Something like that. Is your mistress in?'

'Sleeping. You want a wench?'

'No, just business.'

The eunuch inclined his head. 'That's business.'

'Tell her I have what she asked for, and more, if she can afford it. When she's free. If I'm not at the Unicorn, I'll leave word as to where we can meet.'

'I know what it is,' the eunuch said in a singsong voice.

'Instant maidenhead.' One-Thumb hefted the leather-wrapped brick. 'One pinch, properly inserted, turns you into a girl again.'

The eunuch rolled his eyes. 'An improvement over the old method.'

One-Thumb laughed along with him. 'I could spare a pinch or so, if you'd care for it.'

'Oh ... not on duty.' He leaned the sword against the wall and found a square of parchment in his money-belt. 'I could save it for my off time, though.' One-Thumb gave him a pinch. He stared at it before folding it up. 'Black ... Caronne?'

'The best.'

'You have that much of it.' He didn't reach towards his weapon.

One-Thumb's free hand rested on the pommel of his rapier. 'For sale, twenty *grimales*.'

'A man with no scruples would kill you for it.'

Gap-toothed smile. 'I'm doubly safe with you, then.'

The eunuch nodded and tucked away the krrf, then retrieved the broadsword. 'Safe with anyone not a stranger.' Everyone in the Maze knew of the curse that One-Thumb expensively maintained to protect his life: if he were killed, his murderer would never die, but live forever in helpless agony:

> Burn as the stars burn;
> Burn on after they die.
> Never to the peace of ashes.
> Out of sight and succour
> From men or gods or ghost:
> To the ends of time, burn.

One-Thumb himself suspected that the spell would only be effective for as long as the sorcerer who cast it lived, but that was immaterial. The reputation of the sorcerer, Mizraith, as well as the severity of the spell, kept blades in sheaths and poison out of his food.

'I'll pass the message on. Many thanks.'

'Better mix it with snuff, you know. Very strong.' One-Thumb parted a velvet curtain and passed through the foyer, exchanging greetings with some of the women who lounged there in soft veils (the cut and colour of the veils advertised price, and in some cases, curious specialties), and stepped out into the waning light of the end of day.

The afternoon had been an interesting array of sensations for a man whose nose was as refined as it was large. First the banquet, with all its aromatic Twand delicacies, then the good rare wine with a delicate tang of half-poison, then the astringent krrf sting, the rich charnel smell of butchery, the musty sweat of the tunnel's rock walls, perfume and incense in the foyer, and now the familiar stink of the street. As he walked through the gate into the city proper, he could tell the wind was westering; the earthy smell from the animal pens had a slight advantage over the tanners' vats of rotting urine. He even sorted out the delicate cucumber fragrance of freshly butchered fish, like a whisper in a jabbering crowd; not many snouts had such powers of discrimination. As ever, he enjoyed the first few minutes within the city walls, before the reek stunned even his nose to dullness.

Most of the stalls in the Farmer's Market were shuttered now, but he was able to trade two coppers for a fresh melon, which he peeled as he walked into the bazaar, the krrf inconspicuous under his arm.

He haggled for a while with a coppersmith, new to the bazaar, for a brace of lamps to replace the ones that had been stolen from the Unicorn last night. He would send one of his urchins around to pick them up. He watched the acrobats for a while, then went to the various wine merchants for bids on the next week's ordinaries. He ordered a hundredweight of salt meat, sliced into snacks, to be delivered that night, and checked the guild hall of the mercenaries to find a hall guard more sober than the one who had allowed the lamps to be stolen. Then he went down to the Wideway and had an early dinner of raw fish and crab fritters. Fortified, he entered the Maze.

As the eunuch had said, One-Thumb had nothing to fear from the regular denizens of the Maze. Desperadoes who would dis-

embowel children for sport (a sport sadly declining since the intro-
duction of a foolproof herbal abortifacient) tipped their hats res-
pectfully, or stayed out of his way. Still, he was careful. There
were always strangers, often hot to prove themselves, or desperate
for the price of bread or wine; and although One-Thumb was a
formidable opponent with or without his rapier, he knew he looked
rather like an overweight merchant whose ugliness interfered with
his trade.

He also knew evil well, from the inside, which is why he dressed
shabbily and displayed no outward sign of wealth. Not to prevent
violence, since he knew the poor were more often victims than
the rich, but to restrict the class of his possible opponents to those
who would kill for coppers. They generally lacked skill.

On the way to the Unicorn, on Serpentine, a man with the con-
spicuously casual air of a beginner pickpocket fell in behind him.
One-Thumb knew that the alley was coming up and would be in
deep shadow, and it had a hiding-niche a few paces inside. He
turned into the alley and, drawing the dagger from his boot, slipped
into the niche and set the krrf between his feet.

The man did follow, proof enough, and when his steps faltered
at the darkness, One-Thumb spun out of the niche behind him,
clamped a strong hand over his mouth and nose, and methodically
slammed the stiletto into his back, time and again, aiming for
kidneys. When the man's knees buckled, One-Thumb let him down
slowly, slitting his throat for silence. He took the money-belt and
a bag of coin from the still-twitching body, cleaned and replaced
his dagger, picked up the krrf, and resumed his stroll down the
Serpentine. There were a few bright spatters of blood on his
houppelande, but no one on that street would be troubled by it.
Sometimes guardsmen came through, but not to harass the good
citizens nor criticize their quaint customs.

Two in one day, he thought; it had been a year or more since
the last time that happened. He felt vaguely good about it, though
neither man had been much of a challenge. The cutpurse was a
clumsy amateur and the young noble from Ranke a trusting fool
(whose assassination had been commissioned by one of his father's
ministers).

He came up the street south of the Vulgar Unicorn's entrance

161

and let himself in the back door. He glanced at the inventory in the storeroom and noted that it must have been a slow day, and went through to his office. He locked up the krrf in a strongbox and then poured himself a small glass of lemony aperitif, and sat down at the one-way mirror that allowed him to watch the bar unseen.

For an hour he watched money and drink change hands. The bar-tender, who had been the cook aboard a pirate vessel until he'd lost a leg, seemed good with the customers and reasonably honest, though he gave short measures to some of the more intoxicated patrons – probably not out of concern for their welfare. He started to pour a third glass of the liqueur and saw Amoli, the Lily Garden's mistress, come into the place, along with the eunuch and another bodyguard. He went out to meet them.

'Wine over here,' he said to a serving wench, and escorted the three to a curtained-off table.

Amoli was almost beautiful, though she was scarcely younger than One-Thumb, in a trade that normally aged one rapidly. She came to the point at once: 'Kalem tells me you have twenty *grimales* of Caronne for sale.'

'Prime and pure.'

'That's a rare amount.' One-Thumb nodded. 'Where, may I ask, did it come from?'

'I'd rather not say.'

'You'd better say. I had a twenty-*grimale* block in my bedroom safe. Yesterday it was stolen.'

One-Thumb didn't move or change expression. 'That's an interesting coincidence.'

She snorted. They sat without speaking while a pitcher of wine and four glasses were slipped through the curtain.

'Of course I'm not accusing you of theft,' she said. 'But you can understand why I'm interested in the person you bought it from.'

'In the first place, I didn't buy it. In the second, it didn't come from Sanctuary.'

'I can't afford riddles, One-Thumb. Who was it?'

'That has to remain secret. It involves a murder.'

'You might be involved in another,' she said tightly.

One-Thumb slowly reached down and brought out his dagger. The bodyguards tensed. He smiled, and pushed it across the table to Amoli. 'Go ahead, kill me. What happens to you will be rather worse than going without krrf.'

'Oh –' She knocked the knife back to him. 'My temper is short nowadays. I'm sorry. But the krrf's not just for me; most of my women use it, and take part of their pay in it, which is why I like to buy in large amounts.' One-Thumb was pouring the wine; he nodded. 'Do you have any idea how much of my capital was tied up in that block?'

He replaced the half-full glasses on the round serving tray and gave it a spin. 'Half?'

'And half again of that. I *will* get it back, One-Thumb!' She selected a glass and drank.

'I hope you do. But it can't be the same block.'

'Let me judge that – have you had it for more than two days?'

'No, but it must have left Ranke more than a week ago. It came on the Anenday caravan. Hidden inside a cheese.'

'You can't know for sure that it was on the caravan all the time. It could have been waiting here until the caravan came.'

'I can hear your logic straining, Amoli.'

'But not without reason. How often have you seen a block as large as twenty *grimales*?'

'Only this time,' he admitted.

'And is a pressed design stamped all over it uniformly, an eagle within a circle?'

'It is. But that only means a common supplier, his mark.'

'Still, I think you owe me information.'

One-Thumb sipped his wine. 'All right. I know I can trust the eunuch. What about the other?'

'I had a vassal spell laid on him when I bought him. Besides ... show him your tongue, Gage.' The slave opened his mouth and showed pink scar tissue nested in bad teeth. 'He can neither speak nor write.'

'We make an interesting table,' he said. 'Missing thumb, tongue, and tamale. What are you missing, Amoli?'

'Heart. And a block of krrf.'

'All right.' He drank off the rest of his small glass and refilled it. 'There is a man high in the court of Ranke, old and soon to die. His son, who would inherit his title, is slothful, incompetent, dishonest. The old man's counsellors would rather the daughter succeed; she is not only more able, but easier for them to control.'

'I think I know the family you speak of,' Amoli said.

'When I was in Ranke on other business, one of the counsellors got in touch with me, and commissioned me to dispose of this young pigeon, but to do it in Sanctuary. The twenty *grimales* was my pay, and also the goad, the bait. The boy is no addict, but he is greedy, and the price of krrf is three times higher in the court of Ranke than it is in the Maze. It was arranged for me to befriend him and, eventually, offer to be his wholesaler.

'The counsellor procured the krrf from Caronne and sent word to me. I sent back a tempting offer to the boy. He contrived to make the journey to Sanctuary, supposedly to be introduced to the Emperor's brother. He'll miss the appointment.'

'That's his blood on your sleeve?' the eunuch asked.

'Nothing so direct; that was another matter. When he's supposed to be at the palace tomorrow, he'll be floating in the harbour, disguised as the shit of dogs.'

'So you got the krrf and the boy's money as well,' Amoli said.

'Half the money. He tried to croy me.' He refilled the woman's glass. 'But you see. There can be no connection.'

'I believe there may be. Anenday was when mine disappeared.'

'Did you keep it wrapped in a cheese?'

She ignored that. 'Who delivered yours?'

'Marype, the youngest son of my sorcerer Mizraith. He does all of my caravan deliveries.'

The eunuch and Amoli exchanged glances. 'That's it! It was from Marype I bought the block. Not two hours after the caravan came in.' Her face was growing red with fury.

One-Thumb drummed his fingers on the table. 'I didn't get mine till evening,' he admitted.

'Sorcery?'

'Or some more worldly form of trickery,' One-Thumb said

slowly. 'Marype is studying his father's trade, but I don't think he's adept enough to transport material objects ... could your krrf have been an illusion?'

'It was no illusion. I tried a pinch.'

'Do you recall from what part of the block you took it?'

'The bottom edge, near one corner.'

'Well, we can settle one thing,' he said, standing. 'Let's check mine in that spot.'

She bade the bodyguards stay, and followed One-Thumb. At the door to his office, while he was trying to make the key work, she took his arm and moved softly up against him. 'You never tarry at my place any more. Are you keeping your own woman, out at the estate? Did we do something –'

'You can't have all my secrets, woman.' In fact, for more than a year he had not taken a woman normally, but needed the starch of rape. This was the only part of his evil life that shamed him, and certainly not because of the women he had hurt and twice killed. He dreaded weakness more than death, and wondered which part would fail him next.

Amoli idly looked through the one-way mirror while One-Thumb attended to the strongbox. She turned when she heard him gasp.

'Gods!' The leather wrapping lay limp and empty on the floor of the box.

They both stared for a moment. 'Does Marype have his father's protection?' Amoli asked.

One-Thumb shook his head. 'It was the father that did this.'

Sorcerers are not omnipotent. They can be bargained with. They can even be killed, with stealth and surprise. And spells cannot normally be maintained without effort; a good sorcerer might hold six or a dozen at once. It was Mizraith's fame that he maintained past a hundred, although it was well known that he did this by casting secondary spells on lesser sorcerers, tapping their power unbeknownst. Still, gathering all these strings and holding them, as well as the direct spells that protected his life and fortune, used most of his concentration, giving him a distracted air. The unwary

165

might interpret this as senility – a half-century without sleep had left its mark – and might try to take his purse or life, as their last act.

But Mizraith was rarely seen on the streets, and certainly never near the noise and smell of the Maze. He normally kept to his opulent apartments in the easternmost part of town, flanked by the inns of Wideway, overlooking the sea.

One-Thumb warned the pirate cook that he might have to take a double shift, and took a bottle of finest brandy to give to Mizraith, and a skin of the ordinary kind to keep up their courage as they went to face the man who guarded his life. The emptied skin joined the harbour's flotsam before they'd gone half of Wideway, and they continued in grim silence.

Mizraith's eldest son let them in, not seeming surprised at their visit. 'The bodyguards stay here,' he said, and made a pass with one hand. 'You'll want to leave all your iron here, as well.'

One-Thumb felt the dagger next to his ankle grow warm; he tossed it away and also dropped his rapier and the dagger sheathed to his forearm. There was a similar scattering of weapons from the other three. Amoli turned to the wall and reached inside her skirts, inside herself, to retrieve the ultimate birth-control device, a sort of diaphragm with a spring-loaded razor attached (no one would have her without paying in some coin). The hardware glowed dull red briefly, then cooled.

'Is Marype at home?' One-Thumb asked.

'He was, briefly,' the older brother said. 'You came to see Father, though.' He turned to lead them up a winding flight of stairs.

Velvet and silk embroidered in arcane patterns. A golden samovar bubbling softly in the corner; flower-scented tea. A naked girl, barely of childbearing age, sitting cross-legged by the samovar, staring. A bodyguard much larger than the ones downstairs, but slightly transparent. In the middle of this sat Mizraith, on a pile of pillows, or maybe of gold, bright eyes in dark hollows, smiling open-mouthed at something unseeable.

The brother left them there. Magician, guardian, and girl all ignored them. 'Mizraith?' One-Thumb said.

The sorcerer slowly brought his eyes to bear on him and Amoli.

'I've been waiting for you, Lastel, or what is your name in the Maze, One-Thumb . . . I could grow that back for you, you know.'

'I get along well enough –'

'And you brought me presents! A bottle and a bauble – more my age than this sweetmeat.' He made a grotesque face at the naked girl and winked.

'No, Mizraith, this woman and I, we both believe we've been wronged by you. Cheated and stolen from,' he said boldly, but his voice shook. 'The bottle is a gift.'

The bodyguard moved towards them, its steps making no noise. 'Hold, spirit.' It stopped, glaring. 'Bring that bottle here.'

As One-Thumb and Amoli walked towards Mizraith, a low table materialized in front of him, then three glasses. 'You may serve, Lastel.' Nothing had moved but his head.

One-Thumb poured each glass full; one of them rose a handspan above the table and drained itself, then disappeared. 'Very good. Thank you. Cheated, now? My, oh my. Stolen? Hee. What could you have that I need?'

'It's only we who need it, Mizraith, and I don't know why you would want to cheat us out of it – especially me. You can't have many commissions more lucrative than mine.'

'You might be surprised, Lastel. You might be surprised. *Tea!*' The girl decanted a cup of tea and brought it over, as if in a trance. Mizraith took it and the girl sat at his side, playing with her hair. 'Stolen, eh? What? You haven't told me. What?'

'Krrf,' he said.

Mizraith gestured negligently with his free hand and a small snowstorm of grey powder drifted to the rug, and disappeared.

'No.' One-Thumb rubbed his eyes. When he looked at the pillows, they were pillows; when he looked away, they turned to blocks of gold. 'Not conjured krrf.' It had the same gross effect but no depth, no nuance.

'Twenty *grimales* of black krrf from Caronne,' Amoli said.

'Stolen from both of us,' One-Thumb said. 'It was sent to me by a man in Ranke, payment for services rendered. Your son Marype picked it up at the caravan depot, hidden inside a cheese. He extracted it somehow and sold it to this woman, Amoli –'

'Amoli? You're the mistress of a . . . of the Slippery Lily?'

'No, the Lily Garden. The other place is in the Maze, a good place for pox and slatterns.'

One-Thumb continued. 'After he sold it to her, it disappeared. He brought it to me last night. This evening, it disappeared from my own strongbox.'

'Marype couldn't do that,' Mizraith said.

'The conjuring part, I know he couldn't – which is why I say that you must have been behind it. Why? A joke?'

Mizraith sipped. 'Would you like tea?'

'No. Why?'

He handed the half-empty cup to the girl. 'More tea.' He watched her go to the samovar. 'I bought her for the walk. Isn't that fine? From behind, she could be a boy.'

'Please, Mizraith. This is financial ruin for Amoli and a gross insult to me.'

'A joke, eh? You think I make stupid jokes?'

'I know that you do things for reasons I cannot comprehend,' he said tactfully. 'But this is serious –'

'*I* know that!' He took the tea and fished a flower petal from it; rubbed it away. 'More serious than you think, if my son is involved. Did it all disappear? Is there any tiny bit of it left?'

'The pinch you gave to my eunuch,' Amoli said. 'He may still have it.'

'Fetch it,' Mizraith said. He stared slack-jawed into his tea for a minute. 'I didn't do it, Lastel. Some other did.'

'With Marype's help.'

'Perhaps unwilling. We shall see . . . Marype is adept enough to have sensed the worth of the cheese, and I think he is worldly enough to recognize a block of rare krrf, and know where to sell it. By himself, he would not be able to charm it away.'

'You fear he's betrayed you?'

Mizraith caressed the girl's long hair. 'We have had some argument lately. About his progress . . . he thinks I am teaching him too slowly, withholding . . . mysteries. The truth is, spells are complicated. Being able to generate one is not the same as being able to control it; that takes practice, and maturity. He sees what his brothers can do and is jealous, I think.'

'You can't know his mind directly?'

'No. That's a powerful spell against strangers, but the closer you are to a person, the harder it is. Against your own blood ... no. His mind is closed to me.'

Amoli returned with the square of parchment. She held it out apologetically. 'He shared it with the other bodyguard and your son. Is this enough?' There was a dark patch in the centre of the square.

He took it between thumb and forefinger and grimaced. 'Markmor!' The second most powerful magician in Sanctuary – an upstart not even a century old.

'He's in league with your strongest competitor?' One-Thumb said.

'In league or in thrall.' Mizraith stood up and crossed his arms. The bodyguard disappeared; the cushions became a stack of gold bricks. He mumbled some gibberish and opened his arms wide.

Marype appeared in front of him. He was a handsome lad: flowing silver hair, striking features. He was also furious, naked, and rampant.

'*Father*! I am *busy*!' He made a flinging gesture and disappeared.

Mizraith made the same gesture and the boy came back. 'We can do this all night. Or you can talk to me.'

Noticeably less rampant. 'This is unforgiveable.' He raised his arm to make the pass again; then checked it as Mizraith did the same. 'Clothe me.' A brick disappeared, and Marype was wearing a tunic of woven gold.

'Tell me you are not in the thrall of Markmor.'

The boy's fists were clenched. 'I am not.'

'Are you quite certain?'

'We are friends, partners. He is teaching me things.'

'You know I will teach you everything, eventually. But –'

Marype made a pass and the stack of gold turned to a heap of stinking dung. 'Cheap,' Mizraith said, wrinkling his nose. He held his elbow a certain way and the gold came back. 'Don't you see he wants to take advantage of you?'

'I can see that he wants access to *you*. He was quite open about that.'

'Stefab,' Mizraith whispered. 'Nesteph.'

'You need the help of my brothers?'

The two older brothers appeared, flanking Mizraith. 'What I need is some sense out of you.' To the others: 'Stay him!'

Heavy golden chains bound his wrists and ankles to sudden rings in the floor. He strained and one broke; a block of blue ice encased him. The ice began to melt.

Mizraith turned to One-Thumb and Amoli. 'You weaken us with your presence.' A bar of gold floated over to the woman. 'That will compensate you. Lastel, you will have the krrf, once I take care of this. Be careful for the next few hours. Go.'

As they backed out, other figures began to gather in the room. One-Thumb recognized the outline of Markmor flickering.

In the foyer, Amoli handed the gold to her eunuch. 'Let's get back to the Maze,' she said. 'This place is dangerous.'

One-Thumb sent the pirate cook home and spent the rest of the night in the familiar business of dispensing drink and krrf and haggling over rates of exchange. He took a judicious amount of krrf himself – the domestic kind – to keep alert. But nothing supernatural happened, and nothing more exciting than a routine eye-gouging over a dice dispute. He did have to step over a deceased ex-patron when he went to lock up at dawn. At least he'd had the decency to die outside, so no report had to be made.

One reason he liked to take the death-shift was the interesting ambience of Sanctuary in the early morning. The sunlight was hard, revealing rather than cleansing. Litter and excrement in the gutters. A few exhausted revellers, staggering in small groups or sitting half-awake, blade out, waiting for a bunk to clear at first bell. Dogs nosing the evening's remains. Decadent, stale, worn, mortal. He took dark pleasure in it. Double pleasure this morning, a slight krrf overdose singing death-song in his brain.

He almost went east, to check on Mizraith. 'Be careful the next few hours' – that must have meant his bond to Mizraith made him somehow vulnerable in the weird struggle with Markmor over Marype. But he had to go back to the estate and dispose of the bones in the dogs' troughs, and then be Lastel for a noon meeting.

*

There was one drab whore in the waiting-room of the Lily Garden, who gave him a thick smile and then recognized him and slumped back to doze. He went through the velvet curtain to where the eunuch sat with his back against the wall, glaive across his lap.

He didn't stand. 'Any trouble, One-Thumb?'

'No trouble. No krrf, either.' He heaved aside the bolt on the massive door to the tunnel. 'For all I know, it's still going on. If Mizraith had lost, I'd know by now, I think.'

'Or if he'd won,' the eunuch said.

'Possibly. I'll be in touch with your mistress if I have anything for her.' One-Thumb lit the waiting lamp and swung the door closed behind him.

Before he'd reached the bottom of the stairs, he knew something was wrong. Too much light. He turned the wick all the way down; the air was slightly glowing. At the foot of the stairs, he set down the lamp, drew his rapier, and waited.

The glow coalesced into a fuzzy image of Mizraith. It whispered, 'You are finally in dark, Lastel. One-Thumb. Listen: I may die soon. Your charm, I've transferred to Stefab, and it holds. Pay him as you've paid me ...' He wavered, disappeared, came back. 'Your krrf is in this tunnel. It cost more than you can know.' Darkness again.

One-Thumb waited a few minutes more in the darkness and silence (fifty steps from the light above) before re-lighting the lamp. The block of krrf was at his feet. He tucked it under his left arm and proceeded down the tunnel, rapier in hand. Not that steel would be much use against sorcery, if that was to be the end of this. But an empty hand was less.

The tunnel kinked every fifty steps or so, to restrict line-of-sight. One-Thumb went through three corners and thought he saw light at the fourth. He stopped, doused the lamp again, and listened. No footfalls. He set down the krrf and lamp and filled his left hand with a dagger, then headed for the light. It didn't have to be magic; three times he had surprised interlopers in the tunnel. Their husks were secreted here and there, adding to the musty odour.

But no stranger this time. He peered around the corner and saw Lastel himself, waiting with sword out.

'Don't hold back there,' his alter ego said. 'Only one of us leaves this tunnel.'

One-Thumb raised his rapier slowly. 'Wait ... if you kill me, you die forever. If I kill you, the same. This is a sorcerer's trap.'

'No, Mizraith's dead.'

'His son is holding the spell.'

Lastel advanced, crabwise, dueller's gait. 'Then how am I here?'

One-Thumb struggled with his limited knowledge of the logic of sorcery. Instinct moved him forward, point in line, left-hand weapon ready for side parry or high block. He kept his eye on Lastel's point, krrf-steady as his own. The krrf sang doom, and lifted his spirit.

It was like fencing with a mirror. Every attack drew instant parry, remise, parry, remise, parry, re-remise, break to counter. For several minutes, a swift yet careful ballet, large twins mincing, the tunnel echoing clash:

One-Thumb knew he had to do something random, unpredictable; he lunged with a cut-over, impressing to the right.

Lastel knew he had to do something random, unpredictable; he lunged with a double-disengage, impressing to the right

They missed each other's blades

Slammed home.

One-Thumb saw his red blade emerge from the rich brocade over Lastel's back, tried to shout and coughed blood over his killer's shoulder. Lastel's rapier had cracked breastbone and heart and slit a lung as well.

They clung to each other. One-Thumb watched bright blood spurt from the other's back and heard his own blood falling, as the pain grew. The dagger still in his left hand, he stabbed, almost idly. Again he stabbed. It seemed to take a long time. The pain grew. The other man was doing the same. A third stab, he watched the blade rise and slowly fall, and inching slide back out of the flesh. With every second, the pain seemed to double; with every second, the flow of time slowed by half. Even the splash of blood was slowed, like a viscous oil falling through water as it sprayed away. And now it stopped completely, a thick scarlet web frozen there between his dagger and Lastel's back – his own back – and as the pain spread and grew, marrow itself on fire, he knew he would look at that for ever. For a flickering moment he saw the image of two sorcerers, smiling.

MYRTIS

Christine DeWees

'I feel as young as I look. I could satisfy every man in this house if I took the notion to, or if any one of them had half the magnificence of Lythande.'

So speaking, Myrtis, proprietor of the Aphrodisia House leaned over the banister outside her private parlour and cast judgement on the activity of her establishment below.

'Certainly, madame.'

Her companion on the narrow balcony was a well-dressed young man lately arrived with his parents from the imperial capital. He eased as far from her as possible when she turned to smile at him.

'Do you doubt me, young man?'

The words rolled off Myrtis's tongue with an ease and inflection of majesty. To many of the long-time residents of Sanctuary, Myrtis was the city's unofficial royalty. On the Street of Red Lanterns she reigned supreme.

'Certainly not, madame.'

'You have seen the girls now. Did you have a particular lady in mind, or would you prefer to explore my establishment further?'

Myrtis guided him back into her parlour with slight pressure against his arm. She wore a high-necked dark gown which only hinted at the legendary figure beneath. The madam of the Aphrodisia House was beautiful, more beautiful than any of the girls working for her; fathers told this to their sons who were, in turn, passing this indisputable fact along to their sons. But a ravishing beauty which endured unchanging for three generations was awesome rather than desirable. Myrtis did not compete with the girls who worked for her.

The young man cleared his throat. It was clearly his first visit to any brothel. He fingered the tassels on the side of an immense wine-coloured velvet love-seat before speaking.

'I think I'll go a round with the violet-silks.'

Myrtis stared at him until he fidgeted one of the tassels loose and his face flushed a deep crimson.

'Call Cylene. Tell her the Lavender Room.'

A girl too young to be working jumped up from a cushion where she had waited in silence for such a command. The youth turned to follow her.

'Four pieces of silver – Cylene is *very* talented. And a name – I think that you should be known as Terapis.' Myrtis smiled to reveal her even white teeth.

The youth, who would henceforth be known as Terapis within the walls of the Aphrodisia House, searched his purse to find a single gold piece. He stood arrogant and obviously well-rehearsed while Myrtis counted out his change. The young girl took his hand to lead him to Cylene for two hours of unimaginable bliss.

'Children!' Myrtis mumbled to herself when she was alone in her parlour again.

Four of the nine knobs on the night-candle had melted away. She opened a great leatherbound ledger and entered the youth's true name as well as the one she had just given him, his choice for the evening, and that he had paid in gold. It had been fifteen years or more since she had given the *nom-de-guerre* of Terapis to one of the house's gentlemen. She had a good memory for all those who lingered in the sybaritic luxury of the Aphrodisia House.

A gentle knocking on the parlour door awoke Myrtis late the next morning.

'Your breakfast is ready, madame.'

'Thank you, child. I'll be down for it.'

She lay still for a few moments in the semi-darkness. Lythande had used careful spells to preserve her beauty and give her the longevity of a magician, but there were no spells to numb the memory. The girls, their gentlemen, all passed through Myrtis's mind in a blurred unchanging parade which trapped her beneath the silken bed-clothes.

'Flowers for you, madame.'

The young girl who had sat quietly on the cushion on the previous evening walked nonchalantly into the boudoir bearing a large bouquet of white flowers which she began arranging in a crystal vase.

'A slave from the palace brought them. He said they were from Terapis.'

A surprise. There were always still surprises, and renewed by that comforting knowledge Myrtis threw back the bedcovers. The girl set down the flowers and held an embroidered day-robe of emerald satin for Myrtis to wrap around herself.

Five girls in their linen shifts busied themselves with restoring the studied disorder of the lower rooms as Myrtis passed through them on her way to the kitchen. Five cleaning, one too pregnant to be of any use, another off nursing a newborn; that meant twenty girls were still in the upper rooms. Twenty girls whose time was fully accounted for; in all, a very good night for the Aphrodisia House. Others might be suffering with the new regime, but the foreigners expected a certain style and discretion which in Sanctuary could be found only at the Aphrodisia.

'Madame, Dindan ordered five bottles of our best Aurvesh wine last night. We have only a dozen bottles left ...' A balding man stepped in front of her with a shopping list.

'Then buy more.'

'But, madame, since the prince arrived it is almost impossible to buy Aurvesh wines!'

'Buy them! But first sell the old bottles to Dindan at the new prices.'

'Yes, madame.'

The kitchen was a large, brightly lit room hidden away at the back of the house. Her cooks and an assortment of tradesmen haggled loudly at the back door while the half-dozen or so young children of her working girls raced around the massive centre table. Everyone grew quiet as Myrtis took her seat in a sunlit alcove that faced a tiny garden.

Despite the chaos the children caused, she always let the girls keep them if they wanted to. With the girl-children there was no problem with their earning their keep; no virgin was ever too ugly. But the boy-children were apprenticed off at the earliest possible age. Their wages were garnished to support the on-going concern that was the Aphrodisia House.

'There is a soldier at the front door, Madame.' One of the girls who had been cleaning the lower rooms interrupted as Myrtis spread a thick blue-veined cheese over her bread. 'He demands to see you, madame.'

'Demands to see me?' Myrtis laid down the cheese knife. 'A soldier has nothing that "demands" to see me at the front door. At this hour, soldiers are less use than tradesmen. Send him around to the back.'

The girl ran back up the stairs. Myrtis finished spreading her cheese on the bread. She had eaten half of it when a tall man cast a shadow over her private dining alcove.

'You are blocking my sunlight, young man,' she said without looking up.

'You are Madame Myrtis, proprietress of this ... brothel?' he demanded without moving.

'You are blocking my sunlight and my view of the garden.'

He stepped to one side.

'The girls are not available during the day. Come back this evening.'

'Madame Myrtis, I am Zalbar, captain of Prince Kadakithis's personal guard. I have not come to inquire after the services of your girls.'

'Then what have you come for?' she asked, looking up for the first time.

'By order of Prince Kadakithis, a tax of ten gold pieces for every woman living on the Street of Red Lanterns is to be levied and collected at once if they are to be allowed to continue to practise their trade without incurring official displeasure.'

Only the slight tensing of Myrtis's hand betrayed her indignation at Zalbar's statement. Her voice and face remained dispassionately calm.

'The royal concubines are no longer pleasing?' she replied with a sneering smile. 'You cannot expect every woman on the Street of Red Lanterns to have ten gold pieces. How do you expect them to earn the money for your taxes?'

'We do not expect them to be able to pay the tax, madame.

We expect to close your brothel and every other house like it on the Street. The women, including yourself, will be sent elsewhere to lead more productive lives.'

Myrtis stared at the soldier with a practised contempt that ended their conversation. The soldier fingered the hilt of his sword.

'The tax will be collected, madame. You will have a reasonable amount of time to get the money for yourself and the others. Let us say, three days? I'll return in the evening.'

He turned about without waiting for a reply and left through the back door in complete silence. Myrtis went back to interrupted breakfast while the staff and the girls were hysterical with questions and the seeds of rumour. She let them babble in this manner while she ate; then she strode to the head of the common table.

'Everything shall continue as usual. If it comes to paying their tax, arrangements will be made. You older girls already have ample gold set aside. I will make the necessary adjustments for the newer girls. Unless you doubt me – in which case, I'll arrange a severance for you.'

'But madame, if we pay once, they will levy the tax again and again until we can't pay it. Those Hell Hounds . . .' A girl favoured more by intelligence than beauty spoke up.

'That is certainly their desire. The Street of Red Lanterns is as old as the walls of Sanctuary itself. I can assure you that we have survived much worse than the Hell Hounds.' Myrtis smiled slightly to herself, remembering the others who had tried and failed to shut down the Street. 'Cylene, the others will be coming to see me. Send them up to the parlour. I'll wait for them there.'

The emerald day-robe billowed out from behind her as Myrtis ascended the staircase to the lower rooms and up again to her parlour. In the privacy of her rooms, she allowed her anger to surface as she paced.

'Ambutta!' She shouted, and the young girl who attended her appeared.

'Yes, madame?'

'I have a message for you to carry.' She sat at the writing table composing the message as she spoke to the still-out-of-breath girl. 'It is to be delivered in the special way as before. No one must

178

see you leave it. Do you understand that? If you cannot leave it without being seen, come back here. Don't let yourself become suspicious.'

The girl nodded. She tucked the freshly folded and sealed message into the bodice of her ragged cast-off dress and ran from the room. In time, Myrtis expected her to be a beauty, but she was still very much a child. The message itself was to Lythande, who preferred not to be contacted directly. She would not rely on the magician to solve the Street's problems with the Hell Hounds, but no one else would understand her anger or alleviate it.

The Aphrodisia House dominated the Street. The Hell Hounds would come to her first, then visit the other establishments. As word of the tax spread, the other madams would begin a furtive pilgrimage to the back entrance of the Aphrodisia. They looked to Myrtis for guidance, and she looked out the window for inspiration. She had not found one by the time her guests began to appear.

'It's an outrage. They're trying to put us on the streets like common whores!' Dylan of the artificially flaming red hair exclaimed before sitting in the chair Myrtis indicated to her.

'Nonsense, dear,' Myrtis explained calmly. 'They wish to make us slaves and send us to Ranke. In a way, it is a compliment to Sanctuary.'

'They can't do such a thing!'

'No, but it will be up to us to explain that to them.'

'How?'

'First we'll wait until the others arrive. I hear Amoli in the hall; the others won't be long in coming.'

It was a blatant stall for time on Myrtis's part. Other than her conviction that the Hell Hounds and their prince would not succeed where others had failed in the past, Myrtis had no idea how to approach the utterly incorruptible elite soldiers. The other madams of the Street talked among themselves, exchanging the insight Myrtis had revealed to Dylan, and reacting poorly to it. Myrtis watched their reflections in the rough-cut glass.

They were all old. More than half of them had once worked for her. She had watched them age in the unkind manner that often overtakes youthful beauty and transforms it into grotesquerie. Myrtis might have been the youngest of them – young enough to be working in the houses instead of running one of them. But when she turned from the window to face them, there was the unmistakable glint of experience and wisdom in her eyes.

'Well, it wasn't really a surprise,' she began. It was rumoured before Kittycat got here, and we've seen what has happened to the others the Hell Hounds have been turned loose on. I admit I'd hoped that some of the others would have held their ground better and given us a bit more time.'

'Time wouldn't help. I don't have a hundred gold pieces to give them!' A woman whose white-paste make-up cracked around her eyes as she spoke interrupted Myrtis.

'You don't need a hundred gold pieces!' A similarly made-up woman snarled back.

'The gold is unimportant.' Myrtis's voice rose above the bickering. 'If they can break one of us, they can drive us all out.'

'We could close our doors; then they'd suffer. Half of my men are from Ranke.'

'Half of *all* our men are, Gelicia. They won the war and they've got the money,' Myrtis countered. 'But they'll kowtow to the Hell Hounds, Kittycat, and their wives. The men of Ranke are very ambitious. They'll give up much to preserve their wealth and positions. If the prince is officially frowning on the Street, their loyalties will be less strained if we have closed our doors without putting up a fight.'

Grudgingly the women agreed.

'Then what will we do?'

'Conduct your affairs as always. They'll come to the Aphrodisia first to collect the taxes, just as they came here first to announce it. Keep the back doors open and I'll send word. If they can't collect from me, they won't bother you.'

There was mumbled disagreement, but no one dared to look straight at Myrtis and argue the point of her power on the Street. Seated in her high-backed chair, Myrtis smiled contentedly. She had yet to determine the precise solution, but the house madams of the Street of Red Lanterns controlled much of the gold within

Sanctuary, and she had just confirmed her control of them.

They left her parlour quickly after the decision was rendered. If the Street was to function as usual, they all had work to do. She had work to do. The Hell Hounds would not return for three days. In that time, the Aphrodisia House would earn far more than those three hundred gold pieces the empire wanted, and would spend only slightly less than that amount to maintain itself. Myrtis opened the ledger, making new notations in a clear, educated hand. The household sensed that order had been restored at least temporarily, and one by one they filed into the parlour to report their earnings or debts.

It was well into afternoon and Ambutta had not returned from placing her message behind a loose stone in the wall behind the altar at the temple of Ils. For a moment, Myrtis worried about the girl. The streets of Sanctuary were never truly safe, and perhaps Ambutta no longer seemed as childlike to all eyes. There was always an element of risk. Twice before girls had been lost in the streets, and not even Lythande's magic could find them again.

Myrtis put such thoughts aside and ate dinner alone in her parlour. She had thought a bribe or offer of free privileges might still be the way out of her problem with the taxes. Prince Kadakithis was probably sincere, though, in his determination to make Sanctuary the ideal city of his adviser's philosophies while the capital city of the empire displayed many of the same excesses that Sanctuary did. The young prince had a wife and concubines with whom he was supposedly well pleased. There had never been any suspicion that he might partake of the delights of the Street himself. And as for the Hell Hounds, their first visit had been to announce the taxes.

The élite guard were men made of a finer fibre than most of the soldiers or fighters Sanctuary had known. On reflection, Myrtis doubted that they could be bought or bribed, and knew for certain that they would never relent in their persecution of the Street if the first offer did not succeed in converting them.

It was gathering dusk. The girls could be heard throughout the house, giggling as they prepared for the evening. Myrtis kept no one who showed no aptitude or enjoyment of the profession. Let the other houses bind their girls with poverty or drugs; the Aphrodisia House was the pinnacle of ambition for the working girls of the Street.

'I got your message.' A soft voice called from the drapery-hung doorway near her bed.

'I was beginning to get worried. My girl has not returned.'

Lythande walked to her side, draping an arm about her shoulders and taking hold of her hand.

'I've heard the rumours in the streets. The new regime has chosen its next enemy, it would seem. What is the truth of their demands?'

'They intend to levy a tax of ten gold pieces on every woman living on the Street.'

Lythande's habitual smile faded, and the blue star tattooed forehead wrinkled into a frown. 'Will you be able to pay that?'

'The intent is not that we pay, but that the Street be closed, and that we be sent up to the empire. If I pay it once, they'll keep on levying it until I can't pay.'

'You could close the house . . .'

'Never!' Myrtis pulled her hands away. 'The Aphrodisia House is mine. I was running this house when the Rankan Empire was a collection of half-naked barbaric tribes!'

'But they aren't any longer,' Lythande reminded her gently. 'And the Hell Hounds – if not the prince – are making substantial changes in all our lives.'

'They won't interfere with magic, will they?'

Myrtis's concern for Lythande briefly overshadowed her fears for the Aphrodisia House. The magician's thin-lipped smile returned.

'For now it is doubtful. There are men in Ranke who have the ability to affect us directly, but they have not followed the prince to Sanctuary, and I do not know if he could command their loyalty.'

Myrtis stood up. She walked to the leaded-glass window, with its thick, obscuring panes which revealed movement on the Street but very little else.

'I'll need your help, if it's available,' she said without facing Lythande.

'What can I do?'

'In the past you've prepared a drug for me from a qualis-berry extract. I recall you said it was quite difficult to mix – but I should like enough for two people when it's mixed with pure qualis liqueur.'

'Delicate and precise, but not particularly difficult. It is very subtle. Are you sure you will only need enough to serve two?'

'Yes, Zalbar and myself. I agree; the drug must be subtle.'

'You must be very certain of your methods, then.'

'Of some things, at least. The Street of Red Lanterns does not lie outside the walls of Sanctuary by accident – you know that. The Hell Hounds and their prince have much more to lose by hindering us than by letting the Street exist in peace. If our past purpose were not enough to convince them, then surely the fact that much of the city's gold passes through my hands every year will matter.

'I will use the qualis-berry love potion to open Zalbar's eyes to reality, not to close them.'

'I can have it for you perhaps by tomorrow evening, but more likely the day after. Many of the traders and smugglers of the bazaar are no longer well supplied with the ingredients I will need, but I can investigate other sources. When the Hell Hounds drove the smugglers into the Swamp of Night Secrets, many honest men suffered.'

Myrtis's eyes narrowed, she released the drapery she had clutched.

'And if the Street of Red Lanterns wasn't here ... The mongers and merchants, and even the smugglers, might not want to admit it, but without us to provide them with their gold while "respect-able" people offer promises, they would suffer even more than they do now.'

There was a gentle knocking on the door. Lythande stepped back into the shadows of the room. Ambutta entered, a large bruise visible on the side of her face.

'The men have begun to arrive, Madame Myrtis. Will you collect their money, or shall I take the ledger downstairs?'

'I shall attend to them. Send them up to me and, Ambutta –'

She stopped the girl as she headed out of the parlour. 'Go to the kitchen and find out how many days we could go without buying anything from any of the tradesmen.'

'Yes, madame.'

The room was suddenly empty, except for Myrtis. Only a slight rippling of the wall tapestries showed where Lythande had opened a concealed panel and disappeared into the secret passages of the Aphrodisia House. Myrtis had not expected the magician to stay, but despite all their years together, the magician's sudden comings and goings still unsettled her. Standing in front of a full-length mirror, Myrtis rearranged the pearl-and-gold pins in her hair, rubbed scented oils into her skin, and greeted the first gentleman-caller as if the day had been no different from any other.

Word of the taxation campaign against the Street had spread through the city much as Lythande had observed. The result was that many of their frequent guests and visitors came to the house to pay their last respects to an entertainment that they openly expected would be gone in a very short time. Myrtis smiled at each of them as they arrived, accepted their money, and asked their second choice of the girls before assuring them that the Aphrodisia House would never close its doors.

'Madame?'

Ambutta peered around the doorway when the flow of gentlemen had abated slightly.

'The kitchen says that we have enough food for ten days, but less of ordinary wine and the like.'

Myrtis touched the feather of her pen against her temple.

'Ten days? Someone has grown lax. Our storerooms can hold enough for many months. But ten days is all we will have, and it will have to be enough. Tell the kitchen to place no orders with the tradesmen tomorrow or the next day, and send word to the other backdoors.

'And, Ambutta, Irda will carry my messages in the future. It is time that you were taught more important and useful things.'

A steady stream of merchants and tradesmen made their way through the Aphrodisia House to Myrtis's parlour late the next morning as the effects of her orders began to be felt in the town.

'But Madame Myrtis, the tax isn't due yet, and surely the Aphrodisia House has the resources . . .' The puffy-faced gentleman who sent meat to half the houses on the Street was alternately irate and wheedling.

'In such unsettled times as these, good Mikkun, I cannot look to luxuries like expensive meats. I sincerely wish that this were not true. The taste of salted meat has always reminded me of poverty. But the governor's palace does not care about the poverty of those who live outside its walls, though it sends its forces to tax us,' Myrtis said in feigned helplessness.

In deference to the sad occasion she had not put on one of the brightly embroidered day-robes as was her custom but wore a soberly cut dress of a fashion outdated in Sanctuary at least twenty years before. She had taken off her jewellery, knowing that its absence would cause more rumours than if she had indeed sold a part of it to the gem-cutters. An atmosphere of austerity enveloped the house and every other on the Street, as Mikkun could attest, for he'd visited most of them.

'But madame, I have already slaughtered two cows! For three years I have slaughtered the cows first to assure you the freshest meat early in the day. Today, for no reason, you say you do not want my meat! Madame, you already have a debt to me for those two cows!'

'Mikkun! You have never, in all the years I've known you, extended credit to any house on the Street and now . . . now you're asking me to consider my daily purchases a debt to you!' She smiled disarmingly to calm him, knowing full well that the butcher and the others depended on the hard gold from the Street to pay their own debts.

'There will be credit in the future!'

'But we will not be here to use it!'

Myrtis let her face take on a mournful pout. Let the butcher and his friends start dunning the 'respectable' side of Sanctuary, and word would spread quickly to the palace that something was amiss. A 'something' which she would explain to the Hell Hound captain, Zalbar, when he arrived to collect the tax. The tradesman left her parlour muttering prophecies of doom she hoped would eventually be heard by those in a position to worry about them.

'Madame?'

Ambutta's child-serious face appeared in the doorway moments after the butcher had left. Her ragged dress had already been replaced with one of a more mature cut, brighter colour, and new cloth.

'Amoli waits to speak with you. She is in the kitchen now. Shall I send her up?'

'Yes, bring her up.'

Myrtis sighed after Ambutta left. Amoli was her only rival on the Street. She was a woman who had not learned her trade in the upper rooms of the Aphrodisia, and also one who kept her girls working for her through their addiction to krrf, which she supplied to them. If anyone on the Street was nervous about the tax, though, it was Amoli; she had very little gold to spare. The smugglers had recently been forced by the same Hell Hounds to raise the price of a well-refined brick of the drug to maintain their own profits.

'Amoli, good woman, you look exhausted.'

Myrtis assisted a woman less than a third her age to the loveseat.

'May I get you something to drink?'

'Qualis, if you have any.' Amoli paused while Myrtis passed the request along to Ambutta. 'I can't do it, Myrtis – this whole scheme of yours is impossible. It will ruin me!'

The liqueur arrived. Ambutta carried a finely wrought silver tray with one glass of the deep red liquid. Amoli's hands shook violently as she grasped the glass and emptied it in one gulp. Ambutta looked sagely to her mistress; the other madam was, perhaps, victim of the same addiction as her girls?

'I've been approached by Jubal. For a small fee, he will send his men up here tomorrow night to ambush the Hell Hounds. He has been looking for an opportunity to eliminate them. With them gone, Kittycat won't be able to make trouble for us.'

'So Jubal is supplying the krrf now?' Myrtis replied without sympathy.

'They all have to pay to land their shipments in the Night Secrets, or Jubal will reveal their activities to the Hell Hounds. His plan is fair. I can deal with him directly. So can anyone else – he trades in anything. But you and Lythande will have to unseal the tunnels so his men face no undue risk tomorrow night.'

The remnants of Myrtis's cordiality disappeared. The Golden Lily had been isolated from the rat's nest of passages on the Street when Myrtis realized the extent of krrf addiction within it. Unkind experience warned her against mixing drugs and courtesans. There were always men like Jubal waiting for the first sign of weakness, and soon the houses were nothing more than slaver's dens; the madams forgotten. Jubal feared magic, so she had asked Lythande to seal the tunnels with eerily visible wards. So long as she – Myrtis – lived, the Street would be hers, and not Jubal's, nor the city's.

'There are other suppliers whose prices are not so high. Or perhaps Jubal has promised you a place in his mansion? I have heard he learned things besides fighting in the pits of Ranke. Of course, his home is hardly the place for sensitive people to live.'

Myrtis wrinkled her nose in the accepted way to indicate someone who lived Downwind. Amoli replied with an equally understandable gesture of insult and derision, but she left the parlour without looking back.

The problems with Jubal and the smugglers were only just beginning. Myrtis pondered them after Ambutta removed the tray and glass from the room. Jubal's ruthless ambition was potentially more dangerous than any threat radiating directly from the Hell Hounds. But they were completely distinct from the matters at hand, so Myrtis put them out of her mind.

The second evening was not as lucrative as the first, nor the third day as frantic as the second. Lythande's aphrodisiac potion appeared in the hands of a dazed street urchin. The *geas* the magician had placed on the young beggar dissipated as soon as the vial left his hands. He had glanced around him in confusion and disappeared at a run before the day-steward could hand him a copper coin for his inconvenience.

Myrtis poured the vial into a small bottle of qualis which she then placed between two glasses on the silver tray. The décor of

187

the parlour had been changed subtly during the day. The red liqueur replaced the black-bound ledger which had been banished to the night-steward's cubicle in the lower rooms. The draperies around her bed were tied back, and a padded silk coverlet was creased to show the plump pillows. Musky incense crept into the room from burners hidden in the corners. Beside her bed, a large box containing the three hundred gold pieces sat on a table.

Myrtis hadn't put on any of her jewellery. It would only have detracted from the ebony low-cut, side-slit gown she wore. The image was perfect. No one but Zalbar would see her until the dawn, and she was determined that her efforts and planning would not be in vain.

She waited alone, remembering her first days as a courtesan in Ilsig, when Lythande was a magician's raw apprentice and her own experiences a nightmare adventure. At that time she had lived to fall wildly in love with any young lordling who could offer her the dazzling splendour of privilege. But no man came forward to rescue her from the ethereal, but doomed, world of the courtesan. Before her beauty faded, she had made her pact with Lythande. The magician visited her infrequently, and for all her boasting, there was no passionate love between them. The spells had let Myrtis win for herself the permanent splendour she had wanted as a young girl; a splendour no high-handed barbarian from Ranke was going to strip away.

'Madame Myrtis?'

A peremptory knock on the door forced her from her thoughts. She had impressed the voice in her memory and recognized it though she had only heard it once before.

'Do come in.'

She opened the door for him, pleased to see by the hesitation in his step that he was unaware that he would be entering her parlour and boudoir.

'I have come to collect the taxes!' he said quickly. His military precision did not completely conceal his awe and vague embarrassment at viewing the royal and erotic scene displayed before him.

He did not turn as Myrtis shut the door behind him and quietly slid a concealed bolt into place.

188

'You have very nearly undone me, captain,' she said with downcast eyes and a light touch on his arm. It is not so easy as you might think to raise such a large sum of money.'

She lifted the ebony box inlaid with pearl from the table beside her bed and carried it slowly to him. He hesitated before taking it from her arms.

'I must count it, madame,' he said almost apologetically.

'I understand. You will find that it is all there. My word is good.'

'You ... you are much different now from how you seemed two days ago.'

'It is the difference between night and day.'

He began assembling piles of gold on her ledger table in front of the silver tray with the qualis.

'We have been forced to cut back our orders to the town's merchants in order to pay you.'

From the surprised yet thoughtful look he gave her, Myrtis guessed that the Hell Hounds had begun to hear complaints and anxious whinings from the respectable parts of town as Mikkun and his friends called back their loans and credit.

'Still,' she continued, 'I realize that you are doing only what you have been told to do. It's not you personally who is to blame if any of the merchants and purveyors suffer because the Street no longer functions as it once did.'

Zalbar continued shuffling his piles of coins around, only half-listening to Myrtis. He had half the gold in the box neatly arranged when Myrtis slipped the glass stopper out of the qualis decanter.

'Will you join me in a glass of qualis, since it is not your fault and we still have a few luxuries in our larder. They tell me a damp fog lies heavy on the streets.'

He looked up from his counting and his eyes brightened at the sight of the deep red liqueur. The common variety of qualis, though still expensive, had a duller colour and was inclined to visible sediment. A man of his position might live a full life and never glimpse a fine, pure qualis, much less be offered a glass of it. Clearly the Hell Hound was tempted.

'A small glass, perhaps.'

She poured two equally full glasses and set them both on the table in front of him while she replaced the stopper and took the bottle to the table by her bed. An undetectable glance in a side mirror confirmed that Zalbar lifted the glass farthest from him. Calmly she returned and raised the other.

'A toast then. To the future of your prince and to the Aphrodisia House!'

The glasses clinked.

The potion Lythande had made was brewed in part from the same berries as the qualis itself. The fine liqueur made a perfect concealing dilutant. Myrtis could taste the subtle difference the charm itself made in the normal flavour of the intoxicant, but Zalbar, who had never tasted even the common qualis, assumed that the extra warmth was only a part of the legendary mystique of the liqueur. When he had finished his drink, Myrtis swallowed the last of hers and waited patiently for the faint flush which would confirm that the potion was working.

It appeared in Zalbar first. He became bored with his counting, fondling one coin while his eyes drifted off towards nothingness. Myrtis took the coin from his fingers. The potion took longer to affect her, and its action when it did was lessened by the number of times she had taken it before and by the age-inhibiting spells Lythande wove about her. She had not needed the potion, however, to summon an attraction towards the handsome soldier nor to coax him to his feet and then to her bed.

Zalbar protested that he was not himself and did not understand what was happening to him. Myrtis did not trouble herself to argue with him. Lythande's potion was not one to rouse a wild, blind lust, but one which endowed a lifelong affection in the drinker. The pure qualis played a part in weakening his resistance. She held him behind the curtains of her bed until he had no doubt of his love for her. Then she helped him dress again.

'I'll show you the secrets of the Aphrodisia House,' she whispered in his ear.

'I believe I have already found them.'

'There are more.'

Myrtis took him by the hand, leading him to one of the drapery-covered walls. She pushed aside the fabric; released a well-oiled catch; took a sconce from the wall then led him into a dark, but airy, passage way.

'Walk carefully in my footsteps, Zalbar – I would not want to lose you to the oubliettes. Perhaps you have wondered why the Street is outside the walls and its buildings are so old and well-built? Perhaps you think Sanctuary's founders wished to keep us outside their fair city? What you do not know is that these houses – especially the older ones like the Aphrodisia – are not really outside the walls at all. My house is built of stone four feet thick. The shutters on our windows are aged wood from the mountains. We have our own wells and storerooms which can supply us – and the city – for weeks, if necessary. Other passages lead away from here towards the Swamp of Night Secrets, or into Sanctuary and the governor's palace itself. Whoever has ruled in Sanctuary has always sought our cooperation in moving men and arms if a siege is laid.'

She showed the speechless captain catacombs where a sizeable garrison could wait in complete concealment. He drank water from a deep well whose water had none of the brackish taste so common in the seacoast town. Above he could hear the sounds of parties at the Aphrodisia and the other houses. Zalbar's military eye took all this in, but his mind saw Myrtis, candle-lit in the black gown, as a man's dream come true, and the underground fortress she was revealing to him as a soldier's dream come true. The potion worked its way with him. He wanted both Myrtis and the fortress for his own to protect and control.

'There is so much about Sanctuary that you Rankans know nothing about. You tax the Street and cause havoc with trade in the city. You wish to close the Street and send all of us, including myself, to the slave pens or worse. Your walls will be breachable then. There are men in Sanctuary who would stop at nothing to control these passages, and they know the Swamp and the palace better than you or your children could ever hope to.'

She showed him a wall flickering with runes and magic signs. Zalbar went to touch it and found his fingers singed for his curiosity.

'These warding walls keep us safe now, but they will fade if

191

we are not here to renew them properly. Smugglers and thieves will find the entrances we have kept invulnerable for generations. And you, Zalbar, who wish that Sanctuary will become a place of justice and order, will know in your heart that you are responsible, because you knew what was here and let the others destroy it.'

'No, Myrtis. So long as I live, none of this shall be harmed.'

'There is no other way. Do you not already have your orders to levy a second tax?'

He nodded.

'We have already begun to use the food stored in these basements. The girls are not happy; the merchants are not happy. The Street will die. The merchants will charge higher prices, and the girls will make their way to the streets. There is nowhere else for them to go. Perhaps Jubal will take –'

'I do not think that the Street will suffer such a fate. Once the prince understands the true part you and the others play, he will agree to a nominal tax which would be applied to maintaining the defence of Sanctuary and therefore be returned to you.'

Myrtis smiled to herself. The battle was won. She held his arm tightly and no longer fought the effect of the adulterated qualis in her own emotions. They found an abandoned officer's quarters and made love on its bare wooden-slats bed, and again when they returned to the parlour of the Aphrodisia House.

The night-candle had burned down to its last knob by the time Myrtis released the hidden bolt and let the Hell Hound captain rejoin his men. Lythande was in the room behind her as soon as she shut the door.

'Are you safe now?' the magician asked with a laugh.

'I believe so.'

'The potion?'

'A success, as always. I have not been in love like this for a long time. It is pleasant. I almost do not mind knowing how empty and hurt I will feel as I watch him grow old.'

'Then why use something like the potion? Surely the catacombs themselves would have been enough to convince a Hell Hound?'

'Convince him of what? That the defences of Sanctuary should

192

not be entrusted to whores and courtesans? Except for your potion, there is nothing else to bind him to the idea that we – that I should remain here as I always have. There was no other way!'

'You're right,' Lythande said, nodding. 'Will he return to visit you?'

'He will care, but I do not think he will return. That was not the purpose of the drug.'

She opened the narrow glass-paned doors to the balcony over-looking the emptying lower rooms. The soldiers were gone. She looked back into the room. The three hundred gold pieces still lay half-counted on the table next to the empty decanter. He might return.

'I feel as young as I look,' she whispered to the unnoticing rooms. 'I could satisfy every man in this house if I took the notion to, or if anyone of them had half the magnificence of my Zalbar.'

Myrtis turned back to an empty room and went to sleep alone.

THE SECRET OF THE BLUE STAR

Marion Zimmer Bradley

On a night in Sanctuary, when the streets bore a false glamour in the silver glow of full moon, so that every ruin seemed an enchanted tower and every dark street and square an island of mystery, the mercenary-magician Lythande sallied forth to seek adventure.

Lythande had but recently returned – if the mysterious comings and goings of a magician can be called by so prosaic a name – from guarding a caravan across the Grey Wastes to Twand. Somewhere in the Wastes, a gaggle of desert rats – two-legged rats with poisoned steel teeth – had set upon the caravan, not knowing it was guarded by magic, and had found themselves fighting skeletons that howled and fought with eyes of flame; and at their centre a tall magician with a blue star between blazing eyes, a star that shot lightnings of a cold and paralysing flame. So the desert rats ran, and never stopped running until they reached Aurvesh, and the tales they told did Lythande no harm except in the ears of the pious.

And so there was gold in the pockets of the long, dark, magician's robe, or perhaps concealed in whatever dwelling sheltered Lythande.

For at the end, the caravan master had been almost more afraid of Lythande than he was of the bandits, a situation which added to the generosity with which he rewarded the magician. According to custom, Lythande neither smiled nor frowned, but remarked, days later, to Myrtis, the proprietor of the Aphrodisia House in the Street of Red Lanterns, that sorcery, while a useful skill and filled with many aesthetic delights for the contemplation of the philosopher, in itself put no beans on the table.

A curious remark, that, Myrtis pondered, putting away the ounce of gold Lythande had bestowed upon her in consideration of a secret which lay many years behind them both. Curious that Lythande should speak of beans on the table, when no one but herself had ever seen a bite of food or a drop of drink pass the magician's lips since the blue star had adorned that high and narrow brow. Nor had any woman in the Quarter even been able to boast that a great magician had paid for her favours, or been able to imagine how such a magician behaved in that situation when all men were alike reduced to flesh and blood.

Perhaps Myrtis could have told if she would; some of her girls thought so, when, as sometimes happened, Lythande came to the Aphrodisia House and was closeted long with its owner; even, on rare intervals, for an entire night. It was said, of Lythande, that the Aphrodisia House itself had been the magician's gift to Myrtis, after a famous adventure still whispered in the bazaar, involving an evil wizard, two horse-traders, a caravan master, and a few assorted toughs who had prided themselves upon never giving gold for any woman and thought it funny to cheat an honest working woman. None of them had ever showed their faces – what was left of them – in Sanctuary again, and Myrtis boasted that she need never again sweat to earn her living, and never again entertain a man, but would claim her madam's privilege of a solitary bed.

And then, too, the girls thought, a magician of Lythande's stature could have claimed the most beautiful women from Sanctuary to the mountains beyond Ilsig; not courtesans alone, but princesses and noblewomen and priestesses would have been for Lythande's taking. Myrtis had doubtless been beautiful in her youth, and certainly she boasted enough of the princes and wizards and travellers who had paid great sums for her love. She was beautiful still (and of course there were those who said that Lythande did not pay her, but that, on the contrary, Myrtis paid the magician great sums to maintain her ageing beauty with strong magic) but her hair had gone grey and she no longer troubled to dye it with henna or goldenwash from Tyrisis-beyond-the-sea.

But if Myrtis were not the woman who knew how Lythande

behaved in that most elemental of situations, then there was no woman in Sanctuary who could say. Rumour said also that Lythande called up female demons from the Grey Wastes, to couple in lechery, and certainly Lythande was neither the first nor the last magician of whom that could be said.

But on this night Lythande sought neither food nor drink nor the delights of amorous entertainment; although Lythande was a great frequenter of taverns, no man had ever yet seen a drop of ale or mead or fire-drink pass the barrier of the magician's lips. Lythande walked along the far edge of the bazaar, skirting the old rim of the governor's palace, keeping to the shadows in defiance of footpads and cutpurses, that love for shadows which made the folk of the city say that Lythande could appear and disappear into thin air.

Tall and thin, Lythande, above the height of a tall man, lean to emaciation, with the blue star-shaped tattoo of the magician-adept above thin, arching eyebrows; wearing a long, hooded robe which melted into the shadows. Clean-shaven, the face of Lythande, or beardless – none had come close enough, in living memory, to say whether this was the whim of an effeminate or the hairlessness of a freak. The hair beneath the hood was as long and luxuriant as a woman's, but greying, as no woman in this city of harlots would have allowed it to do.

Striding quickly along a shadowed wall, Lythande stepped through an open door, over which the sandal of Thufir, god of pilgrims, had been nailed up for luck; but the footsteps were so soft, and the hooded robe blended so well into the shadows, that eyewitnesses would later swear, truthfully, that they had seen Lythande appear from the air, protected by sorceries, or by a cloak of invisibility.

Around the hearth fire, a group of men were banging their mugs together noisily to the sound of a rowdy drinking-song, strummed on a worn and tinny lute – Lythande knew it belonged to the tavern-keeper, and could be borrowed – by a young man, dressed in fragments of foppish finery, torn and slashed by the chances of the road. He was sitting lazily, with one knee crossed over the other; and when the rowdy song died away, the young man drifted

196

into another, a quiet love-song from another time and another country. Lythande had known the song, more years ago than bore remembering, and in those days Lythande the magician had borne another name and had known little of sorcery. When the song died, Lythande had stepped from the shadows, visible, and the firelight glinted on the blue star, mocking at the centre of the high forehead.

There was a little muttering in the tavern, but they were not unaccustomed to Lythande's invisible comings and goings. The young man raised eyes which were surprisingly blue beneath the black hair elaborately curled above his brow. He was slender and agile, and Lythande marked the rapier at his side, which looked well handled, and the amulet, in the form of a coiled snake, at his throat. The young man said, 'Who are you, who has the habit of coming and going into thin air like that?'

'One who compliments your skill at song.' Lythande flung a coin to the tapster's boy. 'Will you drink?'

'A minstrel never refuses such an invitation. Singing is dry work.' But when the drink was brought, he said, 'Not drinking with me, then?'

'No man has ever seen Lythande eat or drink,' muttered one of the men in the circle round them.

'Why, then, I hold that unfriendly,' cried the young minstrel. 'A friendly drink between comrades shared is one thing; but I am no servant to sing for pay or to drink except as a friendly gesture!'

Lythande shrugged, and the blue star above the high brow began to shimmer and give forth blue light. The onlookers slowly edged backward, for when a wizard who wore the blue star was angered, bystanders did well to be out of the way. The minstrel set down the lute, so it would be well out of range if he must leap to his feet. Lythande knew, by the excruciating slowness of his movements and great care, that he had already shared a good many drinks with chance-met comrades. But the minstrel's hand did not go to his sword-hilt but instead closed like a fist over the amulet in the form of a snake.

'You are like no man I have ever met before,' he observed mildly, and Lythande, feeling inside the little ripple, nerve-long, that told a magician he was in the presence of spell-casting, hazarded quickly that the amulet was one of those which would not protect its master unless the wearer first stated a set number of truths – usually three or five – about the owner's attacker or foe. Wary, but amused, Lythande said, 'A true word. Nor am I like any man you will ever meet, live you never so long, minstrel.'

The minstrel saw, beyond the angry blue glare of the star, a curl of friendly mockery in Lythande's mouth. He said, letting the amulet go, 'And I wish you no ill; and you wish me none, and those are true sayings too, wizard, hey? And there's an end of that. But although perhaps you are like to no other, you are not the only wizard I have seen in Sanctuary who bears a blue star about his forehead.'

Now the blue star blazed rage, but not for the minstrel. They both knew it. The crowd around them had all mysteriously discovered that they had business elsewhere. The minstrel looked at the empty benches.

'I must go elsewhere to sing for my supper, it seems.'

'I meant you no offence when I refused to share a drink,' said Lythande. 'A magician's vow is not as lightly overset as a lute. Yet I may guest-gift you with dinner and drink in plenty without loss of dignity, and in return ask a service of a friend, may I not?'

'Such is the custom of my country. Cappen Varra thanks you, magician.'

'Tapster! Your best dinner for my guest, and all he can drink tonight!'

'For such liberal guesting I'll not haggle about the service,' Cappen Varra said, and set to the smoking dishes brought before him. As he ate, Lythande drew from the folds of his robe a small pouch containing a quantity of sweet-smelling herbs, rolled them into a blue-grey leaf, and touched his ring to spark the roll alight. He drew on the smoke, which drifted up sweet and greyish.

'As for the service, it is nothing so great; tell me all you know of this other wizard who wears the blue star. I know of none other of my order south of Azehur, and I would be certain you did not see me, nor my wraith.'

Cappen Varra sucked at a marrow-bone and wiped his fingers

fastidiously on the tray-cloth beneath the meats. He bit into a ginger-fruit before replying.

'Not you, wizard, nor your fetch or *doppelgänger*; this one had shoulders brawnier by half, and he wore no sword, but two daggers cross-girt astride his hips. His beard was black; and his left hand missing three fingers.'

'Ils of the Thousand Eyes! Rabben the Half-handed, here in Sanctuary! Where did you see him, minstrel?'

'I saw him crossing the bazaar; but he bought nothing that I saw. And I saw him in the Street of Red Lanterns, talking to a woman. What service am I to do for you, magician?'

'You have done it.' Lythande gave silver to the tavern keeper – so much that the surly man bade Shalpa's cloak cover him as he went – and laid another coin, gold this time, beside the borrowed lute.

'Redeem your harp; that one will do your voice no boon.' But when the minstrel raised his head in thanks, the magician had gone unseen into the shadows.

Pocketing the gold, the minstrel asked, 'How did he know that? And how did he go out?'

'Shalpa the swift alone knows,' the tapster said. 'Flew out by the smoke-hole in the chimney, for all I ken! That one needs not the night-dark cloak of Shalpa to cover him, for he has one of his own. He paid for your drinks, good sir; what will you have?' And Cappen Varra proceeded to get very drunk, that being the wisest thing to do when one becomes entangled unawares in the private affairs of a wizard.

Outside in the street, Lythande paused to consider. Rabben the Half-handed was no friend; yet there was no reason his presence in Sanctuary must deal with Lythande, or personal revenge. If it were business concerned with the Order of the Blue Star, if Lythande must lend Rabben aid, or the Half-handed had been sent to summon all the members of the Order, the star they both wore would have given warning.

Yet it would do no harm to make certain. Walking swiftly, the magician had reached a line of old stables behind the governor's

199

palace. There was silence and secrecy for magic. Lythande stepped into one of the little side alleys, drawing up the magician's cloak until no light remained, slowly withdrawing farther and farther into the silence until nothing remained anywhere in the world – anywhere in the universe but the light of the blue star ever glowing in front. Lythande remembered how it had been set there, and at what cost – the price an adept paid for power.

The blue glow gathered, fulminated in many-coloured patterns, pulsing and glowing, until Lythande stood *within* the light; and there, in the Place That Is Not, seated upon a throne carved apparently from sapphire, was the Master of the Star.

'Greetings to you, fellow star, star-born, *shyryu*.' The terms of endearment could mean fellow, companion, brother, sister, beloved, equal, pilgrim; its literal meaning was *sharer of starlight*. 'What brings you into the Pilgrim Place this night from afar?'

'The need for knowledge, star-sharer. Have you sent one to seek me out in Sanctuary?'

'Not so, *shyryu*. All is well in the Temple of the Star-sharers; you have not yet been summoned; the hour is not yet come.'

For every adept of the Blue Star knows; it is one of the prices of power. At the world's end, when all the doings of mankind and mortals are done, the last to fall under the assault of Chaos will be the Temple of the Star; and then, in the Place That Is Not, the Master of the Star will summon all of the Pilgrim Adepts from the farthest corners of the world, to fight with all their magic against Chaos; but until that day, they have such freedom as will best strengthen their powers. The Master of the Star repeated, reassuringly, 'The hour has not come. You are free to walk as you will in the world.'

The blue glow faded, and Lythande stood shivering. So Rabben had not been sent in that final summoning. Yet the end and Chaos might well be at hand for Lythande before the hour appointed, if Rabben the Half-handed had his way.

It was a fair test of strength, ordained by our masters, Rabben should bear me no ill-will ... Rabben's presence in Sanctuary need not have to do with Lythande. He might be here upon his lawful occasions – if anything of Rabben's could be said to be lawful;

for it was only upon the last day of all that the Pilgrim Adepts were pledged to fight upon the side of Law against Chaos. And Rabben had not chosen to do so before then.

Caution would be needed, and yet Lythande knew that Rabben was near . . .

South and east of the governor's palace, there is a little triangular park, across from the Street of Temples. By day the gravelled walks and turns of shrubbery are given over to predicants and priests who find not enough worship or offerings for their liking; by night the place is the haunt of women who worship no goddess except She of the filled purse and the empty womb. And for both reasons the place is called, in irony, the Promise of Heaven; in Sanctuary, as elsewhere, it is well known that those who promise do not always perform.

Lythande, who frequented neither women nor priests as a usual thing, did not often walk here. The park seemed deserted; the evil winds had begun to blow, whipping bushes and shrubbery into the shapes of strange beasts performing unnatural acts; and moaning weirdly around the walls and eaves of the Temples across the street, the wind that was said in Sanctuary to be the moaning of Azyuna in Vashanka's bed. Lythande moved swiftly, skirting the darkness of the paths. And then a woman's scream rent the air. From the shadows Lythande could see the frail form of a young girl in a torn and ragged dress; she was barefoot and her ear was bleeding where one jewelled earring had been torn from the lobe. She was struggling in the iron grip of a huge burly black-bearded man, and the first thing Lythande saw was the hand gripped around the girl's thin, bony wrist, dragging her; two fingers missing and the other cut away to the first joint. Only then – when it was no longer needed – did Lythande see the blue star between the black bristling brows, the cat-yellow eyes of Rabben the Half-handed!

Lythande knew him of old, from the Temple of the Star. Even then Rabben had been a vicious man, his lecheries notorious. Why, Lythande wondered, had the Masters not demanded that he renounce them as the price of his power? Lythande's lips tightened in a mirthless grimace; so notorious had been Rabben's lecheries that if he renounced them, everyone would know the Secret of his Power.

For the powers of an Adept of the Blue Star depended upon a secret. As in the old legend of the giant who kept his heart in a secret place outside his body, and with it his immortality, so the Adept of the Blue Star poured all his psychic force into a single Secret; and the one who discovered the Secret would acquire all of that adept's power. So Rabben's Secret must be something else ... Lythande did not speculate on it.

The girl cried out pitifully as Rabben jerked at her wrist; as the burly magician's star began to glow, she thrust her free hand over her eyes to shield them from it. Without fully intending to intervene, Lythande stepped from the shadows, and the rich voice that had made the prentice-magicians in the outer court of the Blue Star call Lythande 'minstrel' rather than 'magician', rang out:

'By Shipri the All-Mother, release that woman!'

Rabben whirled. 'By the nine-hundred-and-ninety-ninth eye of Ils! Lythande!'

'Are there not enough women in the Street of Red Lanterns, that you must mishandle girl-children in the Street of Temples?' For Lythande could see how young she was, the thin arms and childish legs and ankles, the breasts not yet full-formed beneath the dirty, torn tunic.

Rabben turned on Lythande and sneered, 'You were always squeamish, *shyryu*. No woman walks here unless she is for sale. Do you want her for yourself? Have you tired of your fat madame in the Aphrodisia House?'

'You will not take her name into your mouth, *shyryu*!'

'So tender for the honour of a harlot?'

Lythande ignored that. 'Let the girl go, or stand to my challenge.'

Rabben's star shot lightnings; he shoved the girl to one side. She fell nerveless to the pavement and lay without moving. 'She'll stay there until we've done. Did you think she could run away while we fought? Come to think of it, I never did see you with a woman, Lythande – is that your Secret, Lythande, that you've no use for women?'

Lythande maintained an impassive face; but whatever came,

202

Rabben must not be allowed to pursue *that* line. 'You may couple like an animal in the streets of Sanctuary, Rabben, but I do not. Will you yield her up, or fight?'

'Perhaps I should yield her to you; this is unheard of, that Lythande should fight in the streets over a woman! You see, I know your habits well, Lythande!'

Damnation of Vashanka! Now indeed I shall have to fight for the girl!

Lythande's rapier snicked from its scabbard and thrust at Rabben as if of its own will.

'Ha! Do you think Rabben fights street-brawls with the sword like any mercenary?' Lythande's sword-tip exploded in the blue star-glow, and became a shimmering snake, twisting back on itself to climb past the hilt, fangs dripping venom as it sought to coil around Lythande's fist. Lythande's own star blazed. The sword was metal again but twisted and useless, in the shape of the snake it had been, coiling back toward the scabbard. Enraged, Lythande jerked free of the twisted metal, sent a spitting rain of fire in Rabben's direction. Quickly the huge adept covered himself in fog, and the fire-spray extinguished itself. Somewhere outside consciousness Lythande was aware of a crowd gathering; not twice in a lifetime did two adepts of the Blue Star battle by sorcery in the streets of Sanctuary. The blaze of the stars, blazing from each magician's brow, raged lightnings in the square.

On a howling wind came little torches ravening, that flickered and whipped at Lythande; they touched the tall form of the magician and vanished. Then a wild whirlwind sent trees lashing, leaves swirling bare from branches, battered Rabben to his knees. Lythande was bored; this must be finished quickly. Not one of the goggling onlookers in the crowd knew afterwards what had been done, but Rabben bent, slowly, slowly, forced inch by inch down and down, to his knees, to all fours, prone, pressing and grinding his face further and further into the dust, rocking back and forth, pressing harder and harder into the sand ...

Lythande turned and lifted the girl. She stared in disbelief at the burly sorcerer grinding his black beard frantically into the dirt.

'What did you –'

'Never mind – let's get out of here. The spell will not hold him long, and when he wakes from it he will be angry.' Neutral mockery edged. Lythande's voice, and the girl could see it, too, Rabben with beard and eyes and blue star covered with the dirt and dust –

She scurried along in the wake of the magician's robe; when they were well away from the Promise of Heaven, Lythande halted, so abruptly that the girl stumbled.

'Who are you, girl?'

'My name is Bercy. And yours?'

'A magician's name is not lightly given. In Sanctuary they call me Lythande.' Looking down at the girl, the magician noted, with a pang, that beneath the dirt and dishevelment she was very beautiful and very young. 'You can go, Bercy. He will not touch you again; I have bested him fairly upon challenge.'

She flung herself on to Lythande's shoulder, clinging. 'Don't send me away!' she begged, clutching, eyes filled with adoration. Lythande scowled.

Predictable, of course, Bercy believed, and who in Sanctuary would have disbelieved, that the duel had been fought for the girl as prize, and she was ready to give herself to the winner. Lythande made a gesture of protest.

'No –'

The girl narrowed her eyes in pity. 'Is it then with you as Rabben said – that your secret is that you have been deprived of manhood?' But beyond the pity was a delicious flicker of amusement – what a tidbit of gossip! A juicy bit for the Street of Women.

'Silence!' Lythande's glance was imperative. 'Come.'

She followed, along the twisting streets that led into the Street of Red Lanterns. Lythande strode with confidence, now, past the House of Mermaids, where, it was said, delights as exotic as the name promised were to be found; past the House of Whips, shunned by all except those who refused to go elsewhere; and at last, beneath the face of the Green Lady as she was worshipped far away and beyond Ranke, the Aphrodisia House.

Bercy looked around, eyes wide, at the pillared lobby, the brilliance of a hundred lanterns, the exquisitely dressed women lounging on cushions till they were summoned. They were finely dressed and bejewelled – Myrtis knew her trade, and how to present her wares – and Lythande guessed that the ragged Bercy's glance was one of envy; she had probably sold herself in the bazaars for a few coppers or for a loaf of bread, since she was old enough. Yet somehow, like flowers covering a dungheap, she had kept an exquisite fresh beauty, all gold and white, flowerlike. Even ragged and half-starved, she touched Lythande's heart.

'Bercy, have you eaten today?'

'No, master.'

Lythande summoned the huge eunuch Jiro, whose business it was to conduct the favoured customers to the chambers of their chosen women, and throw out the drunks and abusive customers into the street. He came – huge-bellied, naked except for a skimpy loincloth and a dozen rings in his ear – he had once had a lover who was an earring-seller and had used him to display her wares.

'How may we serve the magician Lythande?'

The women on the couches and cushions were twittering at one another in surprise and dismay, and Lythande could almost hear their thoughts;

None of us has been able to attract or seduce the great magician, and this ragged street wench has caught his eyes? And, being women, Lythande knew they could see the unclouded beauty that shone through the girl's rags.

'Is Madame Myrtis available, Jiro?'

'She's sleeping, O great wizard, but for you she's given orders she's to be waked at any hour. Is this –' no one alive can be quite so supercilious as the chief eunuch of a fashionable brothel – 'yours, Lythande, or a gift for my madame?'

'Both, perhaps. Give her something to eat and find her a place to spend the night.'

'And a bath, magician? She has fleas enough to louse a floorful of cushions!'

'A bath, certainly, and a bath-woman with scents and oils,' Lythande said, 'and something in the nature of a whole garment.'

'Leave it to me,' said Jiro expansively, and Bercy looked at Lythande in dread, but went when the magician gestured to her

205

to go. As Jiro took her away, Lythande saw Myrtis standing in the doorway; a heavy woman, no longer young, but with the frozen beauty of a spell. Through the perfect spelled features, her eyes were warm and welcoming as she smiled at Lythande.

'My dear, I had not expected to see you here. Is that yours?' She moved her head towards the door through which Jiro had conducted the frightened Bercy. 'She'll probably run away, you know, once you take your eyes off her.'

'I wish I thought so, Myrtis. But no such luck, I fear.'

'You had better tell me the whole story,' Myrtis said, and listened to Lythande's brief, succinct account of the affair.

'And if you laugh, Myrtis, I take back my spell and leave your grey hairs and wrinkles open to the mockery of everyone in Sanctuary!'

But Myrtis had known Lythande too long to take that threat very seriously. 'So the maiden you rescued is all maddened with desire for the love of Lythande!' She chuckled. 'It is like an old ballad, indeed!'

'But what am I to do, Myrtis? By the paps of Shipri the All-Mother, this is a dilemma!'

'Take her into your confidence and tell her why your love cannot be hers,' Myrtis said.

Lythande frowned. 'You hold my Secret, since I had no choice; you knew me before I was made magician, or bore the blue star –'

'And before I was a harlot,' Myrtis agreed.

'But if I make this girl feel like a fool for loving me, she will hate me as much as she loves; and I cannot confide in anyone I cannot trust with my life and my power. All I have is yours, Myrtis, because of that past we shared. And that includes my power, if you ever should need it. But I cannot entrust it to this girl.'

'Still she owes you something, for delivering her out of the hands of Rabben.'

Lythande said, 'I will think about it; and now make haste to bring me food, for I am hungry and athirst.' Taken to a private room, Lythande ate and drank, served by Myrtis's own hands. And Myrtis said, 'I could never have sworn your vow – to eat and drink in the sight of no man!'

'If you sought the power of a magician, you would keep it well enough,' said Lythande. 'I am seldom tempted now to break it; I fear only lest I break it unawares; I cannot drink in a tavern lest among the women there might be some one of those strange men who find diversion in putting on the garments of a female; even here I will not eat or drink among your women, for that reason. All power depends on the vows and the secret.'

'Then I cannot aid you,' Myrtis said, 'but you are not bound to speak truth to her; tell her you have vowed to live without women.'

'I may do that,' Lythande said, and finished the food, scowling.

Later Bercy was brought in, wide-eyed, enthralled by her fine gown and her freshly washed hair, softly curling about her pink-and-white face and the sweet scent of bath oils and perfumes that hung about her.

'The girls here wear such pretty clothes, and one of them told me they could eat twice a day if they wished! Am I pretty enough, do you think, that Madame Myrtis would have me here?'

'If that is what you wish. You are more than beautiful.'

Bercy said boldly, 'I would rather belong to *you*, magician,' and flung herself again on Lythande, her hands clutching and clinging, dragging the lean face down to hers. Lythande, who rarely touched anything living, held her gently, trying not to reveal consternation.

'Bercy, child, this is only a fancy. It will pass.'

'No,' she wept. 'I love you, I want only you!'

And then, unmistakably, along the magician's nerves, Lythande felt that little ripple, that warning thrill of tension which said: *spell-casting is in use.* Not against Lythande. That could have been countered. But somewhere within the room.

Here, in the Aphrodisia House? Myrtis, Lythande knew, could be trusted with life, reputation, fortune, the magical power of the Blue Star itself; she had been tested before this. Had she altered enough to turn betrayer, it would have been apparent in her aura when Lythande came near.

That left only the girl, who was clinging and whimpering, 'I will die if you do not love me! I will die! Tell me it is not true, Lythande, that you are unable to love! Tell me it is an evil lie that magicians are emasculated, incapable of loving woman ...'

'That is certainly an evil lie,' Lythande agreed gravely. 'I give you my solemn assurance that I have never been emasculated.' But Lythande's nerves tingled as the words were spoken. A magician might lie, and most of them did. Lythande would lie as readily as any other, in a good cause. But the law of the Blue Star was this: when questioned directly on a matter bearing directly on the Secret, the adept might not tell a direct lie. And Bercy, unknowing, was only one question away from the fatal one hiding the Secret.

With a mighty effort, Lythande's magic wrenched at the very fabric of Time itself; the girl stood motionless, aware of no lapse, as Lythande stepped away far enough to read her aura. And yes, there within the traces of that vibrating field was the shadow of the blue star. Rabben's; overpowering her will.

Rabben. Rabben the Half-handed, who had set his will on the girl, who had staged and contrived the whole thing, including the encounter where the girl had needed rescue; put the girl under a spell to attract and bespell Lythande.

The law of the Blue Star forbade one adept of the Star to kill another; for all would be needed to fight side by side, on the last day, against Chaos. Yet if one adept could prise forth the secret of another's power ... then the powerless one was not needed against Chaos and could be killed.

What could be done now? Kill the girl? Rabben would take that, too, as an answer; Bercy had been so bespelled as to be irresistible to any man; if Lythande sent her away untouched, Rabben would know that Lythande's secret lay in that area and would never rest in his attempts to uncover it. For if Lythande was untouched by this sex-spell to make Bercy irresistible, then Lythande was a eunuch, or a homosexual, or ... sweating, Lythande dared not even think beyond that. The Secret was safe only if never questioned. It would not be read in the aura; but one simple question, and all was ended.

I should kill her, Lythande thought. *For now I am fighting, not for my magic alone, but for my secret and for my life. For surely, with my power gone, Rabben would lose no time in making an end of me, in revenge for the loss of half a hand.*

The girl was still motionless, entranced. How easily she could be killed! Then Lythande recalled an old fairy-tale, which might be used to save the Secret of the Star.

The light flickered as Time returned to the chamber. Bercy was still clinging and weeping, unaware of the lapse; Lythande had resolved what to do, and the girl felt Lythande's arms enfolding her, and the magician's kiss on her welcoming mouth.

'You must love me or I shall die!' Bercy wept.

Lythande said, 'You shall be mine.' The soft neutral voice was very gentle. 'But even a magician is vulnerable in love, and I must protect myself. A place shall be made ready for us without light or sound save for what I provide with my magic; and you must swear that you will not seek to see or to touch me except by that magical light. Will you swear it by the All-Mother, Bercy? For if you swear this, I shall love you as no woman has ever been loved before.'

Trembling, she whispered, 'I swear.' And Lythande's heart went out in pity, for Rabben had used her ruthlessly; so that she burned alive with her unslaked and bewitched love for the magician, that she was all caught up in her passion for Lythande. Painfully, Lythande thought; *if she had only loved me, without the spell; then I could have loved . . .*

Would that I could trust her with my secret! But she is only Rabben's tool; her love for me is his doing, and none of her own will . . . and not real . . . And so everything which would pass between them now must be only a drama staged for Rabben.

'I shall make all ready for you with my magic.'

Lythande went and confided to Myrtis what was needed; the woman began to laugh, but a single glance at Lythande's bleak face stopped her cold. She had known Lythande since long before the blue star was set between those eyes; and she kept the Secret for love of Lythande. It wrung her heart to see one she loved in the grip of such suffering. So she said, 'All will be prepared. Shall I give her a drug in her wine to weaken her will, that you may the more readily throw a glamour upon her?'

Lythande's voice held a terrible bitterness. 'Rabben has done that already for us, when he put a spell upon her to love me.'

'You would have it otherwise?' Myrtis asked, hesitating.

'All the gods of Sanctuary – they laugh at me! All-Mother, help me! But I would have it otherwise; I could love her, if she were not Rabben's tool.'

When all was prepared, Lythande entered the darkened room. There was no light but the light of the Blue Star. The girl lay on a bed, stretching up her arms to the magician with exalted abandon.

'Come to me, come to me, my love!'

'Soon,' said Lythande, sitting beside her, stroking her hair with a tenderness even Myrtis would never have guessed. 'I will sing to you a love-song of my people, far away.'

She writhed in erotic ecstasy. 'All you do is good to me, my love, my magician!'

Lythande felt the blankness of utter despair. She was beautiful, and she was in love. She lay in a bed spread for the two of them, and they were separated by the breadth of the world. The magician could not endure it.

Lythande sang, in that rich and beautiful voice; a voice lovelier than any spell;

> 'Half the night is spent; and the crown of moonlight
> Fades, and now the crown of the stars is paling;
> Yields the sky reluctant to coming morning;
> Still I lie lonely.'

Lythande could see tears on Bercy's cheeks.

> 'I will love you as no woman has ever been loved.'

Between the girl on the bed, and the motionless form of the magician, as the magician's robe fell heavily to the floor, a wraith-form grew, the very wraith and fetch, at first, of Lythande, tall and lean, with blazing eyes and a star between its brows and a body white and unscarred; the form of the magician, but this one triumphant in virility, advancing on the motionless woman, waiting. Her mind fluttered away in arousal, was caught, captured, be-spelled. Lythande let her see the image for a moment; she could not see the true Lythande behind; then, as her eyes closed in ecstatic awareness of the touch, Lythande smoothed light fingers over her closed eyes.

'See – what I bid you to see!

'Hear – what I bid you hear!

'Feel only what I bid you feel, Bercy!'

And now she was wholly under the spell of the wraith. Unmoving, stony-eyed, Lythande watched as her lips closed on emptiness and she kissed invisible lips; and moment by moment Lythande knew what touched her, what caressed her. Rapt and ravished by illusion that brought her again and again to the heights of ecstasy, till she cried out in abandonment. Only to Lythande that cry was bitter; for she cried out not to Lythande but to the man-wraith who possessed her.

At last she lay all but unconscious, satiated; and Lythande watched in agony. When she opened her eyes again, Lythande was looking down at her, sorrowfully.

Bercy stretched up languid arms. 'Truly, my beloved, you have loved me as no woman has ever been loved before.'

For the first and last time, Lythande bent over her and pressed her lips in a long, infinitely tender kiss. 'Sleep, my darling.'

And as she sank into ecstatic, exhausted sleep, Lythande wept.

Long before she woke, Lythande stood, girt for travel, in the little room belonging to Myrtis.

'The spell will hold. She will make all haste to carry her tale to Rabben – the tale of Lythande, the incomparable lover! Of Lythande, of untiring virility, who can love a maiden into exhaustion!' The rich voice of Lythande was harsh with bitterness.

'And long before you return to Sanctuary, once freed of the spell, she will have forgotten you in many other lovers,' Myrtis agreed. 'It is better and safer that it should be so.'

'True.' But Lythande's voice broke. 'Take care of her, Myrtis. Be kind to her.'

'I swear it, Lythande.'

'If only she could have loved *me*' – the magician broke and sobbed again for a moment; Myrtis looked away, wrung with pain, knowing not what comfort to offer.

'If only she could have loved me as I am, freed of Rabben's spell! Loved me without pretence! But I feared I could not master the spell Rabben had put on her ... nor trust her not to betray me, knowing ...'

Myrtis put her plump arms around Lythande, tenderly.

'Do you regret?'

The question was ambiguous. It might have meant: *Do you regret that you did not kill the girl?* Or even: *Do you regret your oath and the secret you must bear to the last day?* Lythande chose to answer the last.

'Regret? How can I regret? One day I shall fight against Chaos with all of my order; even at the side of Rabben, if he lives un-murdered as long as that. And that alone must justify my existence and my secret. But now I must leave Sanctuary, and who knows when the chances of the world will bring me this way again? Kiss me farewell, my sister.'

Myrtis stood on tiptoe. Her lips met the lips of the magician.

'Until we meet again, Lythande. May She attend and guard you for ever. Farewell, my beloved, my sister.'

Then the magician Lythande girded on her sword, and went silently and by unseen ways out of the city of Sanctuary, just as the dawn was breaking. And on her forehead the glow of the Blue Star was dimmed by the rising sun. Never once did she look back.

THE MAKING OF
THIEVES' WORLD

Robert Lynn Asprin

It was a dark and stormy night ...

Actually, that Thursday night before Boskone '78 was a very pleasant night. Lynn Abbey, Gordy Dickson, and I were enjoying a quiet dinner in the Boston Sheraton's Mermaid Restaurant prior to the chaos which inevitably surrounds a major science fiction convention.

As so often happens when several authors gather socially, the conversation turned to the subject of writing in general and specifically to problems encountered and pet peeves. Not to be outdone by my dinner companions, I voiced one of my long-standing gripes: that whenever one set out to write heroic fantasy, it was first necessary to re-invent the universe from scratch regardless of what had gone before. Despite the carefully crafted Hyborean world of Howard or even the delightfully complex town of Lankhmar which Leiber created, every author was expected to beat his head against the writing table and devise a world of his own. Imagine, I proposed, if our favourite sword-and-sorcery characters shared the same settings and time-frames. Imagine the story potentials. Imagine the tie-ins. What if ...

What if Fafhrd and Mouser had just finished a successful heist. With an angry crowd on their heels, they pull one of their notorious doubleback escapes and elude the pursuing throng. Now suppose this angry, torch-waving pack runs headlong into Conan, hot and tired from the trail, his dead horse a day's walk behind him. All he wants is a jug of wine and a wench. Instead, he's confronted with a lynch mob. What if his saddlebags are full of loot from one of his own ventures, yet undiscovered?

Or what if Kane and Elric took jobs marshalling opposite armies in the same war?

Why, I proclaimed, the possibilities are endless. Pouring a little more wine, I admitted that one of my pet projects under consideration was to do a collection of fantasy stories featuring not one, but an array of central characters. They would all share the same terrain and be peripherally aware of each other's existence as their paths crossed. The only problem: my writing schedule was filling up so fast I wasn't sure when or if I'd ever get a chance to write it.

More wine flowed.

Gordy sympathized eloquently, pointing out that this was a problem all writers encountered as they grew more and more successful. Time! Time to fulfil your commitments and still be able to write the fun things you really want to write. As an example, he pointed out that there were countless story potentials in his Dorsai universe, but that he was barely able to find the time to complete the Childe Cycle novels, much less pursue all the spin-offs.

More wine flowed.

The ideal thing, Lynn suggested, was to be able to franchise one's ideas and worlds out to other authors. The danger there, Gordy pointed out, was the danger of losing control. None of us were particularly wild about letting any Tom, Dick, or Harry play around with our pet ideas.

More wine flowed.

Anthologies! If we went to an anthology format, we could invite authors to participate, as well as having final say as to the acceptability of the stories submitted.

Gordy ordered a bottle of champagne.

Of course, he observed, you'll be able to get some top-flight authors for this because it'll be fun. They'll do it more for the love of the idea than for the money.

I remarked on the ease with which *'our'* idea had become *'my'* anthology. As the weight of the project had suddenly come to rest on my shoulders, I asked whether he intended to assist or at least contribute to the anthology. His reply set the classic pattern for nearly all the contributors to *Thieves' World:*

I'd love to, but I don't have the time. It's a lovely idea, though.

(Five minutes later) I just thought of a character who would fit into this perfectly.

(Fifteen minutes later . . . thoughtful stare into nothingness converting into a smug grin) I've got my story!

During this last exchange, Lynn was saying very little. Unbeknownst to me, she had mentally dealt herself out of the project when Gordy proposed 'established writers only'. At that point in time, she had in her suitcase the manuscript for *Daughter of the Bright Moon*, hoping to find an interested editor at Boskone. She was far from being 'established'. It is to her credit, however, that she successfully hid her disappointment at being excluded, and accompanied Gordy and me as we finished the last of the champagne and went 'trolling for editors'.

It may seem to you that it was rather early to try to find a publisher for such a nebulous work. That's how it struck me at the time. Gordy pointed out, however, that if we could find an editor and nudge him into an appraisal of the dollar value of the idea, I would have a better feel for what my budget would be when I went to line up my authors. (The fact that this made sense to me at the time will serve as an indication of the lateness of the hour and the amount of wine we had consumed.)

To this end, we devised a subtle tactic. We would try to find an author and an editor in the same room, preferably in the same conversation. We would then pitch the idea to the author as a potential contributor and see if the editor showed interest.

We found such a duo and launched into our song and dance. The editor yawned, but the author thought it was a great idea. Of course, he didn't have the time to write anything . . . Then he thought of a character! That's how John Brunner came on board.

The next morning, the effects of our dinner wine dissipated and I began to realize what I had let myself in for. A brand-new author, barely published, and I was going to try to edit an anthology? Soliciting contributions from the best in the field, yet! That revelation sobered me up faster than a bucket of ice water and a five-day hotel bill.

Still, the ball was already rolling, and I had story commitments from Gordy and John. I might as well see how far things could go.

FRIDAY: I ambushed Joe Haldeman over a glass of lunch. He thought it was a terrific idea, but he didn't have any time. Besides, he pointed out, he had never written heroic fantasy. I countered by reminding him of his stay in Vietnam, courtesy of the US Army. Surely, I pressed, there must be one or two characters he had encountered who would fit into a sword-and-sorcery setting with minimal rewriting. His eyes cleared. He had his character.

SATURDAY: I finally found out what was bothering Lynn and assured her of a place on the *Thieves' World* roster. I was confident she would be 'established' before the anthology came out, and even if she wasn't, I knew she could produce a solid story. No, I don't have a crystal ball. Lynn and I both live in Ann Arbor and share workspace when we're writing. As such, I had been reading the manuscript of *Daughter of the Bright Moon* as she was writing it, and knew her writing style even before the editors saw it. (My prophecy proved correct. Ace/Sunridge bought her manuscript, and a major promo campaign is currently underway. The book should be on the stands when you see this anthology.)

SUNDAY: Wonder of wonders. Over cognac at the Ace dead-dog party, Jim Baen expresses a solid interest in the anthology ... *if* I succeed in filling the remaining slots with authors of an equal quality to those already committed. Leaving the party, I encounter Jim Odbert in the hall and do a little bragging. He brings me down to earth by asking about the street map. I hadn't even thought about it, but he was right! It would be absolutely necessary for internal continuity. Thinking fast, I commission him on the spot and retire, harbouring a nagging hunch that this project might be a bit more involved than I had imagined.

Back in Ann Arbor, I face the task of filling the remaining openings for the anthology. My magic wand for this feat is a telephone. Having been a fan for many years, I have had passing contact with several prominent authors, many of whom don't know that I'm writing now. I figure it will be easier to jog their memories over the phone than trying to do the same thing by letter.

The problem now is ... who? Solid authors ... that's a must. Authors who know me well enough that they won't hang up when I call. Authors who *don't* know me so well that they'll hang up when I call.

Andy! Andy Offutt. Our paths had crossed several times at cons, and I know we share a mutual admiration of Genghis Khan.

Andy doesn't have any time, but is super enthusiastic over the idea and has his character. Yes, that's all one sentence. If anything, I've condensed it. If you've ever talked to Andy on the phone, you'll understand.

Next will be Poul Anderson. Poul and I know each other mostly by reputation through Gordy and through a medieval re-enactment organization known as the Society for Creative Anachronism, Inc. Sir Bela of Eastmarch and Yang the Nauseating. Hooboy, do we know each other. In spite of that, Poul agrees to do a story for me ... if he gets the time ... in fact, he has a character in mind.

The list is growing. Confident now that the impressive array of authors submitting stories will offset my own relative obscurity, I go for a few who may not remember me.

Roger Zelazny was Pro Guest of Honour at a convention in Little Rock, Arkansas, where I was Fan Guest of Honour. He remembers and listens to my pitch.

I spoke briefly with Marion Zimmer Bradley about the sword-work in *Hunter of the Red Moon* – when we passed in the hall at a Wester-Con in Los Angeles – two years ago. She remembers me and listens to my pitch.

Philip José Farmer and I have seen each other twice: once in Milwaukee and once in Minneapolis. Both times we were at opposite ends of a table with half a dozen people crowded between us. He acknowledges the memory, then listens in silence for fifteen minutes while I do my spiel. When I finally grind to a halt, he says okay and hangs up. I find out later that this is his way of expressing enthusiasm. If he hadn't been enthusiastic, he would have said no and hung up.

By this time it's Minicon. Jim Odbert passes me a set of maps. Then he, Gordy, Joe, Lynn, and I sit around half the night discussing the history of the city and the surrounding continent. A set of house rules is devised and agreed upon: (1) Each contributor is to send me a brief description of the main character of his/her story. (2) These descriptions will be copied and distributed to the other contributors. (3) Any author can use these characters in his/her story, providing they're not killed off or noticeably reformed.

I run all this through a typewriter and mail it out to all the contributors. It occurs to me that this isn't nearly as difficult as I had feared. My only worry is that the mails might slow communication with John Brunner in England, causing him to be late with his submission. Except for that everything was going fine.

Then the fun began ...

Andy, Poul, and John all send me notes in varying degrees of gentleness correcting my grammar and/or word usage in the flier. They are willing to accept without confirmation that my spelling was intended as a joke. These are the people I'm supposed to be editing! Riiiiight!

Poul sends me a copy of his essay, 'On Thud and Blunder', to ensure the realism of the setting, particularly the economic structure of the town. He also wants to know about the judicial system in Sanctuary.

Andy wants to know about the deities worshipped, preferably broken down by nationality and economic class of worshippers. Fortunately, he includes a proposed set of gods, which I gleefully copy and send to the other contributors. He heads his ten-page letters with 'To Colossus: The Asprin Project'. It occurs to me that with his own insight as an anthology editor, this could be more truth than humour.

To make my job a little easier, some of the authors start playing poker with their character sketches: 'I won't show you mine till you show me yours.' They delay submitting their sketches until they see what the other authors turn in. One of these is Gordy. Remember him? He's the one who got me into this in the first place. He's the one who 'had his character' before there was an anthology! Terrific!

John Brunner submits his story – a full year before the stated deadline. So much for transatlantic delays. I haven't gotten all the character descriptions yet. More important, I haven't gotten the advance money yet! His agent begins to prod gently for payment.

Roger reappraises his time commitments and withdraws from the project. Oh, well. You can't win them all.

Poul wants to know about the architectural style of Sanctuary.

Andy and Poul want to know about the structure and nationality of names.

A call comes in from Ace. Jim Baen wants the manuscript a full three months ahead of the contracted deadline. I point out that this is impossible – the new deadline would give me only two weeks between receiving the stories from the authors and submitting the complete manuscript to New York. If I encountered difficulties with any of the stories or if any of the submissions came in late, it would disrupt the schedule completely. They point out that if I can meet the new schedule, they'll make it their lead book for the month it's released. The avaricious side of me is screaming, but I stick to my guns and repeat that it's impossible to guarantee. They offer a contract for a second *Thieves' World* anthology, suggesting that if a couple of stories are late, I can include them in the next book. Under attack now both from my publisher and my own greedy nature, I roll my eyes heavenward, swallow hard, and agree.

A new note is rapidly dispatched to the contributors, politely reminding them of the approaching deadline. Also included is Gordy's character sketch for Jamie the Red which he had finally submitted under mild duress (his arm will heal eventually).

Andy calls and wants to know the prince's name. I haven't given it any thought, but am willing to negotiate. An hour later, I hang up. It occurs to me that I haven't written my story yet.

Gordy notifies me that he can't get his story done in time for the first book. Terrific! With Gordy and Roger both out of the first volume, it's starting to look a little short.

Andy's story comes in, as does Joe's and Poul's.

Andy's story includes a discussion with Joe's One-Thumb character. Joe has killed One-Thumb off in his story. A minor sequencing problem.

Poul's story has Cappen Varra going off on an adventure with Gordy's Jamie the Red. Gordie's Jamie the Red story won't be in the first book! A major sequencing problem! Oh, well. I owe Gordy one for talking me into editing this monster.

I look at the stories already in the bin and decide that the first draft of my story needs some drastic rewriting.

A note arrives from Phil Farmer. He had sent me a letter months ago, which apparently never arrived, withdrawing from the project. (It hadn't!) Realizing that withdrawing at this late date would leave me in a bad spot, he is now rearranging his writing schedule in order to send me 'something'. Of course, it will be a little late. I am grateful, but panicky.

Lynn finishes her story and starts to gloat. I threaten to beat her head in with my Selectric.

Ace calls again. They want additional information for the cover copy. They also want a word count. I explain the situation as calmly as I can. Half-way through my explanation, the phone melts.

Ma Bell fixes my phone in record time (I am rapidly becoming their favourite customer), and I hurriedly call Marion to ask for a rough word-count on her unsubmitted story. She tells me she sent me a letter which must not have arrived. (It didn't.) She tells me she'll have to withdraw from the project because of time pressures in her other writing commitments. She tells me to stop gibbering and say something. I calm myself and explain I'd *really* like to have a story from her. I explain I really *need* her story. I mention that her character is on the cover of the book. She observes that the water gushing from the phone is threatening to flood her living room and agrees to try to squeeze the story into her writing schedule ... before she flies to London in two weeks.

With steady hand but trembling mind, I call Ace and ask for Jim Baen. I explain the situation: I have six stories in hand (yes, I finally finished mine) and two more on the way ... a little late ... maybe. He informs me that with just six stories the book will be too short. He wants at least one more story and an essay from me about how much fun it was to edit the anthology. To calm my hysterics, he suggests I commission a back-up story in case the two en route don't arrive in time. I point out that there are only two weeks remaining before the deadline. He concedes that with such a limited time-frame, I probably won't be able to get a story from a 'name' author. He'll let me work with an 'unknown', but the story had better be good!

Christine DeWees is a kindly, white-haired grandmother who rides a Harley and wants to be a writer. Lynn and I have been criticizing her efforts for some time and have repeatedly encouraged her to submit something to an editor. So far, she has resisted our proddings, insisting that she would be embarrassed to show her work to a professional editor. I decide to kill two birds with one stone.

In my most disarming 'nothing can go wrong' tones, I give my spiel to Christine and pass her a *Thieves' World* package. Three hours later, my phone rings. Christine loves the character of Myrtis, the madam of the Aphrodisia House and is ready to do a story centring around her. I stammer politely and point out that Myrtis is one of Marion's characters and that she might object to someone else writing her characters. Christine cackles and tells me she's already cleared it with Marion (don't ask me how she got the phone number!), and everything is effervescent. Two days later, she hands me the story, and I still haven't gotten around to looking up 'effervescent' in the dictionary.

With seven stories now in hand, I declare *Thieves' World I* to be complete and begin writing my 'fun fun' essay. The stories from Marion and Phil can wait until the second book.

Then Marion's story arrives.

Marion's story interfaces so nicely with Christine's that I decide to use them both in the first book. Rather than cut one of the other stories, the volume is assembled with intros, maps, eight stories, and essay, crated, and shipped off to New York.

Endo volume one! Print it!

The whole whirlwind process of editing this monster child was only vaguely as I had imagined it would be. Still, in hindsight, I loved it. With all the worries and panics, the skyhigh phone bills and the higher bar bills, I loved every minute. I find myself actually looking forward to the next volume ... and that's what worries me!

MORE ABOUT PENGUINS,
PELICANS AND PUFFINS

For further information about books available from Penguins please write to Dept EP, Penguin Books Ltd, Harmondsworth, Middlesex UB7 0DA.

In the U.S.A.: For a complete list of books available from Penguins in the United States write to Dept DG, Penguin Books, 299 Murray Hill Parkway, East Rutherford, New Jersey 07073.

In Canada: For a complete list of books available from Penguins in Canada write to Penguin Books Canada Ltd, 2801 John Street, Markham, Ontario L3R 1B4.

In Australia: For a complete list of books available from Penguins in Australia write to the Marketing Department, Penguin Books Australia Ltd, P.O. Box 257, Ringwood, Victoria 3134.

In New Zealand: For a complete list of books available from Penguins in New Zealand write to the Marketing Department, Penguin Books (N.Z.) Ltd, P.O. Box 4019, Auckland 10.

In India: For a complete list of books available from Penguins in India write to Penguin Overseas Ltd, 706 Eros Apartments, 56 Nehru Place, New Delhi 110019.